FORBIDDEN SURGERIES OF THE HIDEOUS DR·DIVINUS

Other books by S. Craig Zahler

A Congregation of Jackals
Wraiths of the Broken Land
Corpus Chrome, Inc.
Mean Business on North Ganson Street
Hug Chickenpenny: The Panegyric of an Anomalous Child
The Slanted Gutter

FORBIDDEN SURGERIES OF THE HIDEOUS DR·DIVINUS

Written & Illustrated by

S. CRAIG ZAHLER

FLOATING
WORLD COMICS

FORBIDDEN SURGERIES OF THE HIDEOUS DR. DIVINUS

Book design by François Vigneault

Floating World Comics
400 NW Couch St.
Portland, OR 97209
www.floatingworldcomics.com

First paperback edition: December 2020
Printed in China.

ISBN 978-1-942801-05-4

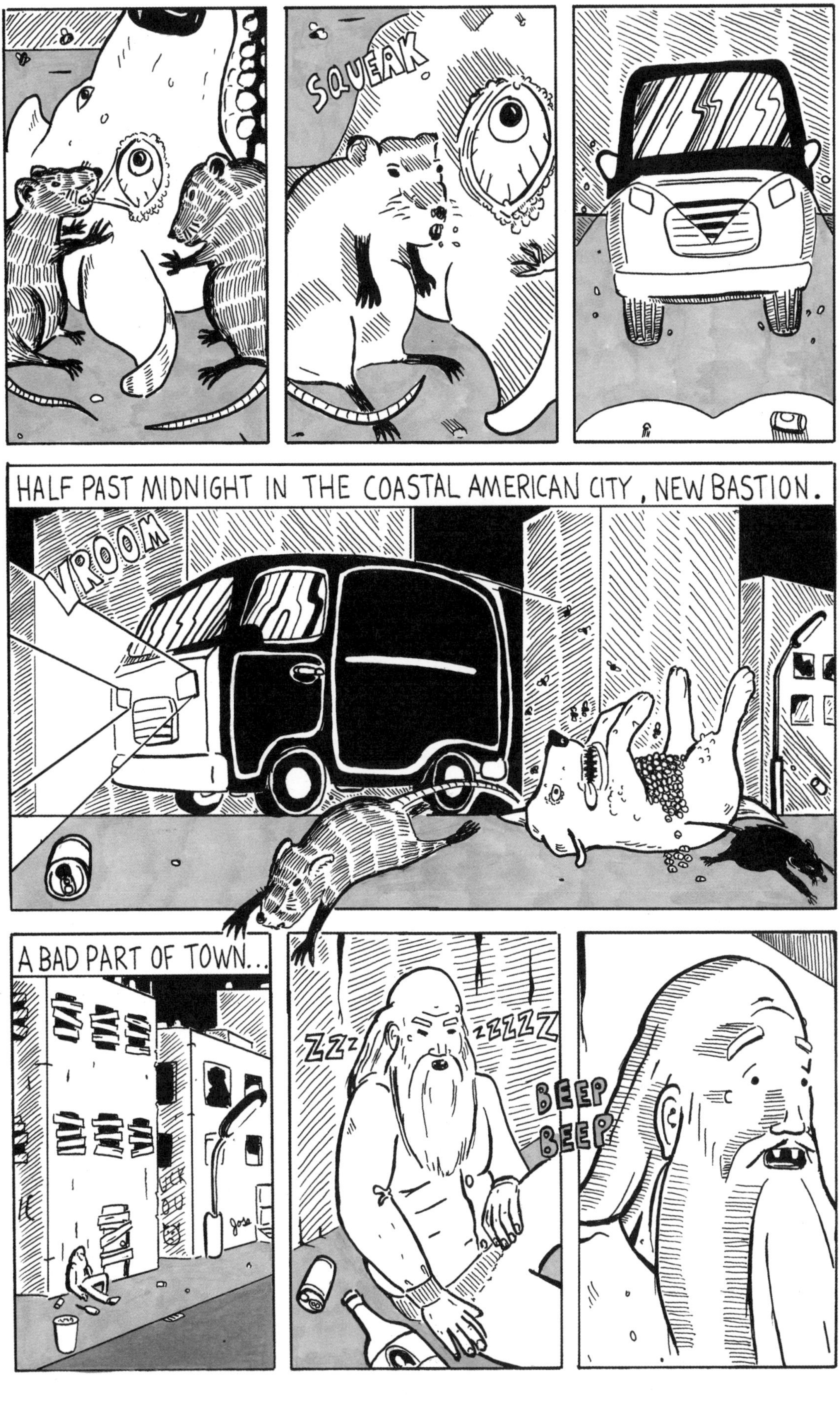
SQUEAK
HALF PAST MIDNIGHT IN THE COASTAL AMERICAN CITY, NEW BASTION.
VROOM
A BAD PART OF TOWN...
ZZz
ZZZZZ
BEEP
BEEP

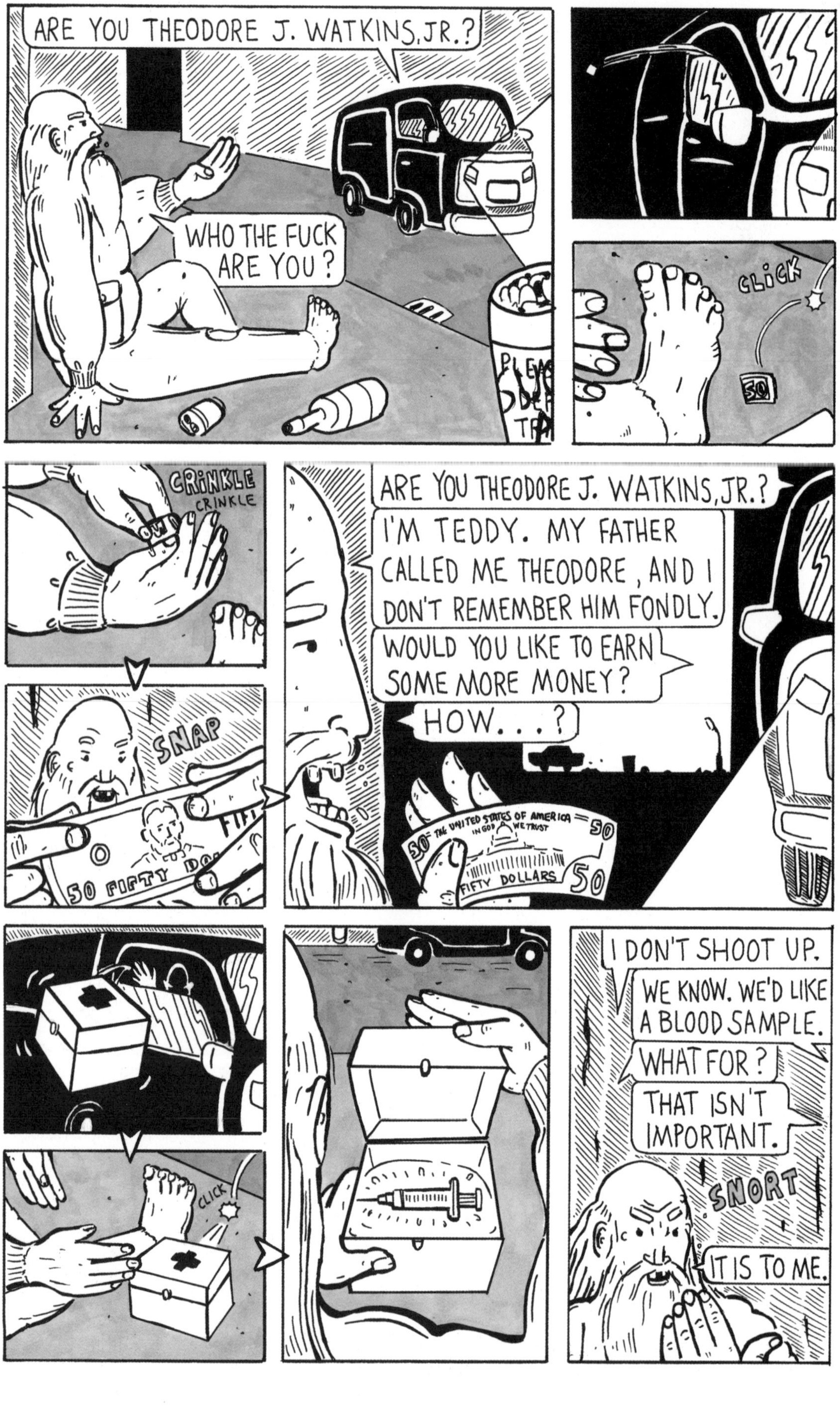
ARE YOU THEODORE J. WATKINS, JR.?
WHO THE FUCK ARE YOU?
CLICK
CRINKLE
CRINKLE
SNAP
50 FIFTY
ARE YOU THEODORE J. WATKINS, JR.?
I'M TEDDY. MY FATHER CALLED ME THEODORE, AND I DON'T REMEMBER HIM FONDLY.
WOULD YOU LIKE TO EARN SOME MORE MONEY?
HOW...?
THE UNITED STATES OF AMERICA
IN GOD WE TRUST
FIFTY DOLLARS
CLICK
I DON'T SHOOT UP.
WE KNOW. WE'D LIKE A BLOOD SAMPLE.
WHAT FOR?
THAT ISN'T IMPORTANT.
SNORT
IT IS TO ME.

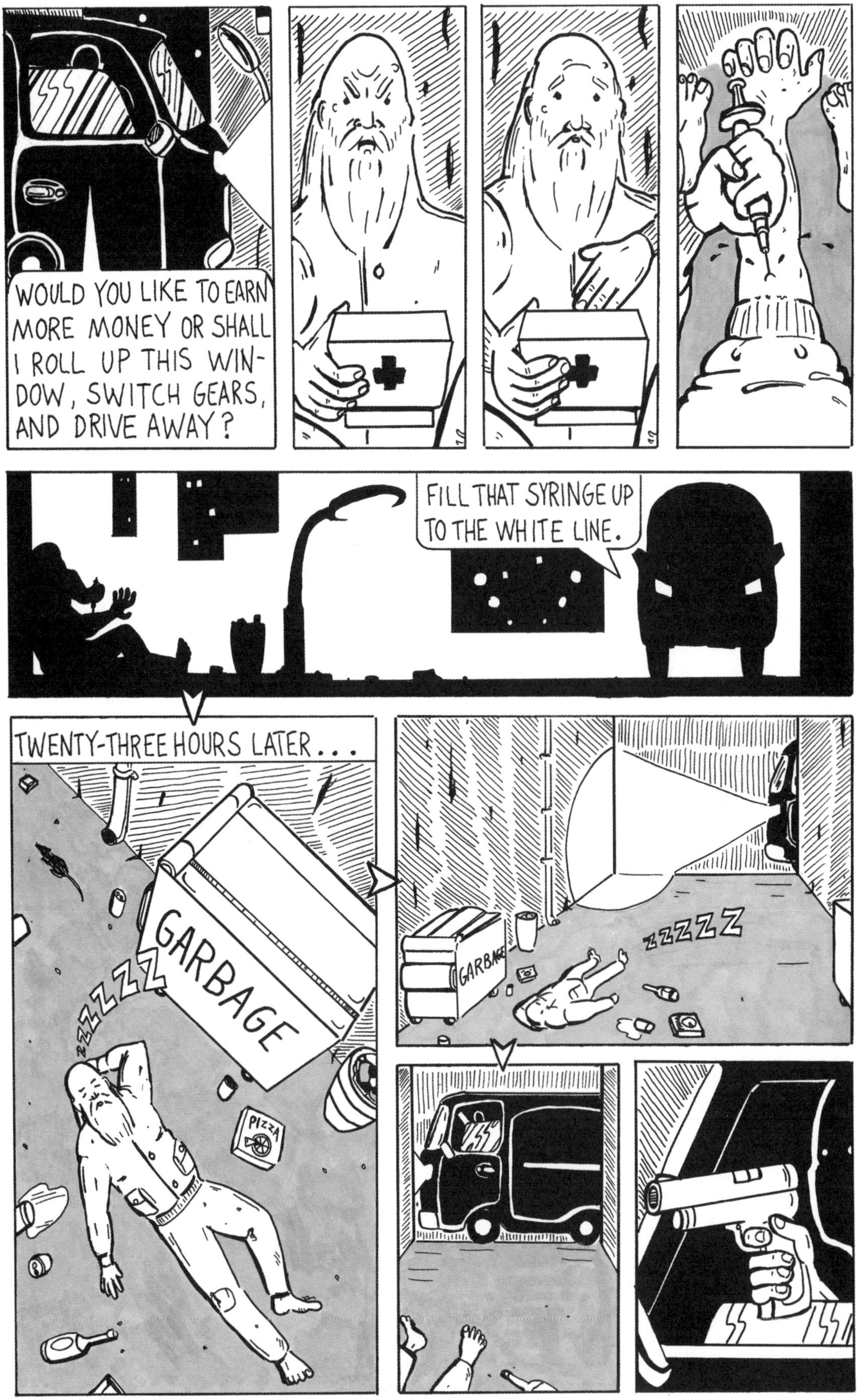
WOULD YOU LIKE TO EARN MORE MONEY OR SHALL I ROLL UP THIS WINDOW, SWITCH GEARS, AND DRIVE AWAY?
FILL THAT SYRINGE UP TO THE WHITE LINE.
TWENTY-THREE HOURS LATER...
GARBAGE
ZZZZZ
PIZZA
GARBAGE
ZZZZZ

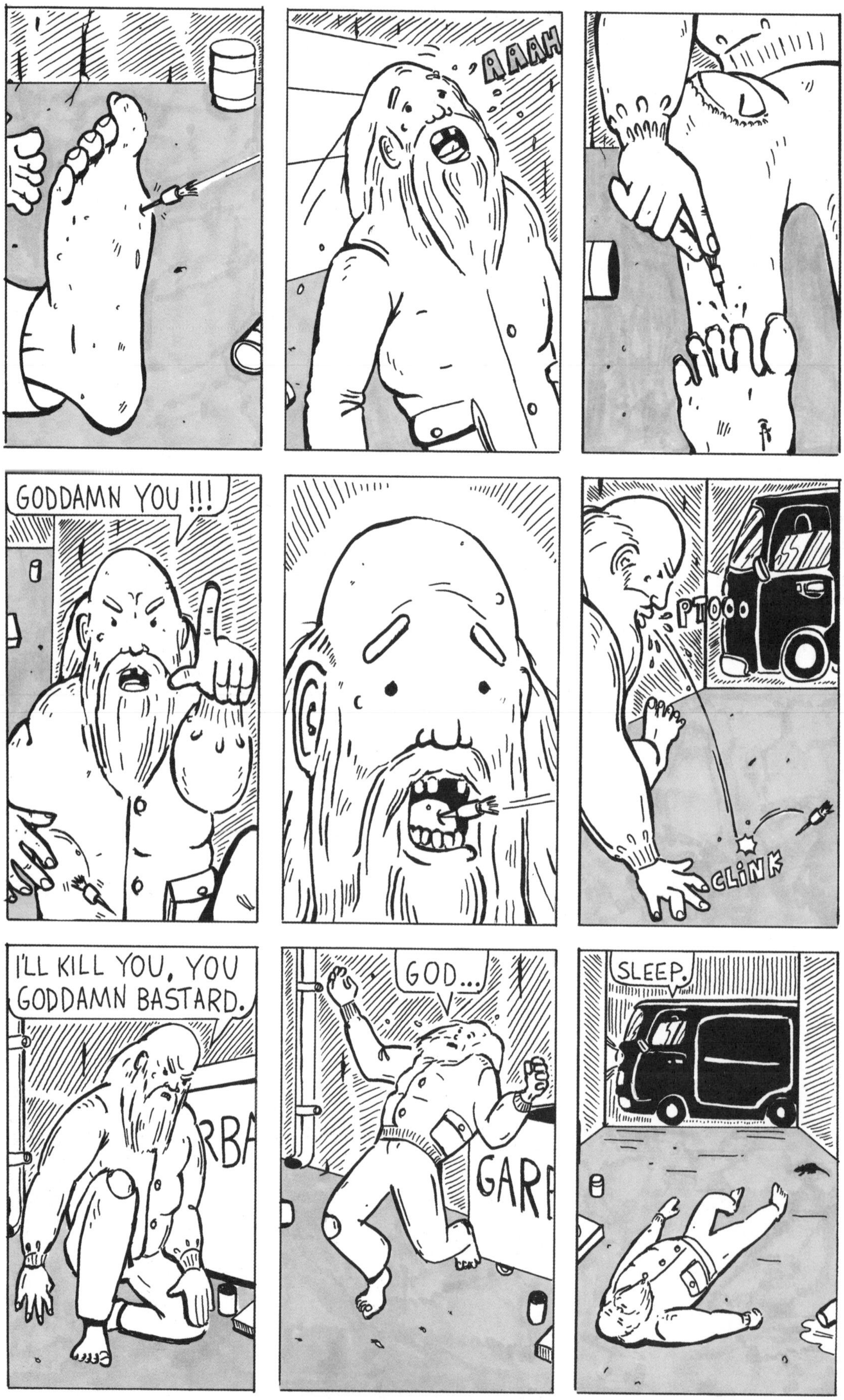
AAAH
GODDAMN YOU !!!
PTOOO
CLINK
I'LL KILL YOU, YOU GODDAMN BASTARD.
RBA
GOD...
GAR
SLEEP.

FIVE DAYS LATER, SOMEWHERE BENEATH NEW BASTION CITY...
ZZZZ
CLICK
YOUR TREMENS HAVE FULLY SUBSIDED...
NO. NO. NO.
YOU WILL BE ANAESTHETIZED BEFORE I COMMENCE.
I AM NOT WITHOUT MERCY.

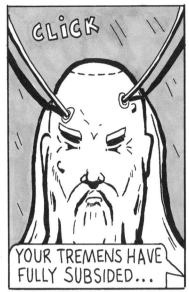

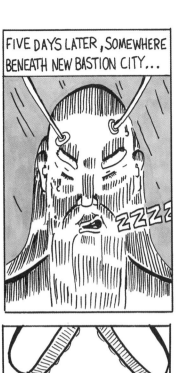

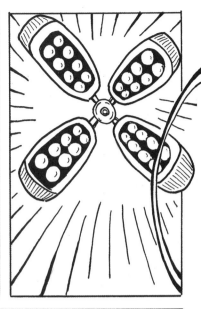

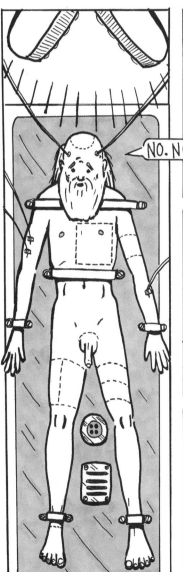

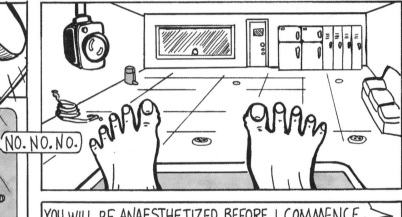

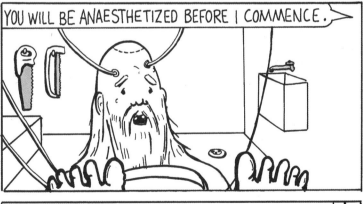

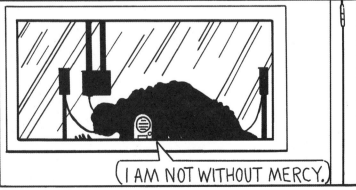

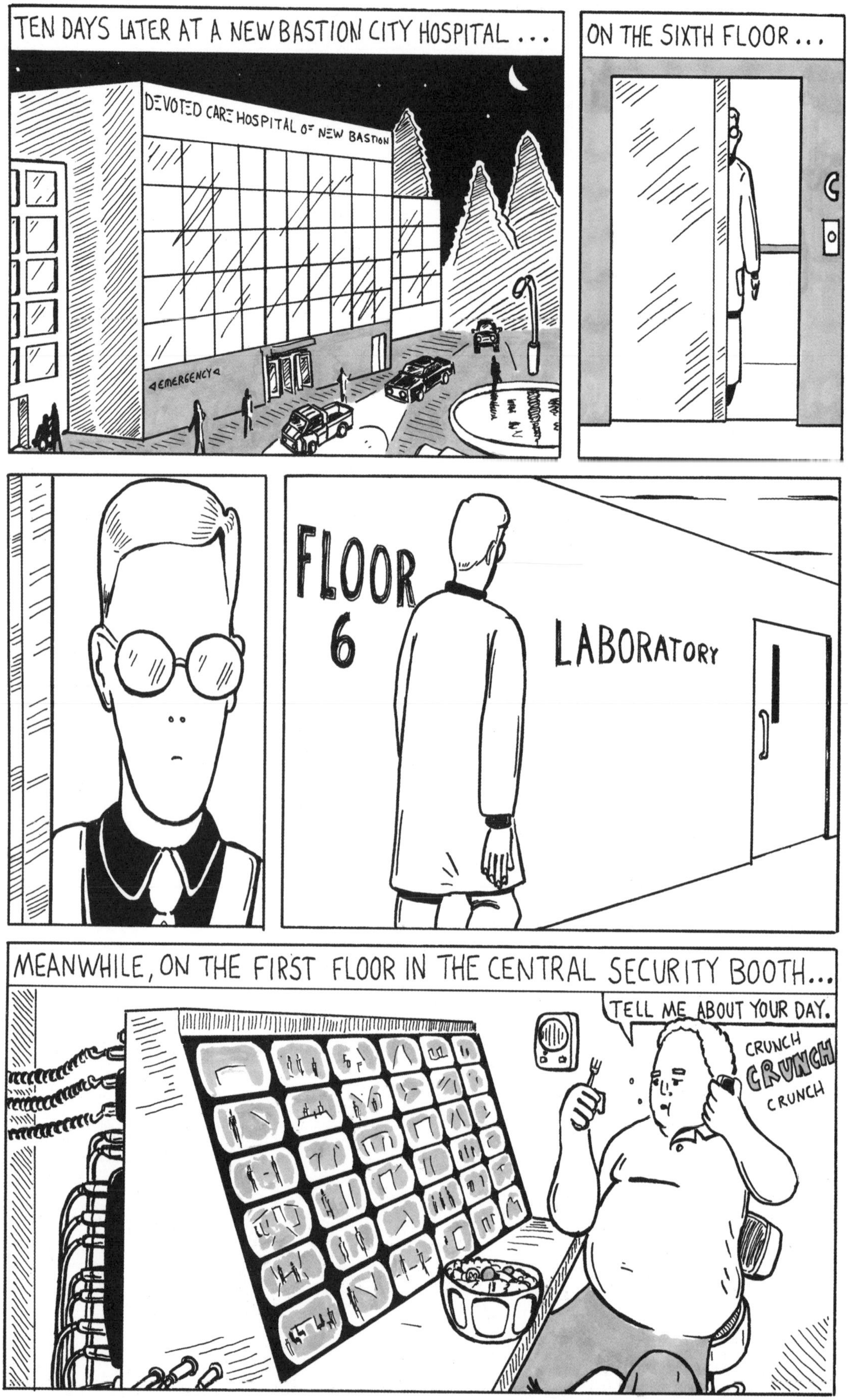
TEN DAYS LATER AT A NEW BASTION CITY HOSPITAL . . .
DEVOTED CARE HOSPITAL OF NEW BASTION
EMERGENCY
ON THE SIXTH FLOOR . . .
FLOOR 6
LABORATORY
MEANWHILE, ON THE FIRST FLOOR IN THE CENTRAL SECURITY BOOTH...
TELL ME ABOUT YOUR DAY.
CRUNCH
CRUNCH
CRUNCH

CRUNCH CRUNCH GRUNCH CRUNCH

C: I'LL WAIT UNTIL AFTER THE CATACLYSM.

CRUNCH CRUNCH GRUNCH CRUNCH

GULP

OKAY.

THIS SALAD'S QUITE GOOD. VERY HEALTHFUL.

C: CONGRATULATIONS.

I BET YOU'D LIKE IT... THERE'S AVOCADO. CAPERS TOO.

MAYBE THEY'RE OLIVES.

C: THIS ISN'T THE MOST RIVETING TOPIC OF CONVERSATION.

HONEY... ALL I'M SAYING IS THAT IT'S HEALTHFUL AND I THINK YOU'D ENJOY IT.

C: YOU'RE THE ONE WHO'S TRYING TO SHED SOME BLUBBER BEFORE YOUR CLASS REUNION, NOT ME.

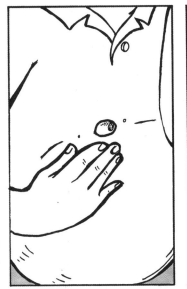

C: NICK....? I DIDN'T MEAN TO OFFEND YOU.

I KNOW THAT YOU MEANT THE WORD BLUBBER COMPLIMENTARILY.

C: DON'T BE SO SENSITIVE.

CRYSTAL, HONEY, YOU KNOW WHAT I'VE NOTICED?

C: WHAT?

INSENSITIVE PEOPLE ARE THE ONES ONLY ONES WHO SAY, 'DON'T BE SO SENSITIVE.'

C: NICK...?

CRUNCH CRUNCH

C: I'M SORRY I SAID THE WORD BLUBBER.

C: ARE YOU SULKING?

A MAN WHOM I DON'T RECOGNIZE IS WHEELING OUR LASER SCALPEL PROTOTYPE FROM THE SURGERY LAB TOWARDS THE ELEVATORS.

C: DEAR, IS—

I HAVE TO GO. NOW.

C: OKAY, OKAY. BUT PLEASE REMEMBER:

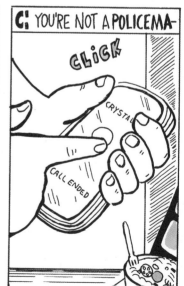

C: YOU'RE NOT A POLICEMA—

CLICK

CRYSTAL

CALL ENDED

8

CLICK
JARED.
NICK?
GET TO THE ELEVATOR BANK. LOOK FOR A MAN IN A SMOCK WHO IS ROLLING AN APPARATUS. CAUCASIAN. GLASSES. GAUNT.
GAUNT?
SKINNY.
GOT IT, BOSS.
ELECTROSHOCK WEAPON
STUNSHOXX
AND YOU?
CLICK
IMMINENT.
C
SECURITY
MEANWHILE, IN ELEVATOR 'C' ON FLOOR SIX...
6
5
6
3
4
L
2

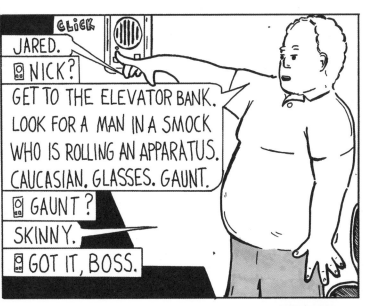

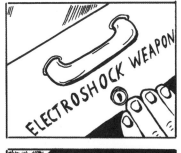

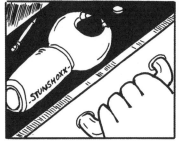

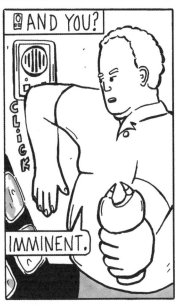

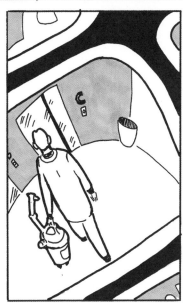

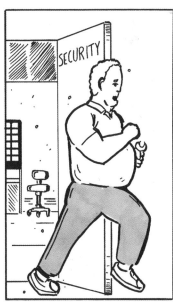

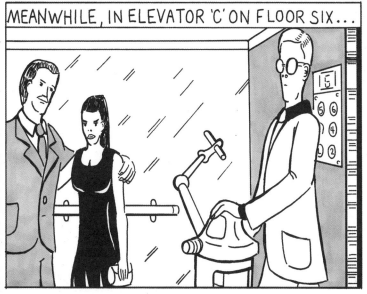

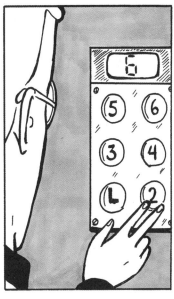

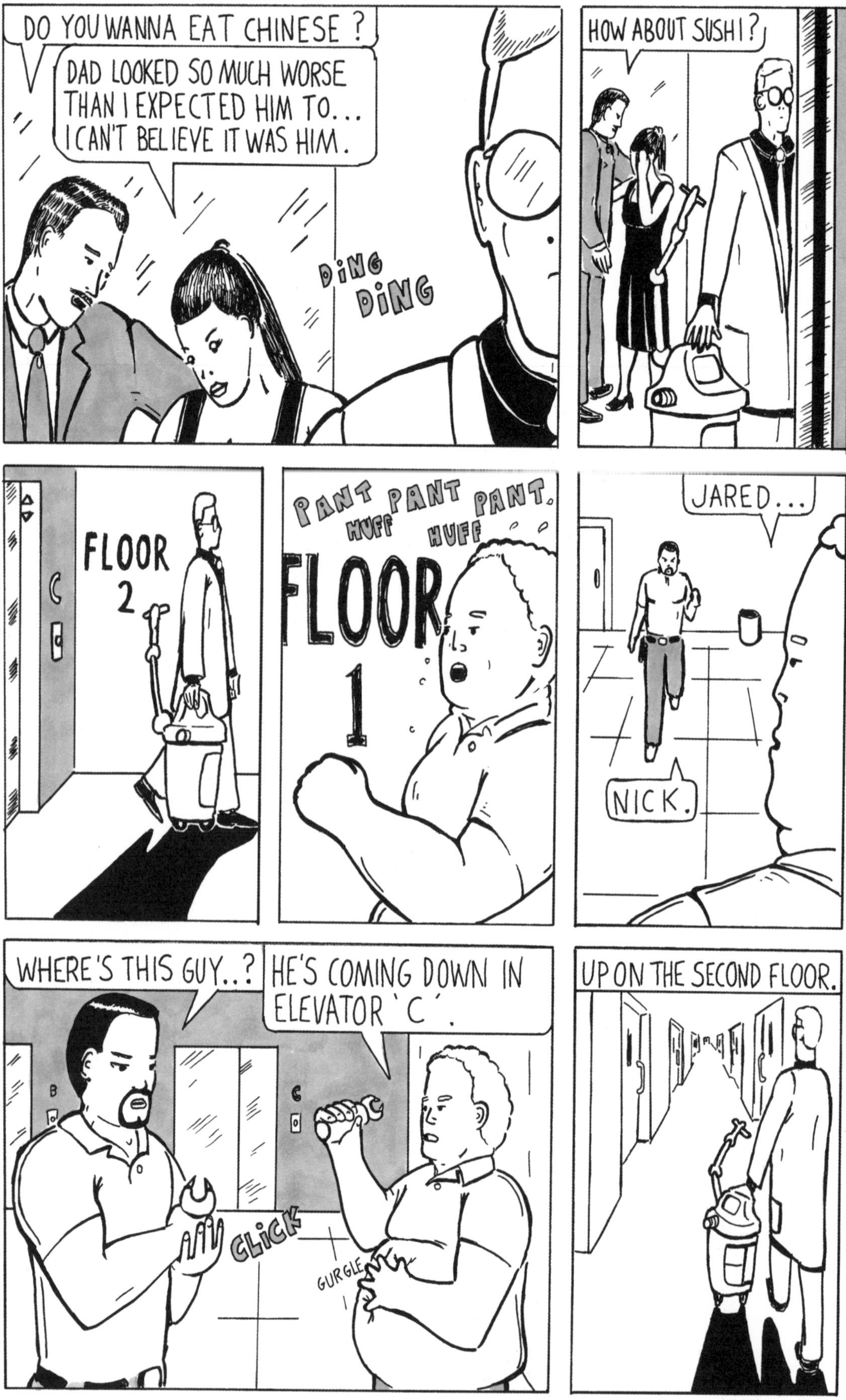
DO YOU WANNA EAT CHINESE ?
DAD LOOKED SO MUCH WORSE THAN I EXPECTED HIM TO... I CAN'T BELIEVE IT WAS HIM.
DING DING
HOW ABOUT SUSHI?
FLOOR 2
PANT PANT PANT.
HUFF HUFF
FLOOR 1
JARED...
NICK.
WHERE'S THIS GUY..?
HE'S COMING DOWN IN ELEVATOR 'C'.
CLICK
GURGLE
UP ON THE SECOND FLOOR.

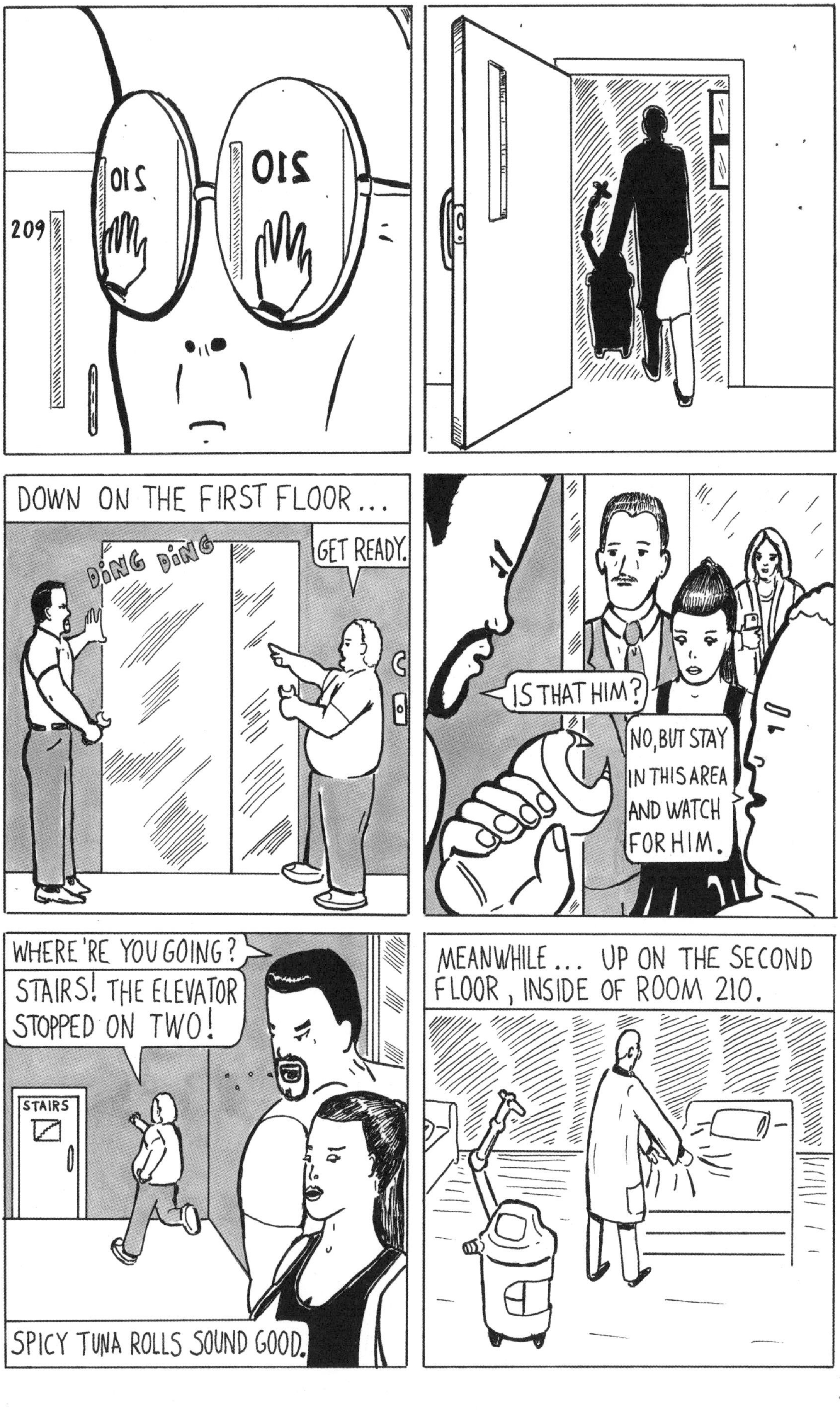
209
DOWN ON THE FIRST FLOOR...
DING DING
GET READY.
IS THAT HIM?
NO, BUT STAY IN THIS AREA AND WATCH FOR HIM.
WHERE'RE YOU GOING?
STAIRS! THE ELEVATOR STOPPED ON TWO!
STAIRS
SPICY TUNA ROLLS SOUND GOOD.
MEANWHILE... UP ON THE SECOND FLOOR, INSIDE OF ROOM 210.

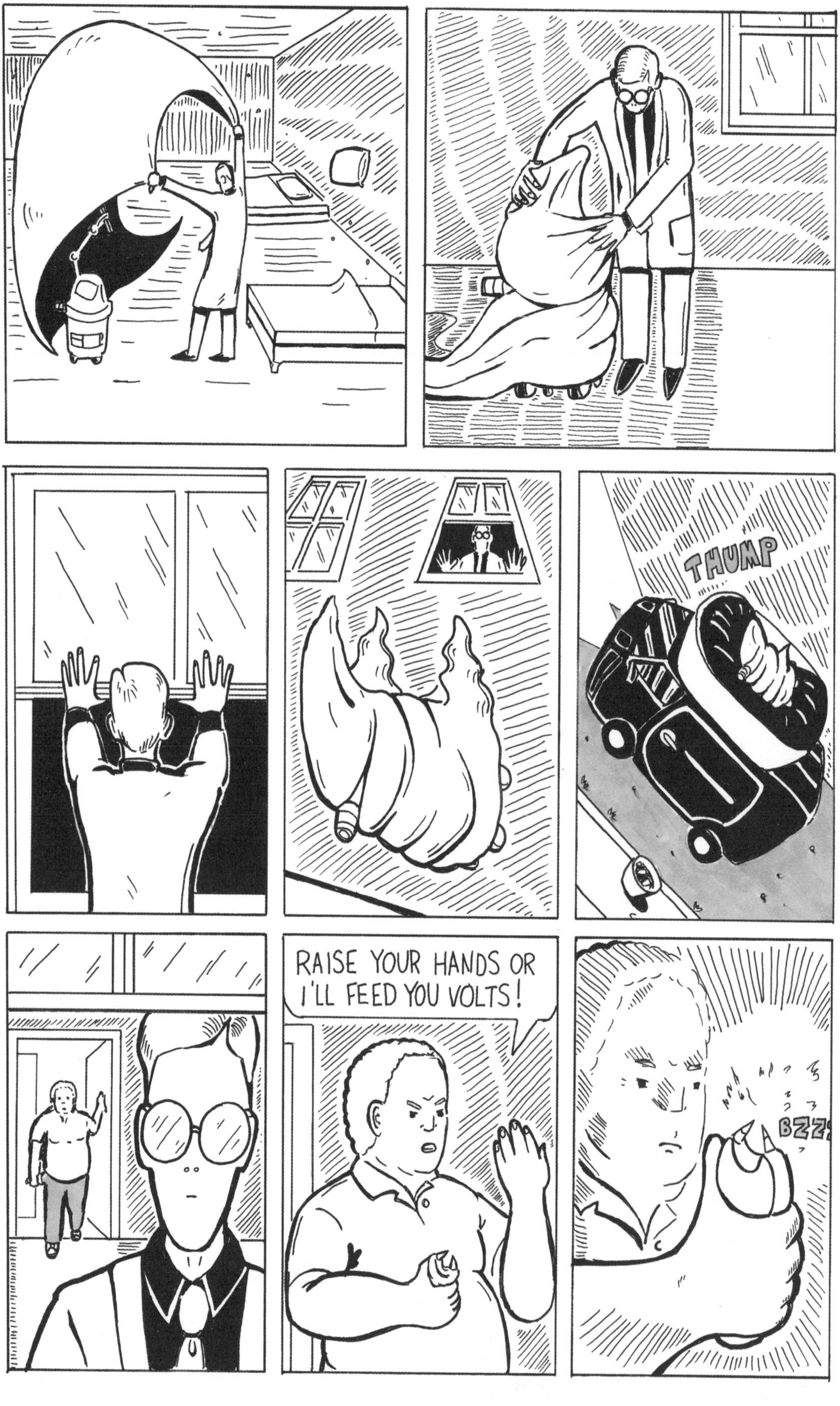
THUMP
RAISE YOUR HANDS OR I'LL FEED YOU VOLTS!
BZZ

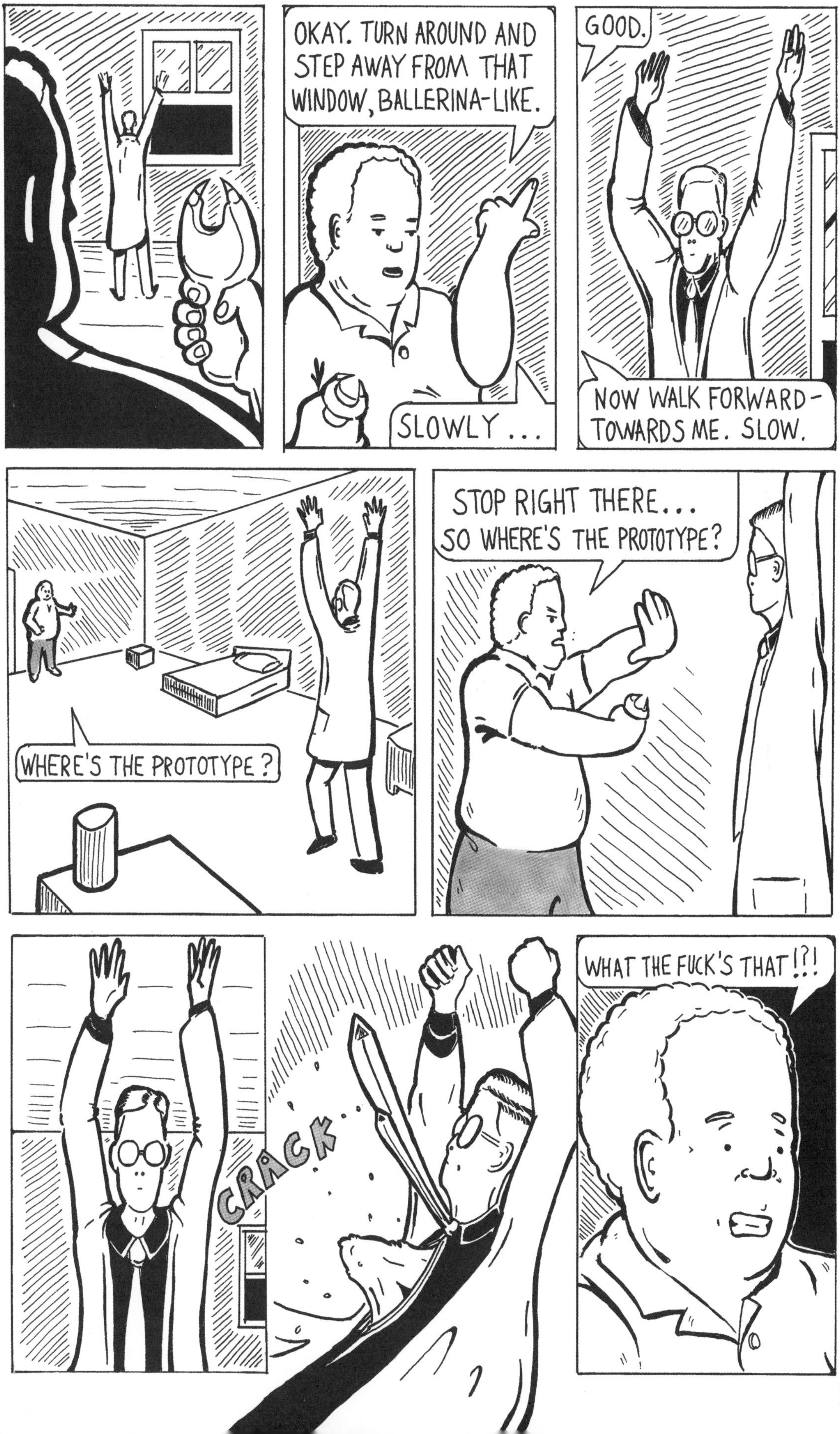
OKAY. TURN AROUND AND STEP AWAY FROM THAT WINDOW, BALLERINA-LIKE.
SLOWLY...
GOOD.
NOW WALK FORWARD- TOWARDS ME. SLOW.
WHERE'S THE PROTOTYPE?
STOP RIGHT THERE... SO WHERE'S THE PROTOTYPE?
CRACK
WHAT THE FUCK'S THAT!?!

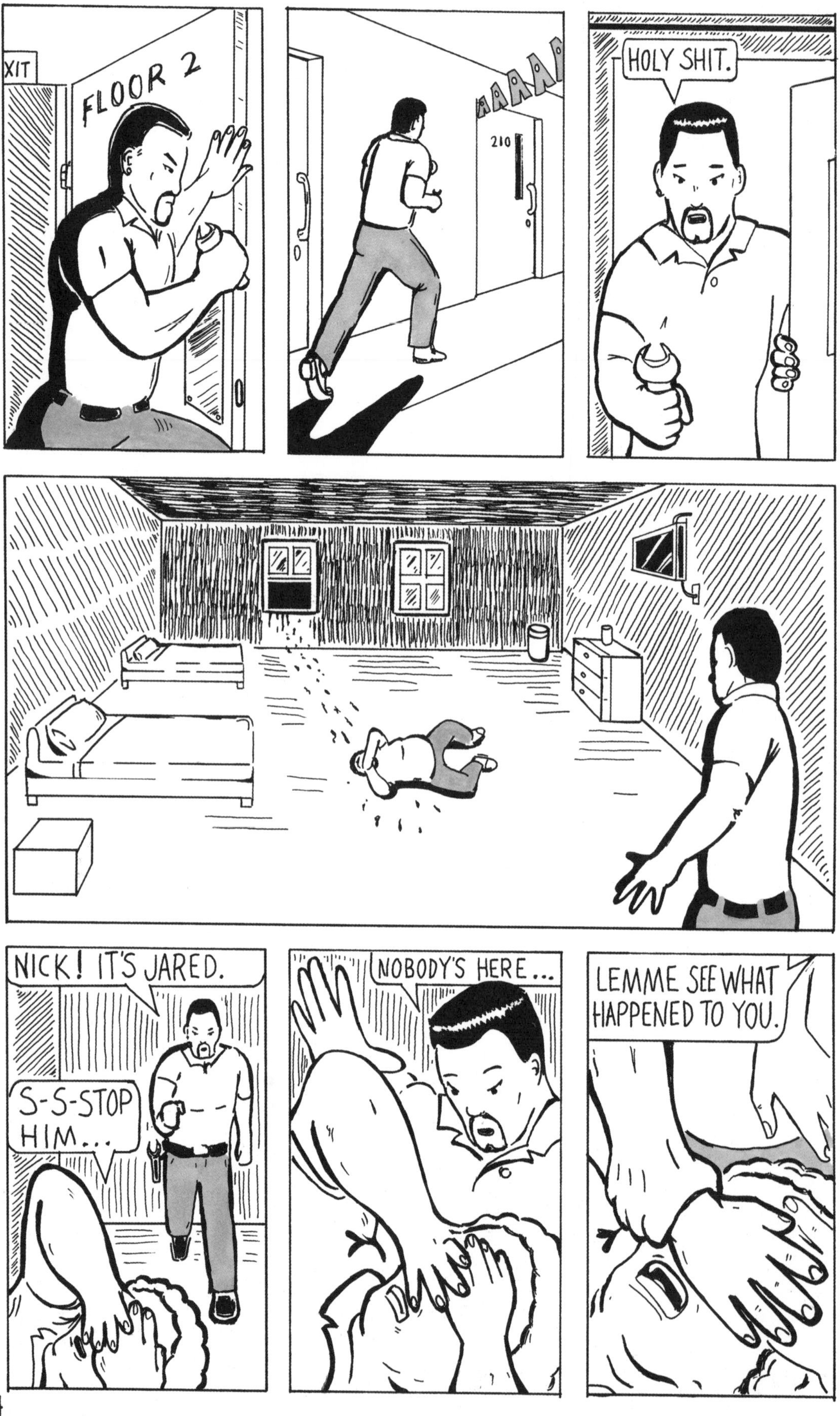
XIT
FLOOR 2
AAAAA
210
HOLY SHIT.
NICK! IT'S JARED.
S-S-STOP HIM...
NOBODY'S HERE...
LEMME SEE WHAT HAPPENED TO YOU.

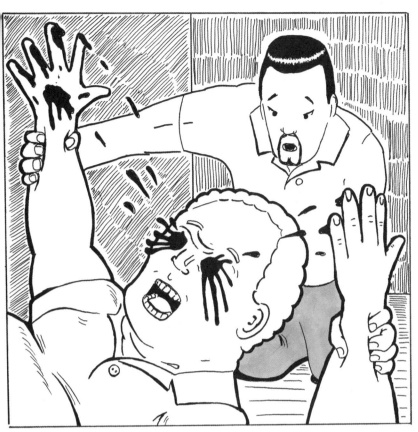

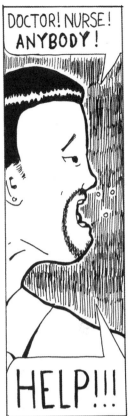

DOCTOR! NURSE! ANYBODY!

HELP!!!

ONE YEAR LATER AT THE DEVOTED CARE HOSPITAL OF NEW BASTION. NOON.

DEVOTED CARE HOSPITAL OF

◁ EMERGENCY ◁

JARED LEUNG IS NOW THE HEAD OF HOSPITAL SECURITY . . .

HIS WEAPON HAS ALSO BEEN UPGRADED.

15

WE FONDLY REMEMBER NICHOLAS DUGAN

$15,000 CASH REW[ARD] FOR HELPFU[L] INFORMATIO[N] REGARDING THE DEATH OF SECURITY NICK DUGAN[...] PLEASE CAL[L]

ON THE FIFTH FLOOR...

TOMMY? ARE YOU STILL THERE?

YEAH. I WAS JUST DISTRACTED BY THE SMELL OF AMMONIA. I'LL CALL YOU BACK LATER.

OKAY. BYE.

ADIOS.

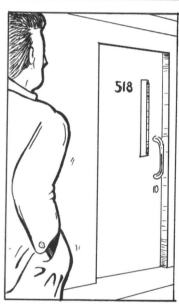

518

LEO.

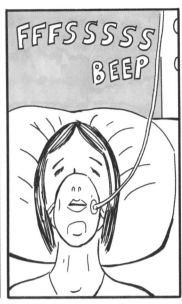

FFFSSSSS BEEP

IS THERE A LUNAR ECLIPSE TODAY? OR MAYBE THAT SHITTY COMET IS FLYING AROUND?

WHAT'RE YOU TALKING ABOUT?

I'M TRYING TO FIGURE OUT WHAT ASTRONOMICAL OCCURENCE COMPELLED YOU TO FINALLY VISIT OUR COMATOSE SISTER.

IT HASN'T BEEN THAT LONG.

BEEP

WELL... MAYBE YOU'RE RIGHT — THE LAST TIME I SAW YOU, YOUR SCALP HAD MORE THAN SIX HAIRS.

EAT MANURE.

AND YOU DIDN'T LOOK PREGNANT.

DROWN IN FECES.

17

SO WE'RE JUST GONNA STAND IN THIS ROOM WITH LILLIAN AND FLING INSULTS?

MAYBE SHE'LL COME OUT OF HER COMA AND TELL US TO SHUT THE HELL UP.

BEEP

I WISH.

FFSSSSSS

YEAH.

BEEP

ANY CHANGES?

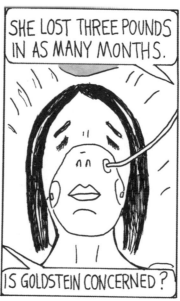

SHE LOST THREE POUNDS IN AS MANY MONTHS.

IS GOLDSTEIN CONCERNED?

NOT ESPECIALLY.

BEEP

THEY'RE STILL DOING HER PHYSICAL THERAPY? MOVING THOSE SKINNY LIMBS AROUND?

WE HAVEN'T GIVEN UP.

BEEP

NONE OF THE NURSES STOLE HER CHARM BRACELET...

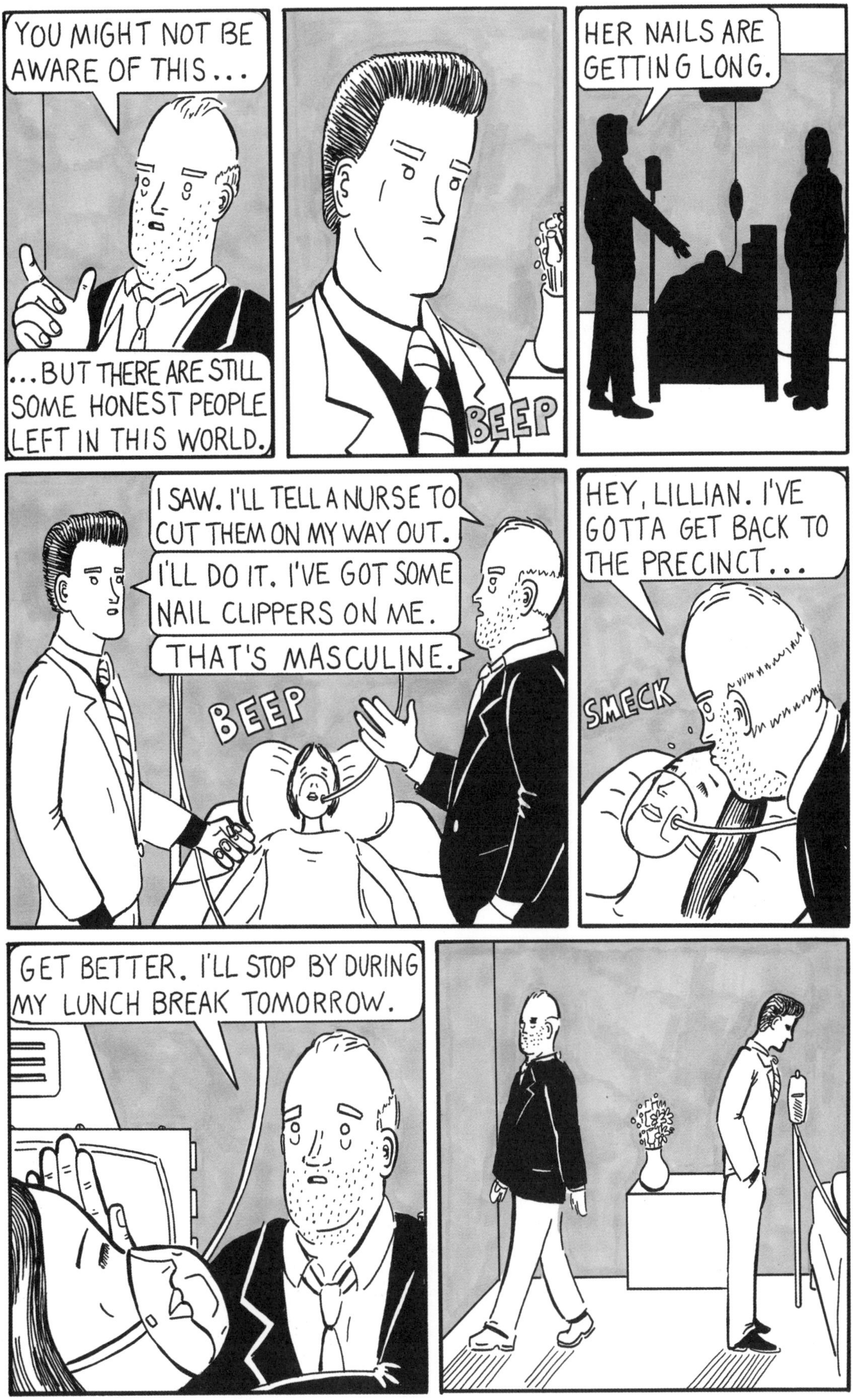
YOU MIGHT NOT BE AWARE OF THIS...
...BUT THERE ARE STILL SOME HONEST PEOPLE LEFT IN THIS WORLD.
BEEP
HER NAILS ARE GETTING LONG.
I SAW. I'LL TELL A NURSE TO CUT THEM ON MY WAY OUT.
I'LL DO IT. I'VE GOT SOME NAIL CLIPPERS ON ME.
THAT'S MASCULINE.
BEEP
HEY, LILLIAN. I'VE GOTTA GET BACK TO THE PRECINCT...
SMECK
GET BETTER. I'LL STOP BY DURING MY LUNCH BREAK TOMORROW.

YOU'VE GOT ANYTHING TO SAY ABOUT A GUY CALLED MANUEL "PLATINO" RODRIGUEZ?

NEVER HEARD OF HIM.

PLATINO DISTRIBUTED PILLS. BAD ONES. THE KIND THAT CONTAIN MORE GRAMS OF CHALK, PLASTER, AND POISON THAN HAPPY STUFF.

I DON'T KNOW HIM.

BEEP

HE'S IN JAIL AND GOING TO PRISON.

YOUR NAME AND NUMBER WERE ON HIS CELLPHONE.

MY BUSINESS IS LEGAL.

YOU'RE ADORABLE.

CLICK

SORRY IT'S BEEN SO LONG...

BEEP

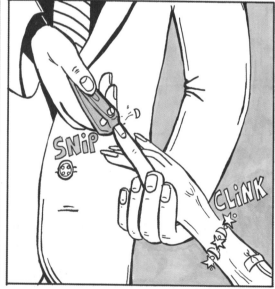

SNIP

CLINK

20

THREE WEEKS LATER, IN A NEW BASTION NEIGHBORHOOD THAT IS NEITHER GOOD NOR BAD...

FINE'S discount gourmet GROCERY

ITALIAN STYLE PIZZA

DETECTIVE LEONARD DRISCOLL SITS DOWN TO A LATE DINNER...

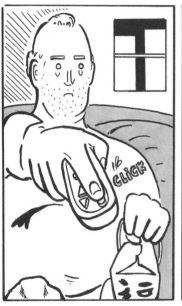
CLICK

—BEEN MISSING SINCE LAST MONTH.

NBLN LATE REPORT LIVE

HE DISAPPEARED AFTER THAT BIG STORM WE HAD.

LIVE

AND SO WHY DO YOU BELIEVE THAT MR. PORTSMITH HAS BEEN ABDUCTED?

I FOUND HIS STASH.

AIN'T NO WAY THAT HE'D ABANDON HIS STUFF LIKE THAT.

AND AFTER TEDDY WAS FOUND ALL CUT UP AND DEAD INSIDE OF A DUMPSTER LAST YEAR—

—I DECIDED TO GO OVER AND TELL THE COPS MY SUSPICIONS.

NBL

FILE PHOTO
DECEASED

THEODORE J. WATKINS, JR.
AKA "TEDDY"

21

DO YOU FEEL THAT THE POLICE ARE SENSITIVE TO THE NEEDS AND SAFETY OF THE HOMELESS—

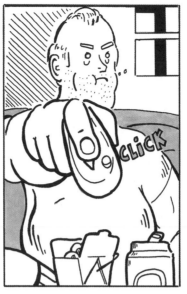

CLICK

OKAY CLASS—

STRETCH THOSE QUADS!

THE VAST CITY OF NEW BASTION DEVOURS ANOTHER WEEK. IT IS MIDNIGHT, AND ILLICIT BUSINESSMAN TOMMY DRISCOLL CANNOT FALL ASLEEP...

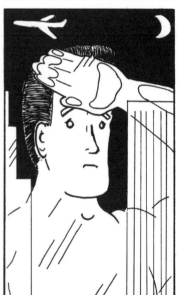

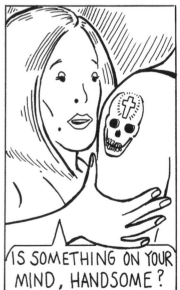

IS SOMETHING ON YOUR MIND, HANDSOME?

22

I'M JUST THINKING ABOUT MY SISTER...

IS SHE DOING ANY BETTER?

I HAVEN'T SEEN HER IN THREE WEEKS.

FOUR, ACTUALLY...

IT'S BEEN SO LONG SINCE THAT BUS HIT HER ... AND IT'S HARD TO REMAIN HOPEFUL.

BUT I SHOULD GO AND SEE HER.

YOU SHOULD. EVEN IF SHE CAN'T HEAR YOU, CONSCIOUSLY, TALKING TO HER MIGHT HELP—LIKE HOW IT'S SUPPOSED TO WORK WITH PLANTS.

I COULD GO WITH YOU IF YOU WANT...

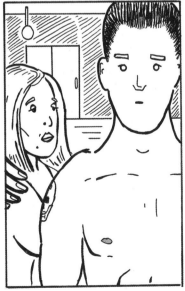

IF YOU WANNA BE ALONE RIGHT NOW, I CAN GO HOME...

23

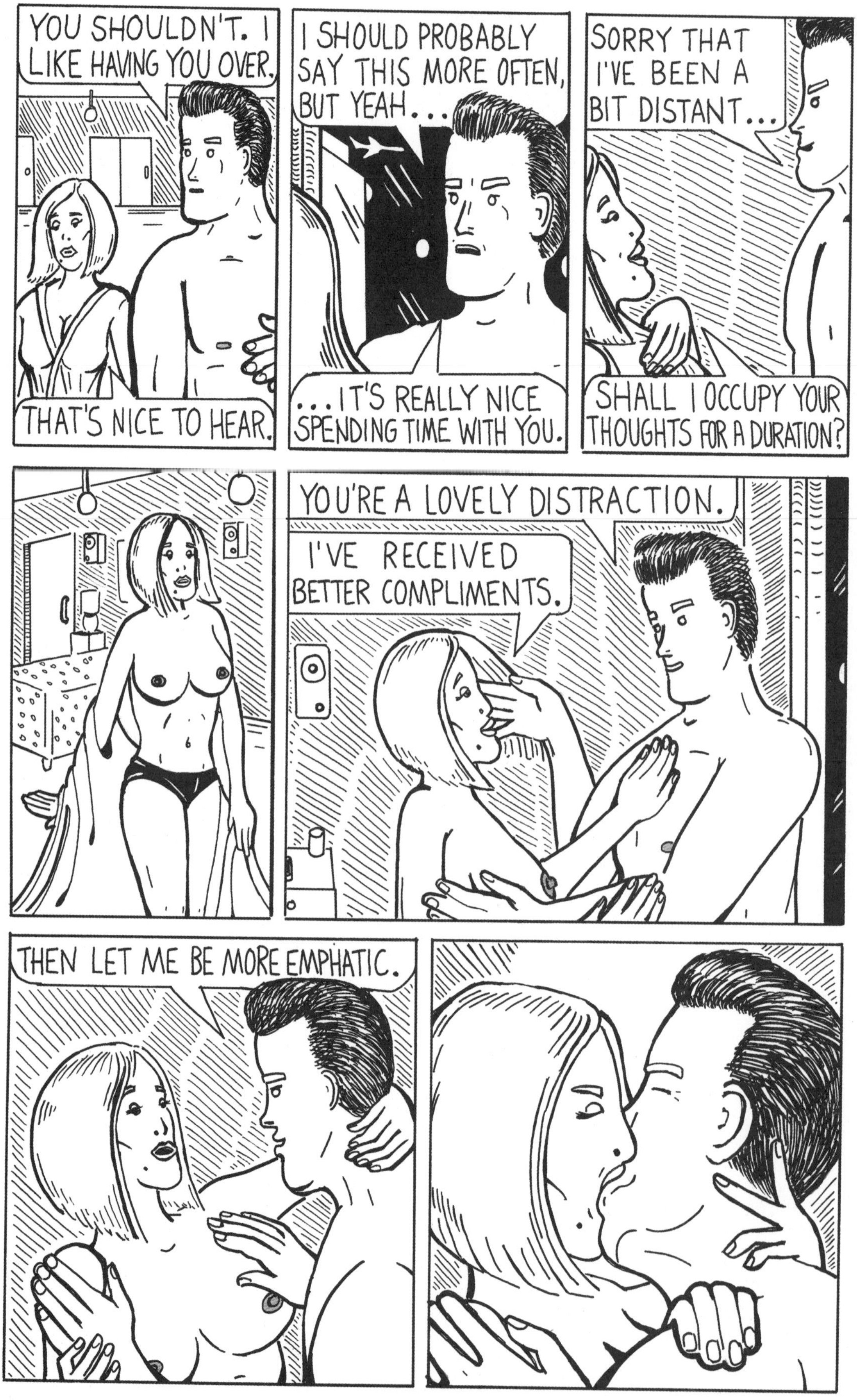
YOU SHOULDN'T. I LIKE HAVING YOU OVER.
THAT'S NICE TO HEAR.
I SHOULD PROBABLY SAY THIS MORE OFTEN, BUT YEAH...
...IT'S REALLY NICE SPENDING TIME WITH YOU.
SORRY THAT I'VE BEEN A BIT DISTANT...
SHALL I OCCUPY YOUR THOUGHTS FOR A DURATION?
YOU'RE A LOVELY DISTRACTION.
I'VE RECEIVED BETTER COMPLIMENTS.
THEN LET ME BE MORE EMPHATIC.

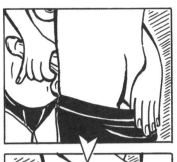

ONE HOUR LATER AT THE DEVOTED CARE HOSPITAL...

THE HEAD OF SECURITY IS WORKING THE LATE SHIFT IN THE CONTROL BOOTH...

CLICK

WILLIAMS...?

YEAH BOSS?

THERE'S A FIGHT IN THE E.R.

I'M ON MY WAY. SEE YOU THERE.

EMERGENCY ROOM

WHY WOULD I STEAL YOUR CELLPHONE?

STAFF ONLY

BLACK PEOPLE RESENT ME BECAUSE I AM WHITE AND BEAUTIFUL!

25

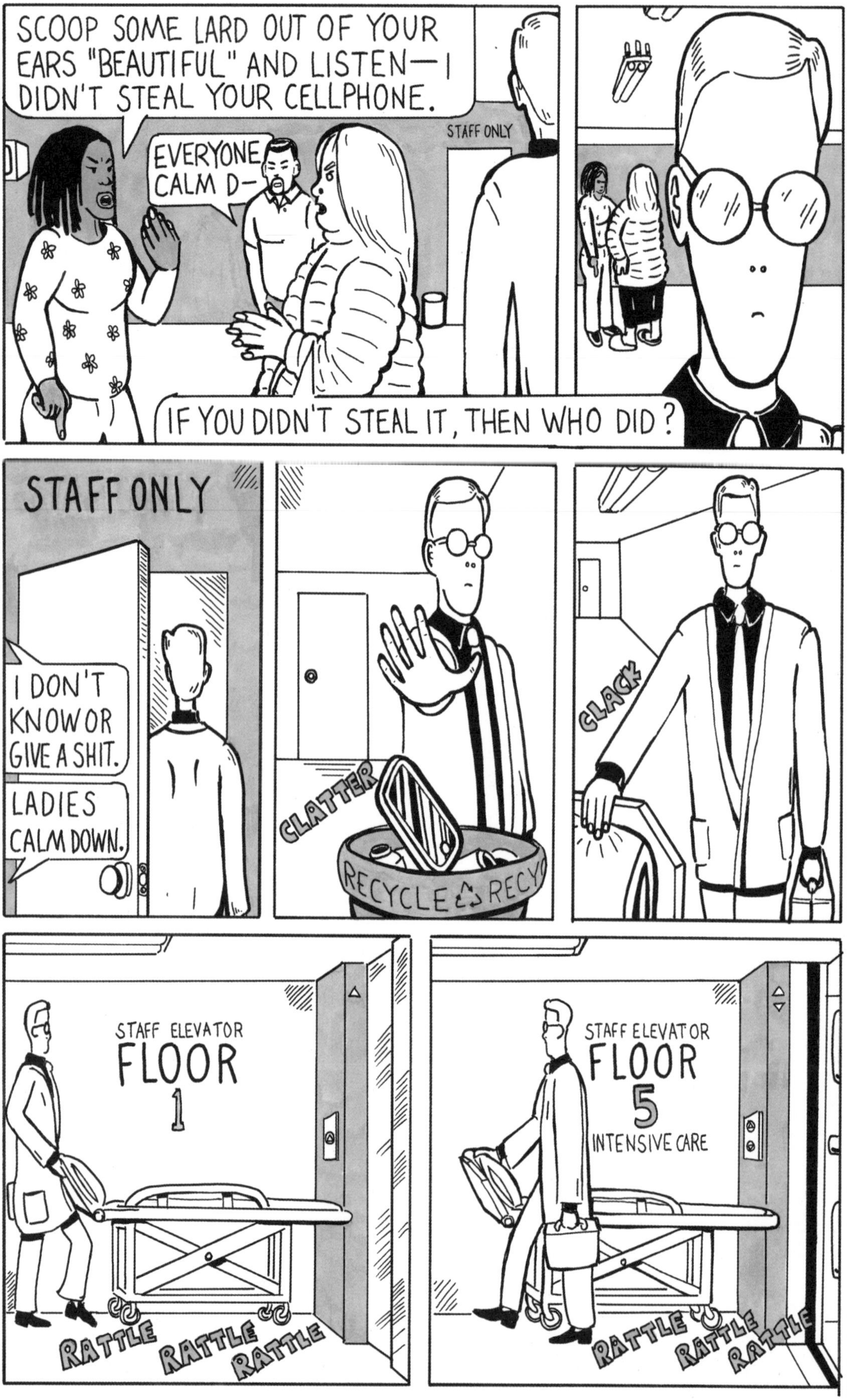
SCOOP SOME LARD OUT OF YOUR EARS "BEAUTIFUL" AND LISTEN—I DIDN'T STEAL YOUR CELLPHONE.
EVERYONE CALM D—
STAFF ONLY
IF YOU DIDN'T STEAL IT, THEN WHO DID?
STAFF ONLY
I DON'T KNOW OR GIVE A SHIT.
LADIES CALM DOWN.
CLATTER
RECYCLE RECY
CLACK
STAFF ELEVATOR
FLOOR
1
RATTLE
RATTLE
RATTLE
STAFF ELEVATOR
FLOOR
5
INTENSIVE CARE
RATTLE
RATTLE
RATTLE

518
520
RATTLE
RATTLE
RATTLE
CLICK
RATTLE
RATTLE
RATTLE
BEEP
SNAP
RIP
MEDICAL GAUZE
SQUEEZE RESPIRATOR
FSSS
518
FSSSSSS
520
RATTLE
RATTLE
RATTLE

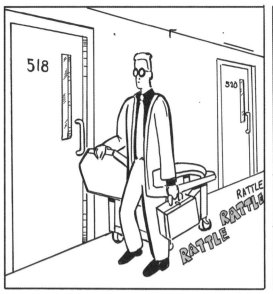

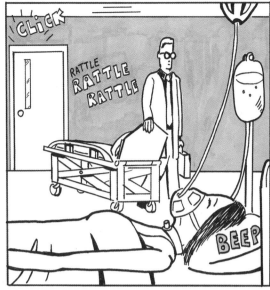

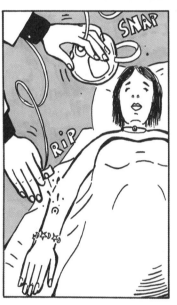

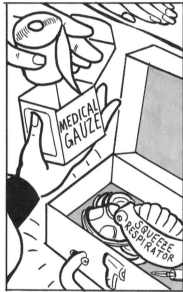

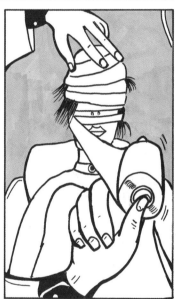

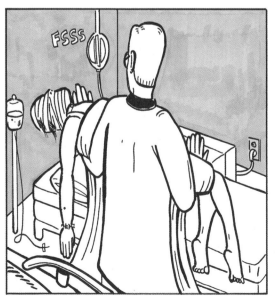

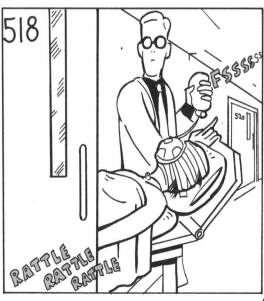

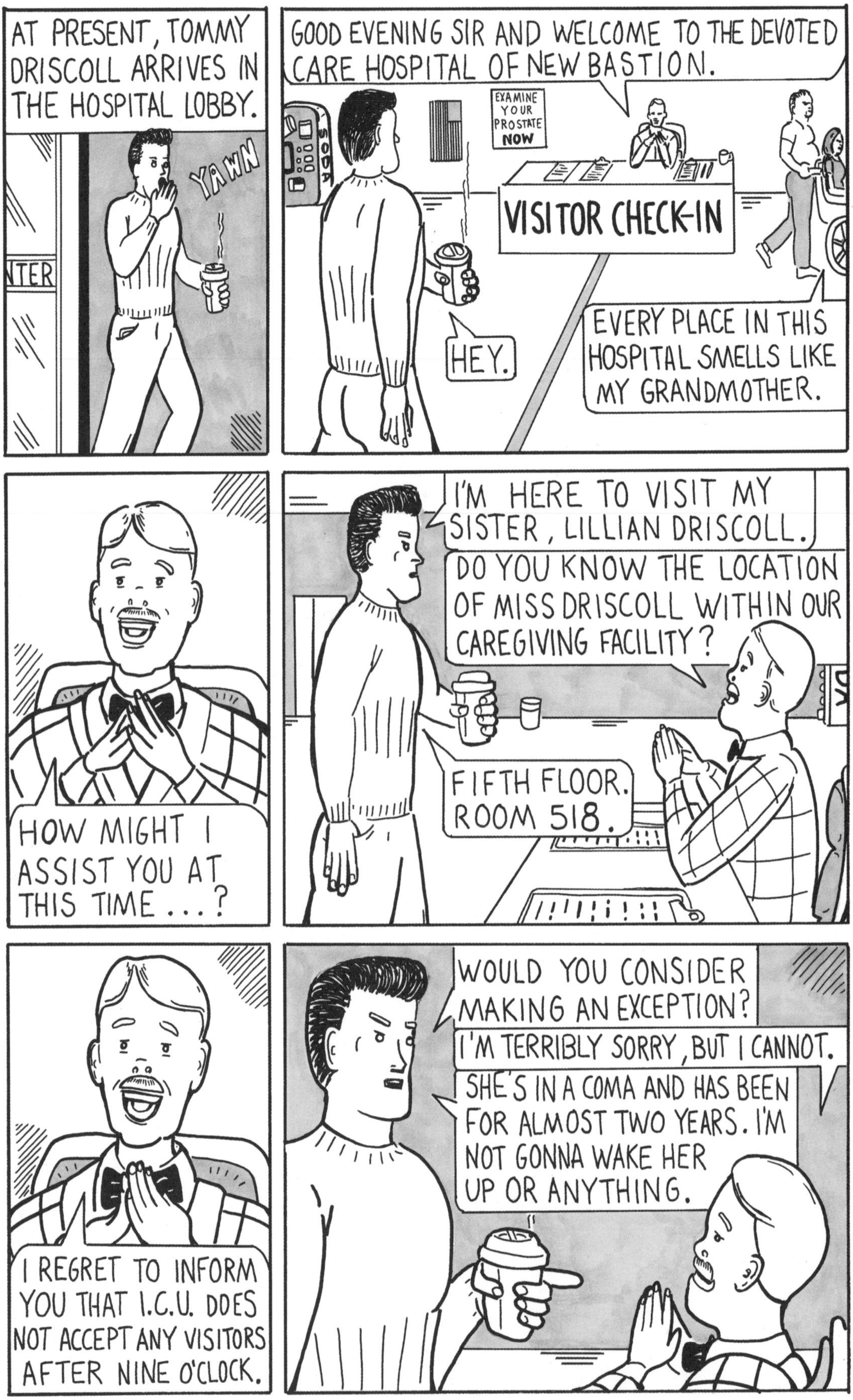
AT PRESENT, TOMMY DRISCOLL ARRIVES IN THE HOSPITAL LOBBY.
YAWN
NTER
GOOD EVENING SIR AND WELCOME TO THE DEVOTED CARE HOSPITAL OF NEW BASTION.
EXAMINE YOUR PROSTATE NOW
SODA
VISITOR CHECK-IN
HEY.
EVERY PLACE IN THIS HOSPITAL SMELLS LIKE MY GRANDMOTHER.
HOW MIGHT I ASSIST YOU AT THIS TIME...?
I'M HERE TO VISIT MY SISTER, LILLIAN DRISCOLL.
DO YOU KNOW THE LOCATION OF MISS DRISCOLL WITHIN OUR CAREGIVING FACILITY?
FIFTH FLOOR. ROOM 518.
I REGRET TO INFORM YOU THAT I.C.U. DOES NOT ACCEPT ANY VISITORS AFTER NINE O'CLOCK.
WOULD YOU CONSIDER MAKING AN EXCEPTION?
I'M TERRIBLY SORRY, BUT I CANNOT.
SHE'S IN A COMA AND HAS BEEN FOR ALMOST TWO YEARS. I'M NOT GONNA WAKE HER UP OR ANYTHING.

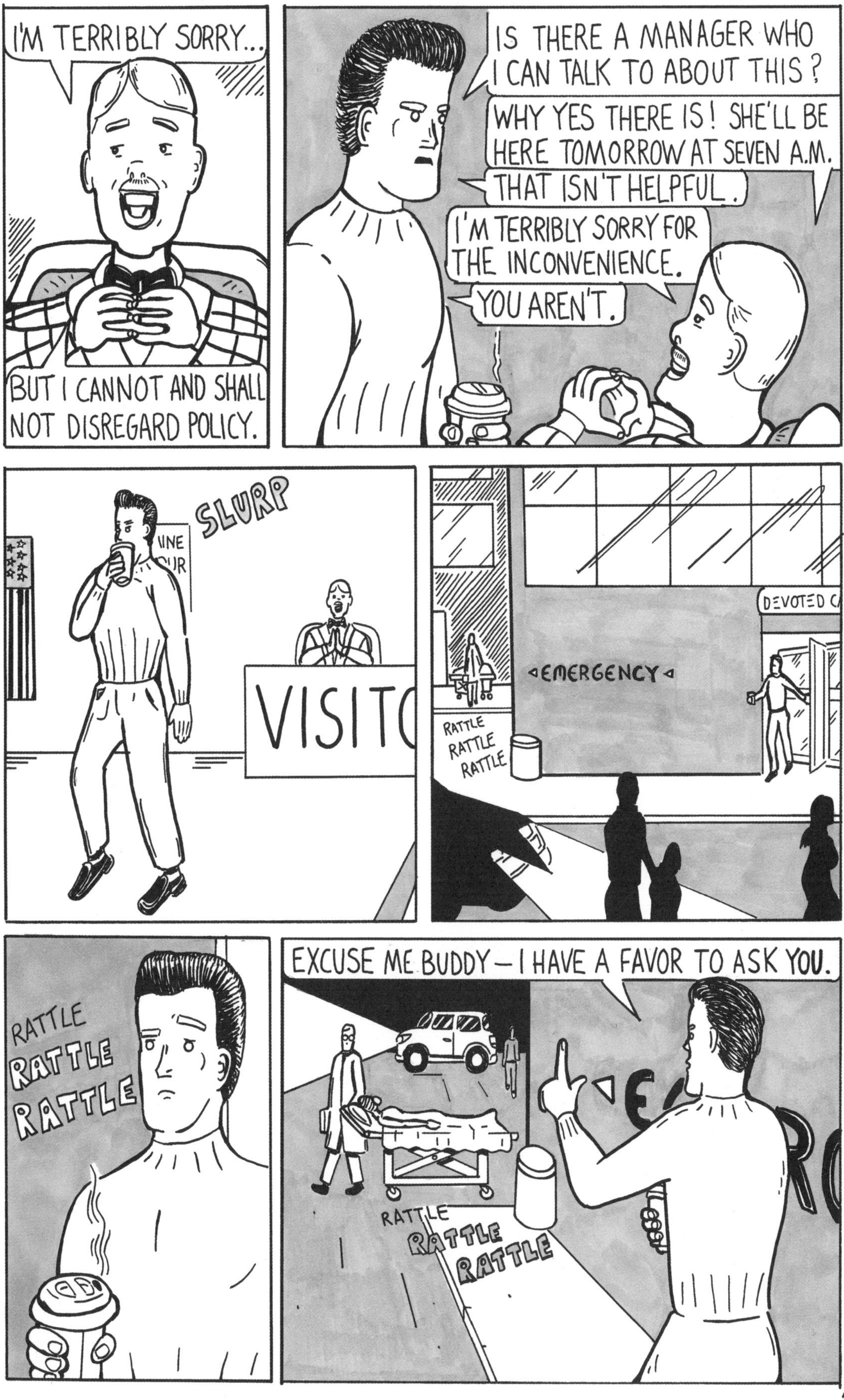
I'M TERRIBLY SORRY...
BUT I CANNOT AND SHALL NOT DISREGARD POLICY.
IS THERE A MANAGER WHO I CAN TALK TO ABOUT THIS?
WHY YES THERE IS! SHE'LL BE HERE TOMORROW AT SEVEN A.M.
THAT ISN'T HELPFUL.
I'M TERRIBLY SORRY FOR THE INCONVENIENCE.
YOU AREN'T.
SLURP
VISITO
DEVOTED C
EMERGENCY
RATTLE RATTLE RATTLE
RATTLE RATTLE RATTLE
EXCUSE ME BUDDY — I HAVE A FAVOR TO ASK YOU.
RATTLE RATTLE RATTLE

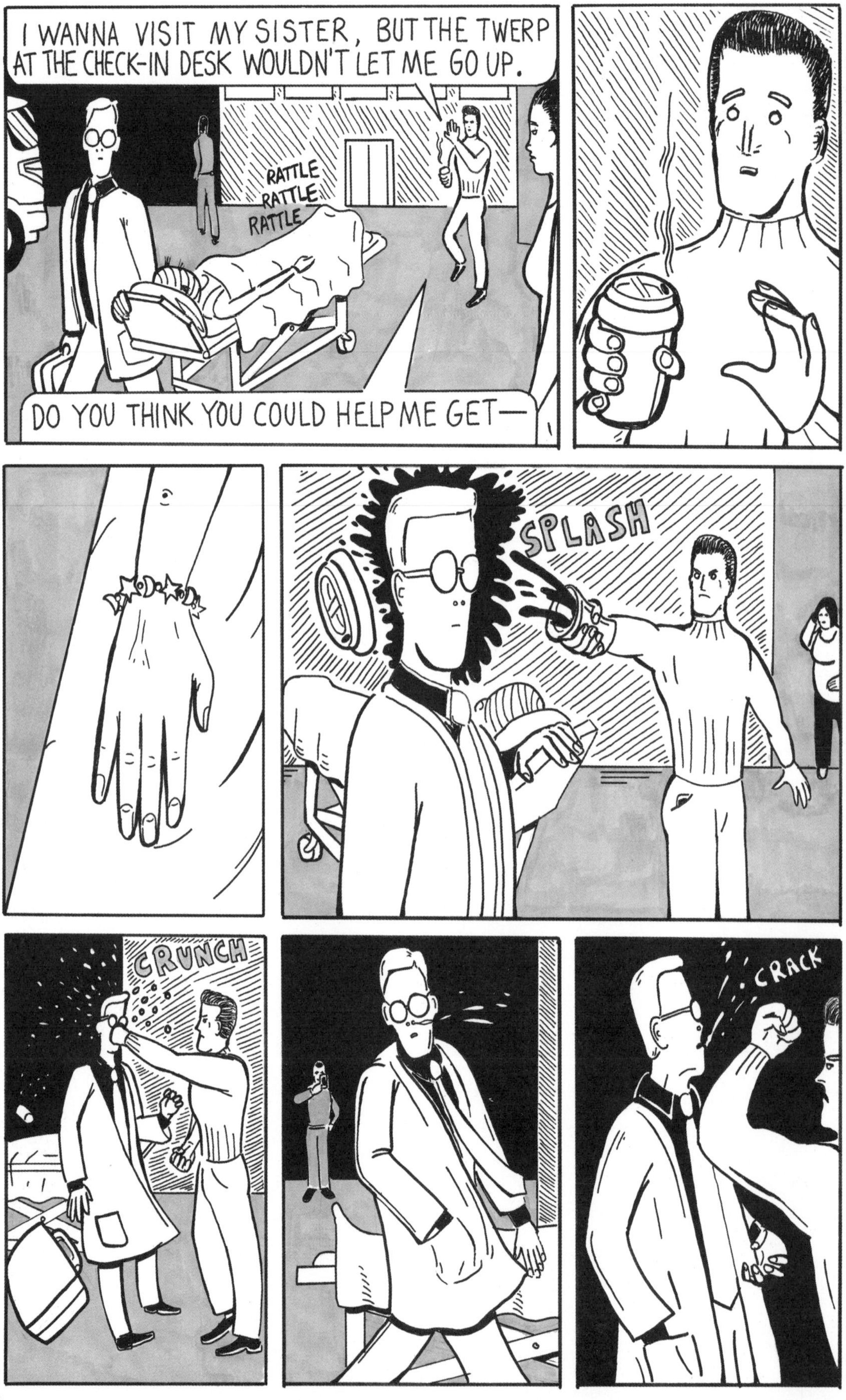
I WANNA VISIT MY SISTER, BUT THE TWERP AT THE CHECK-IN DESK WOULDN'T LET ME GO UP.
RATTLE RATTLE RATTLE
DO YOU THINK YOU COULD HELP ME GET—
SPLASH
CRUNCH
CRACK

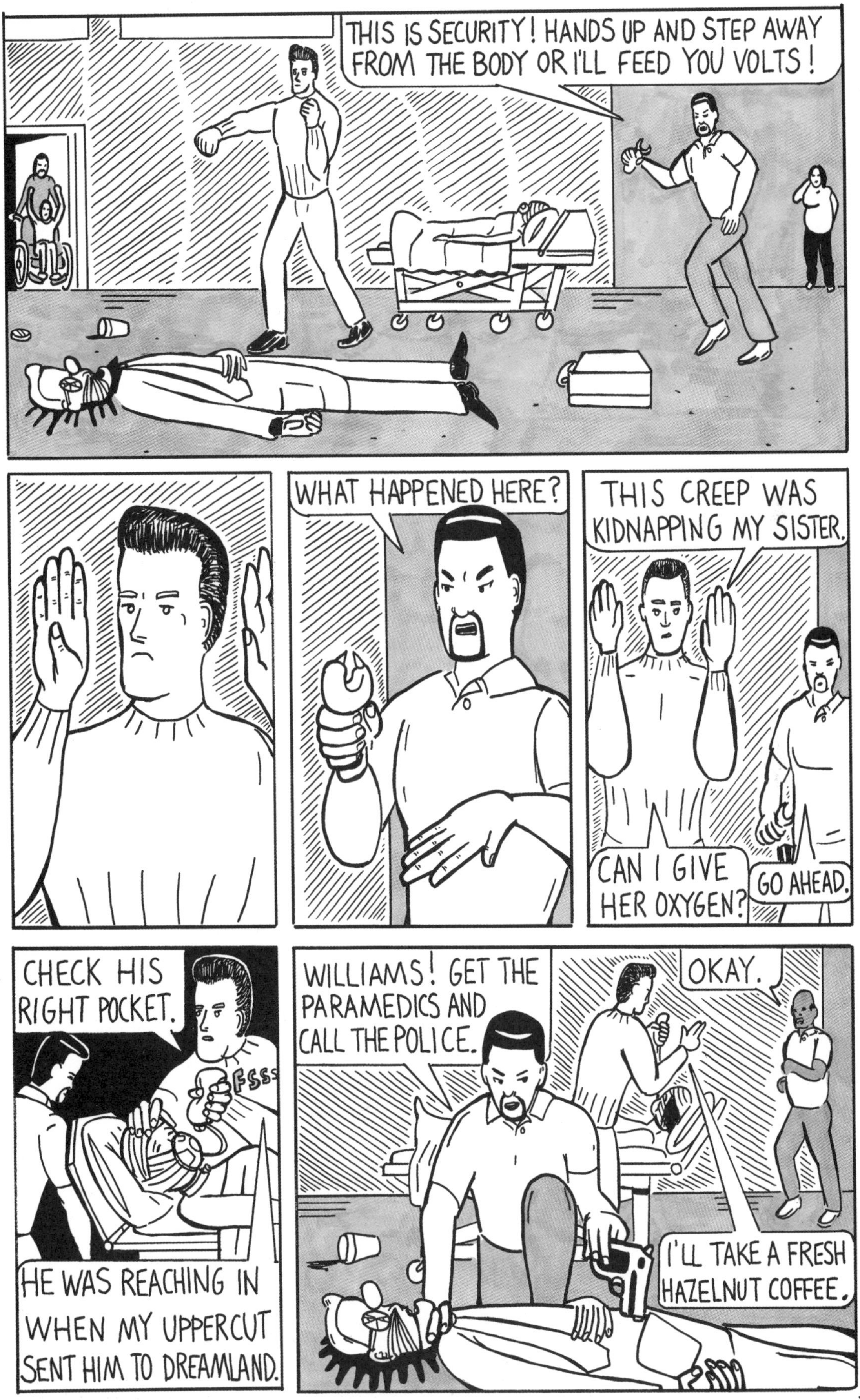
THIS IS SECURITY! HANDS UP AND STEP AWAY FROM THE BODY OR I'LL FEED YOU VOLTS!
WHAT HAPPENED HERE?
THIS CREEP WAS KIDNAPPING MY SISTER.
CAN I GIVE HER OXYGEN?
GO AHEAD.
CHECK HIS RIGHT POCKET.
FSSS
HE WAS REACHING IN WHEN MY UPPERCUT SENT HIM TO DREAMLAND.
WILLIAMS! GET THE PARAMEDICS AND CALL THE POLICE.
OKAY.
I'LL TAKE A FRESH HAZELNUT COFFEE.

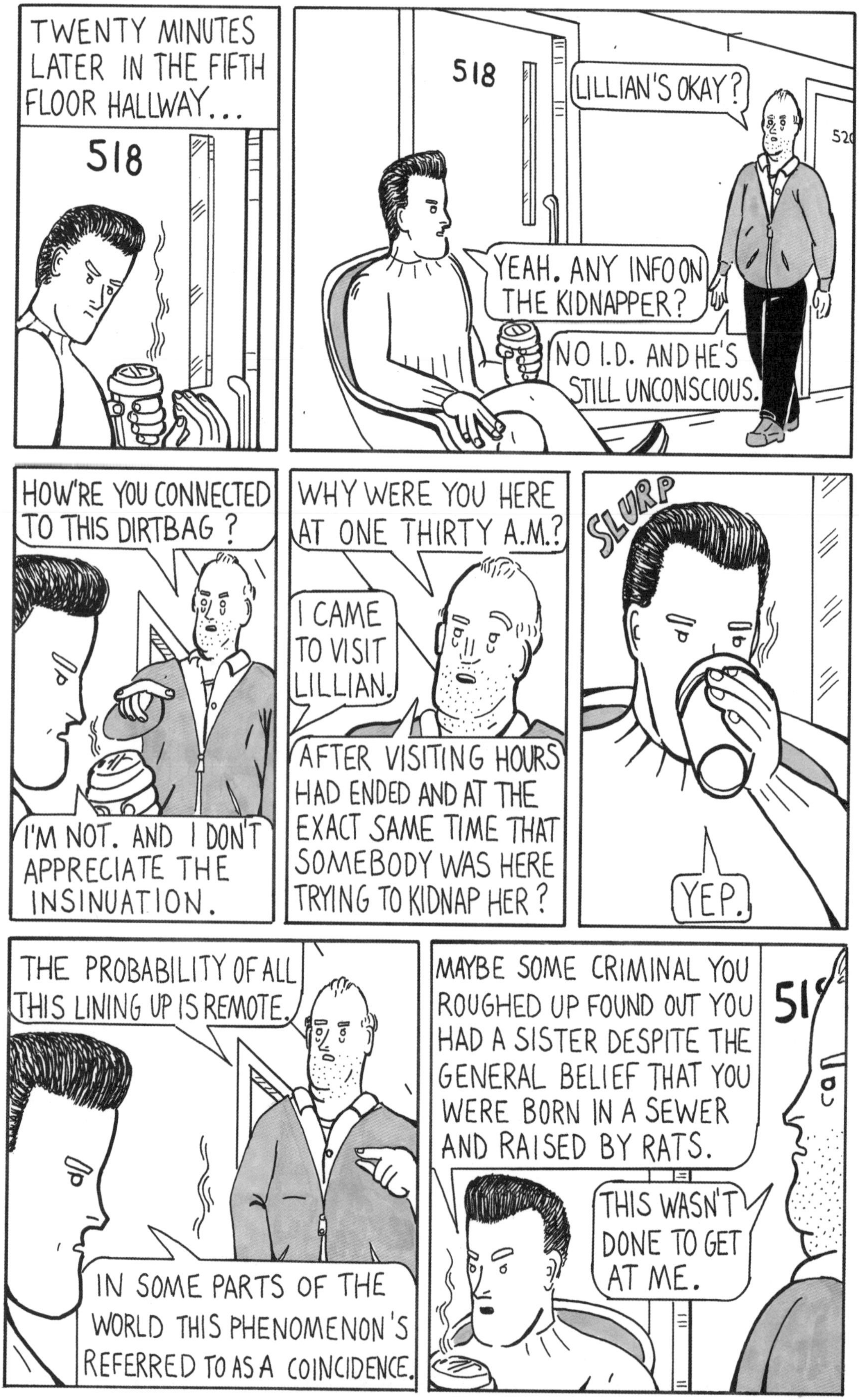
TWENTY MINUTES LATER IN THE FIFTH FLOOR HALLWAY...
518
518
LILLIAN'S OKAY?
YEAH. ANY INFO ON THE KIDNAPPER?
NO I.D. AND HE'S STILL UNCONSCIOUS.
HOW'RE YOU CONNECTED TO THIS DIRTBAG?
I'M NOT. AND I DON'T APPRECIATE THE INSINUATION.
WHY WERE YOU HERE AT ONE THIRTY A.M.?
I CAME TO VISIT LILLIAN.
AFTER VISITING HOURS HAD ENDED AND AT THE EXACT SAME TIME THAT SOMEBODY WAS HERE TRYING TO KIDNAP HER?
SLURP
YEP.
THE PROBABILITY OF ALL THIS LINING UP IS REMOTE.
IN SOME PARTS OF THE WORLD THIS PHENOMENON'S REFERRED TO AS A COINCIDENCE.
MAYBE SOME CRIMINAL YOU ROUGHED UP FOUND OUT YOU HAD A SISTER DESPITE THE GENERAL BELIEF THAT YOU WERE BORN IN A SEWER AND RAISED BY RATS.
THIS WASN'T DONE TO GET AT ME.

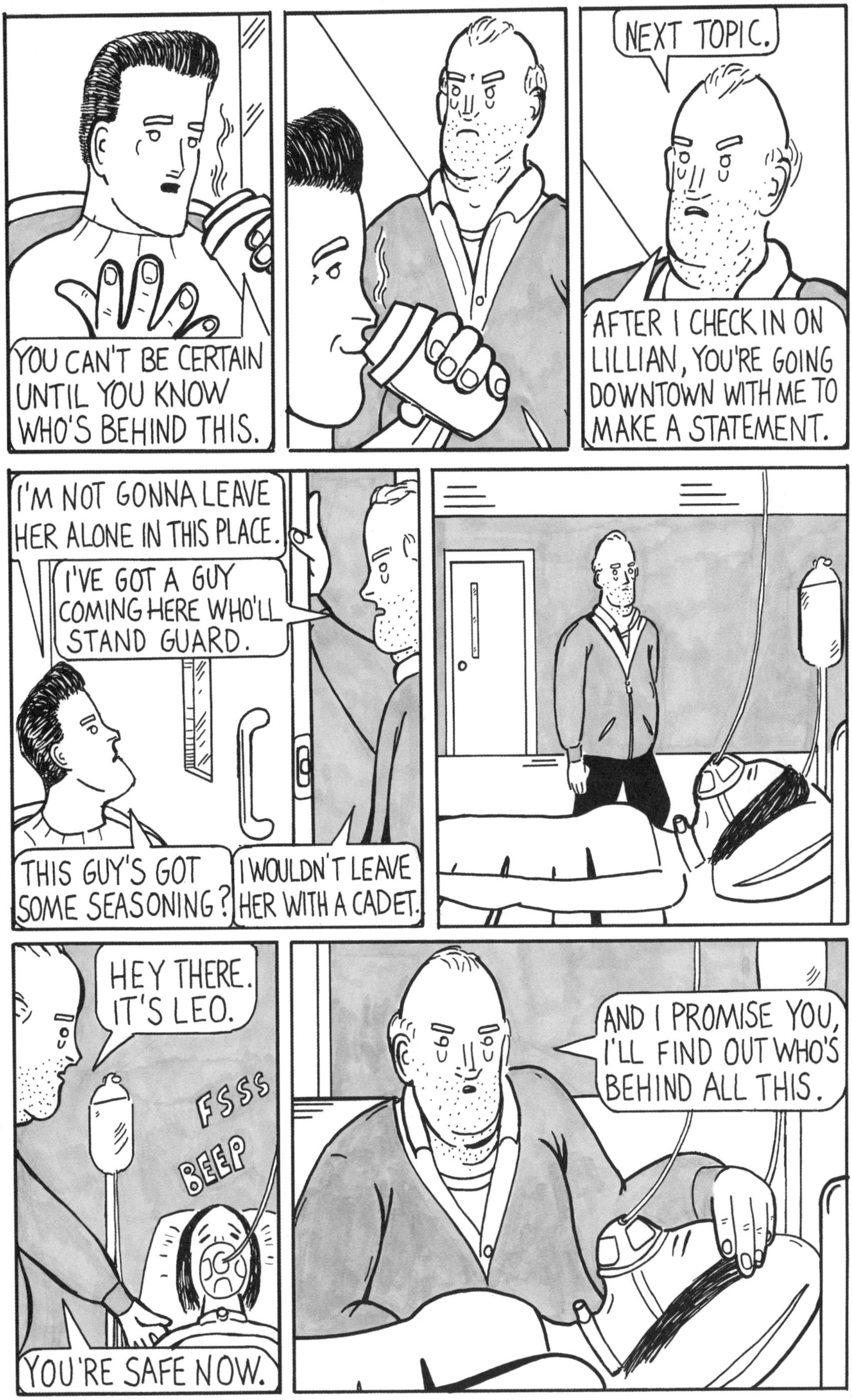
YOU CAN'T BE CERTAIN UNTIL YOU KNOW WHO'S BEHIND THIS.
NEXT TOPIC.
AFTER I CHECK IN ON LILLIAN, YOU'RE GOING DOWNTOWN WITH ME TO MAKE A STATEMENT.
I'M NOT GONNA LEAVE HER ALONE IN THIS PLACE.
I'VE GOT A GUY COMING HERE WHO'LL STAND GUARD.
THIS GUY'S GOT SOME SEASONING?
I WOULDN'T LEAVE HER WITH A CADET.
HEY THERE. IT'S LEO.
FSSS
BEEP
YOU'RE SAFE NOW.
AND I PROMISE YOU, I'LL FIND OUT WHO'S BEHIND ALL THIS.

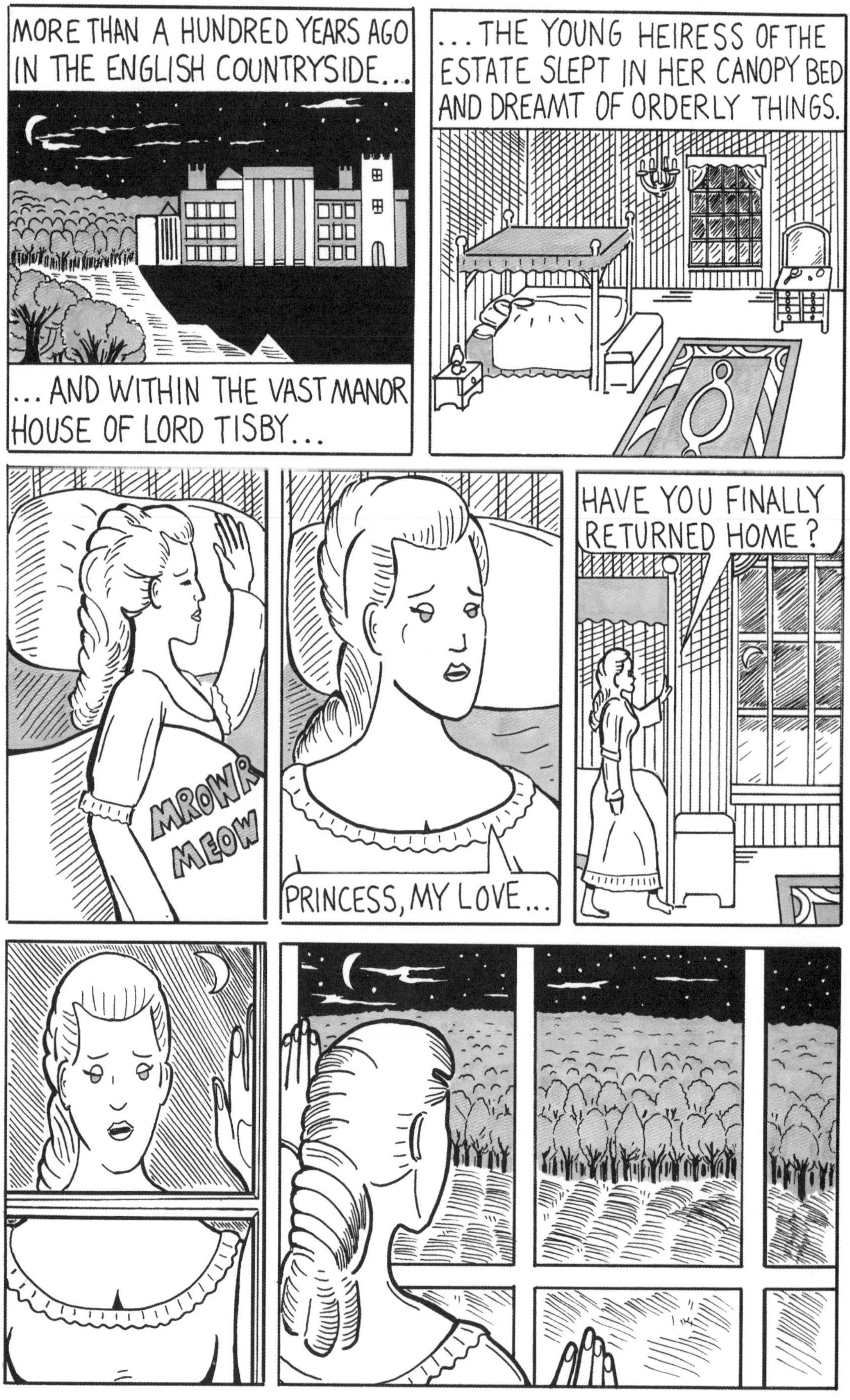
MORE THAN A HUNDRED YEARS AGO IN THE ENGLISH COUNTRYSIDE...
... AND WITHIN THE VAST MANOR HOUSE OF LORD TISBY...
... THE YOUNG HEIRESS OF THE ESTATE SLEPT IN HER CANOPY BED AND DREAMT OF ORDERLY THINGS.
MROWR
MEOW
PRINCESS, MY LOVE...
HAVE YOU FINALLY RETURNED HOME?

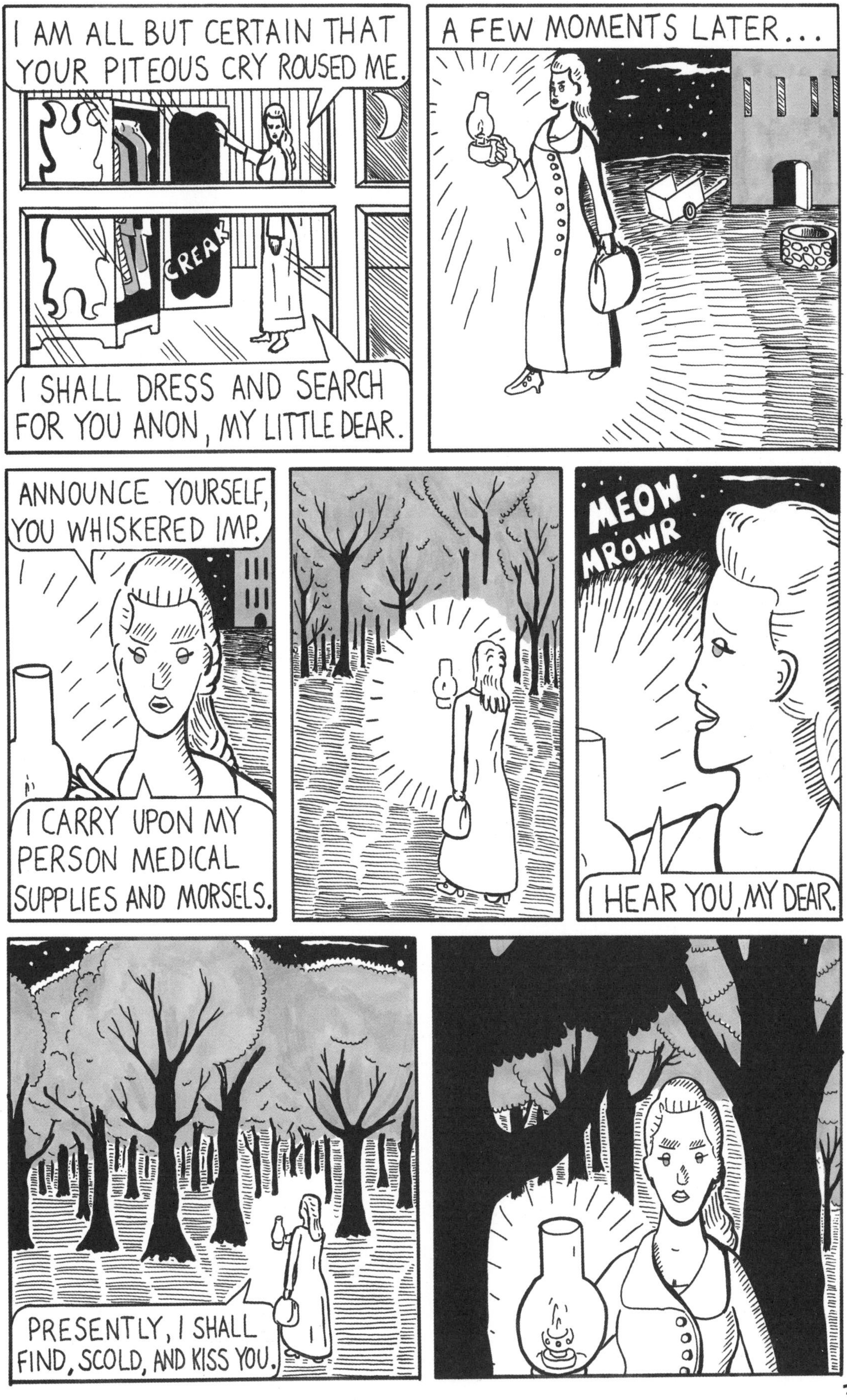
I AM ALL BUT CERTAIN THAT YOUR PITEOUS CRY ROUSED ME.
CREAK
I SHALL DRESS AND SEARCH FOR YOU ANON, MY LITTLE DEAR.
A FEW MOMENTS LATER...
ANNOUNCE YOURSELF, YOU WHISKERED IMP.
I CARRY UPON MY PERSON MEDICAL SUPPLIES AND MORSELS.
MEOW
MROWR
I HEAR YOU, MY DEAR.
PRESENTLY, I SHALL FIND, SCOLD, AND KISS YOU.

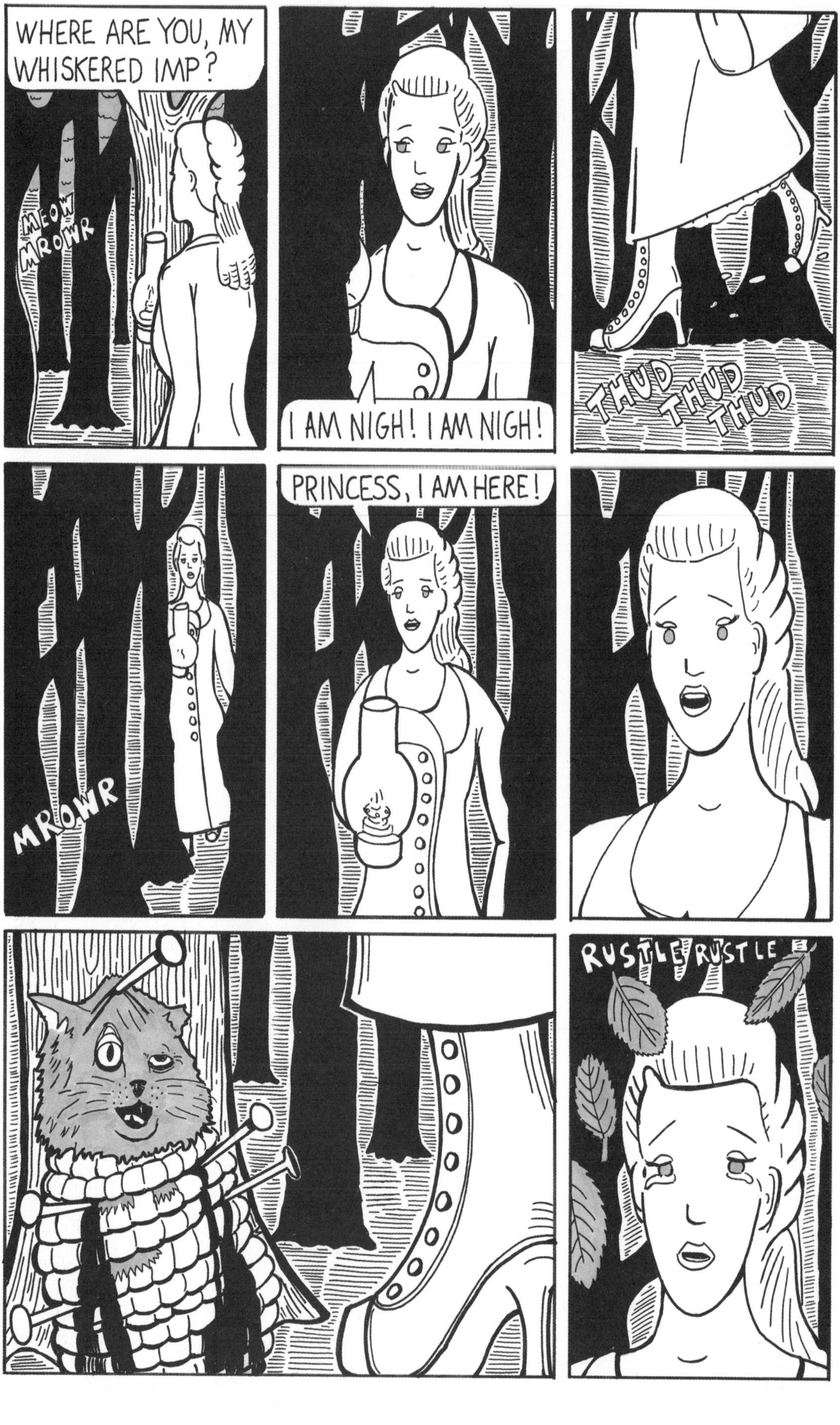
WHERE ARE YOU, MY WHISKERED IMP?
MEOW MROWR
I AM NIGH! I AM NIGH!
THUD THUD THUD
MROWR
PRINCESS, I AM HERE!
RUSTLE RUSTLE

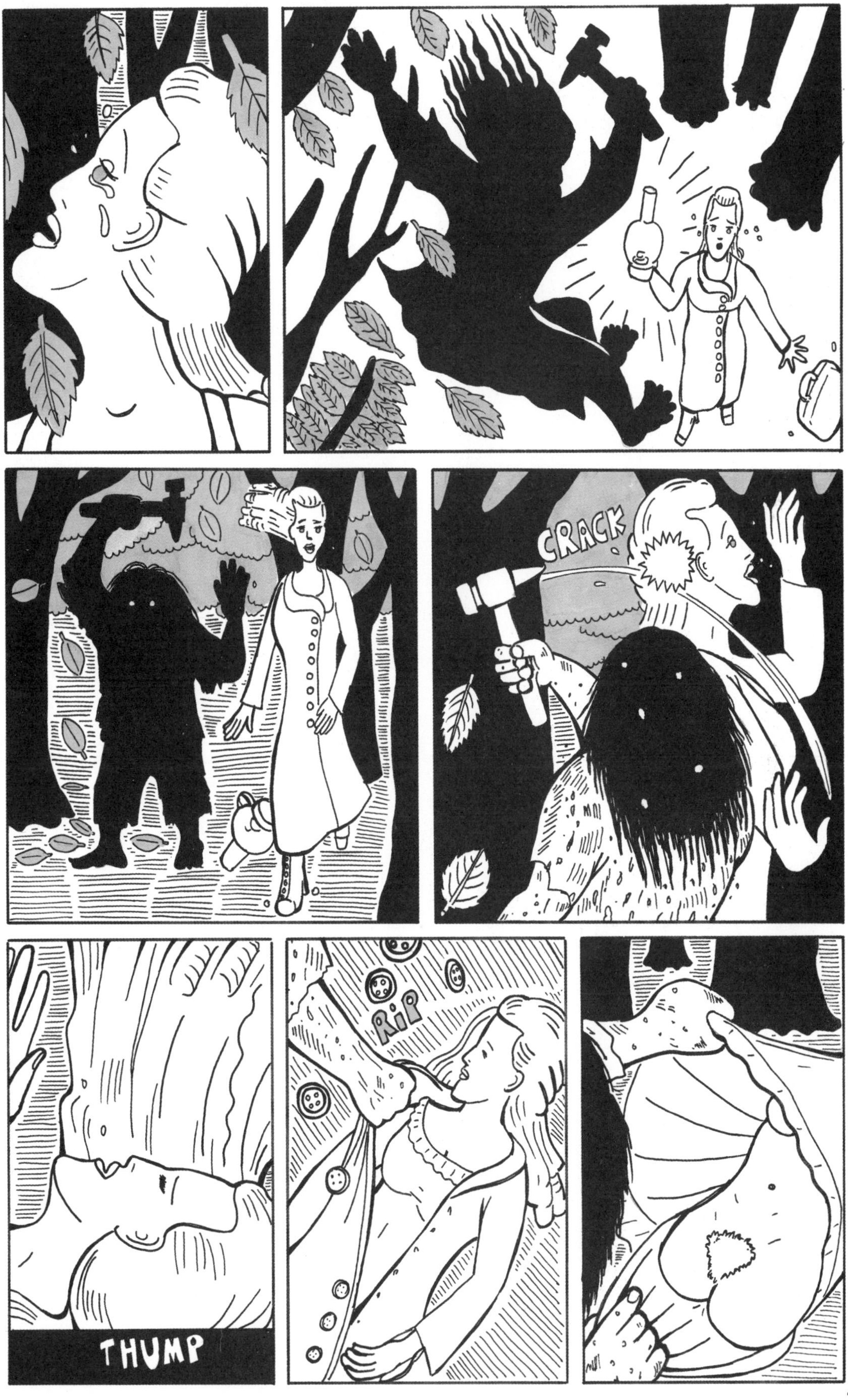
CRACK
THUMP
RIP

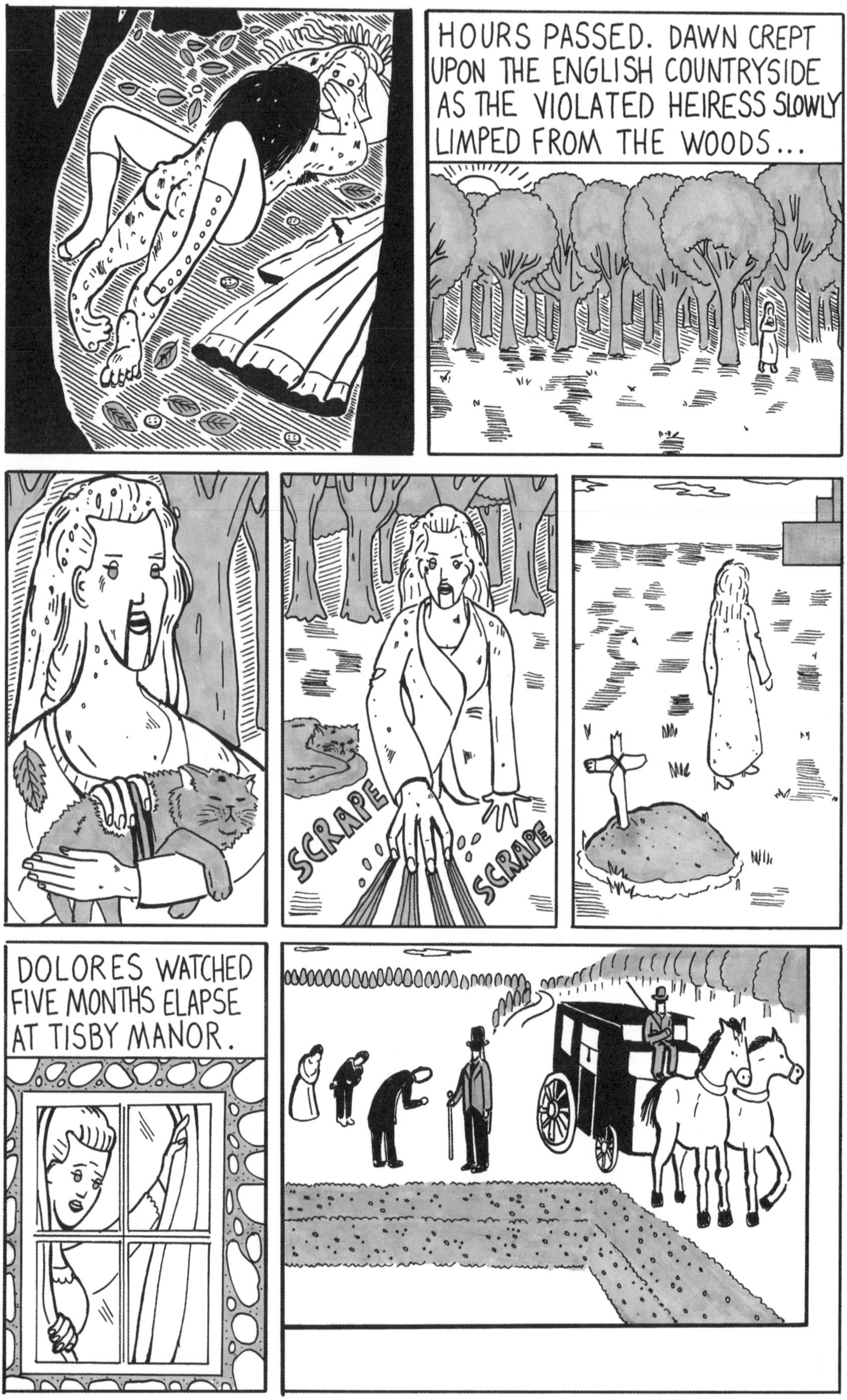
HOURS PASSED. DAWN CREPT UPON THE ENGLISH COUNTRYSIDE AS THE VIOLATED HEIRESS SLOWLY LIMPED FROM THE WOODS...
SCRAPE
SCRAPE
DOLORES WATCHED FIVE MONTHS ELAPSE AT TISBY MANOR.

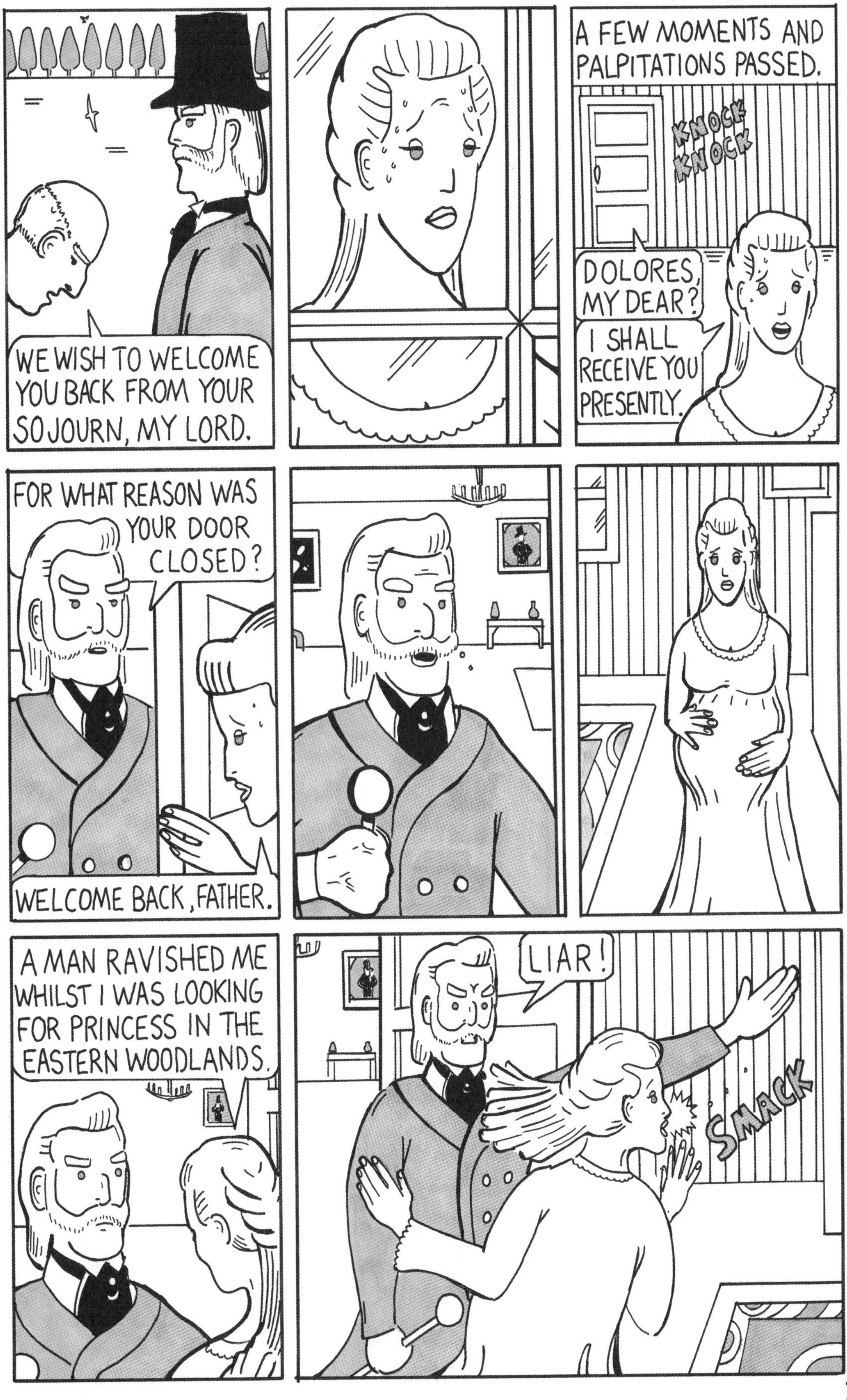
WE WISH TO WELCOME YOU BACK FROM YOUR SOJOURN, MY LORD.
A FEW MOMENTS AND PALPITATIONS PASSED.
KNOCK KNOCK
DOLORES, MY DEAR?
I SHALL RECEIVE YOU PRESENTLY.
FOR WHAT REASON WAS YOUR DOOR CLOSED?
WELCOME BACK, FATHER.
A MAN RAVISHED ME WHILST I WAS LOOKING FOR PRINCESS IN THE EASTERN WOODLANDS.
LIAR!
SMACK

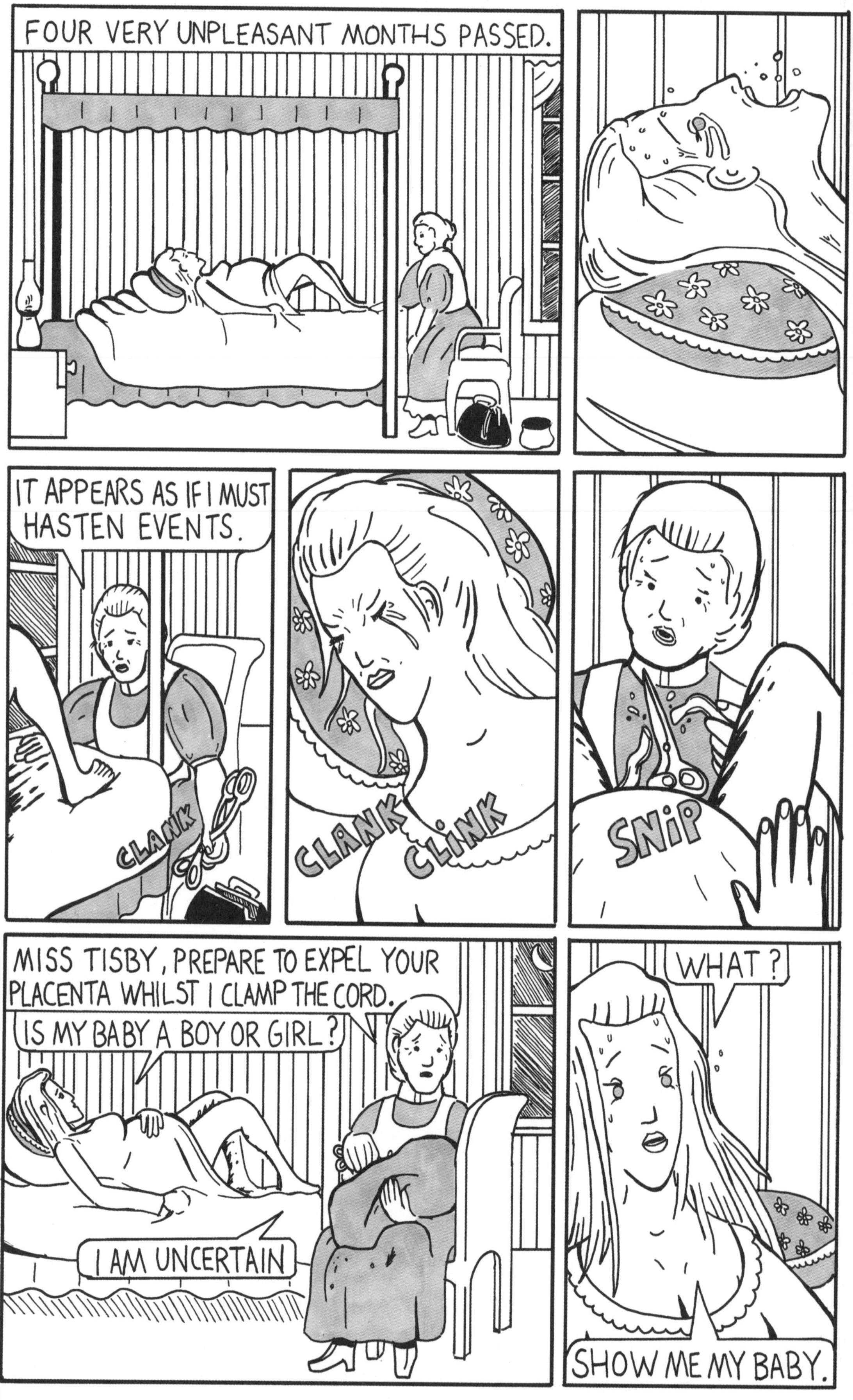
FOUR VERY UNPLEASANT MONTHS PASSED.
IT APPEARS AS IF I MUST HASTEN EVENTS.
CLANK
CLANK
CLINK
SNIP
MISS TISBY, PREPARE TO EXPEL YOUR PLACENTA WHILST I CLAMP THE CORD.
IS MY BABY A BOY OR GIRL?
I AM UNCERTAIN
WHAT?
SHOW ME MY BABY.

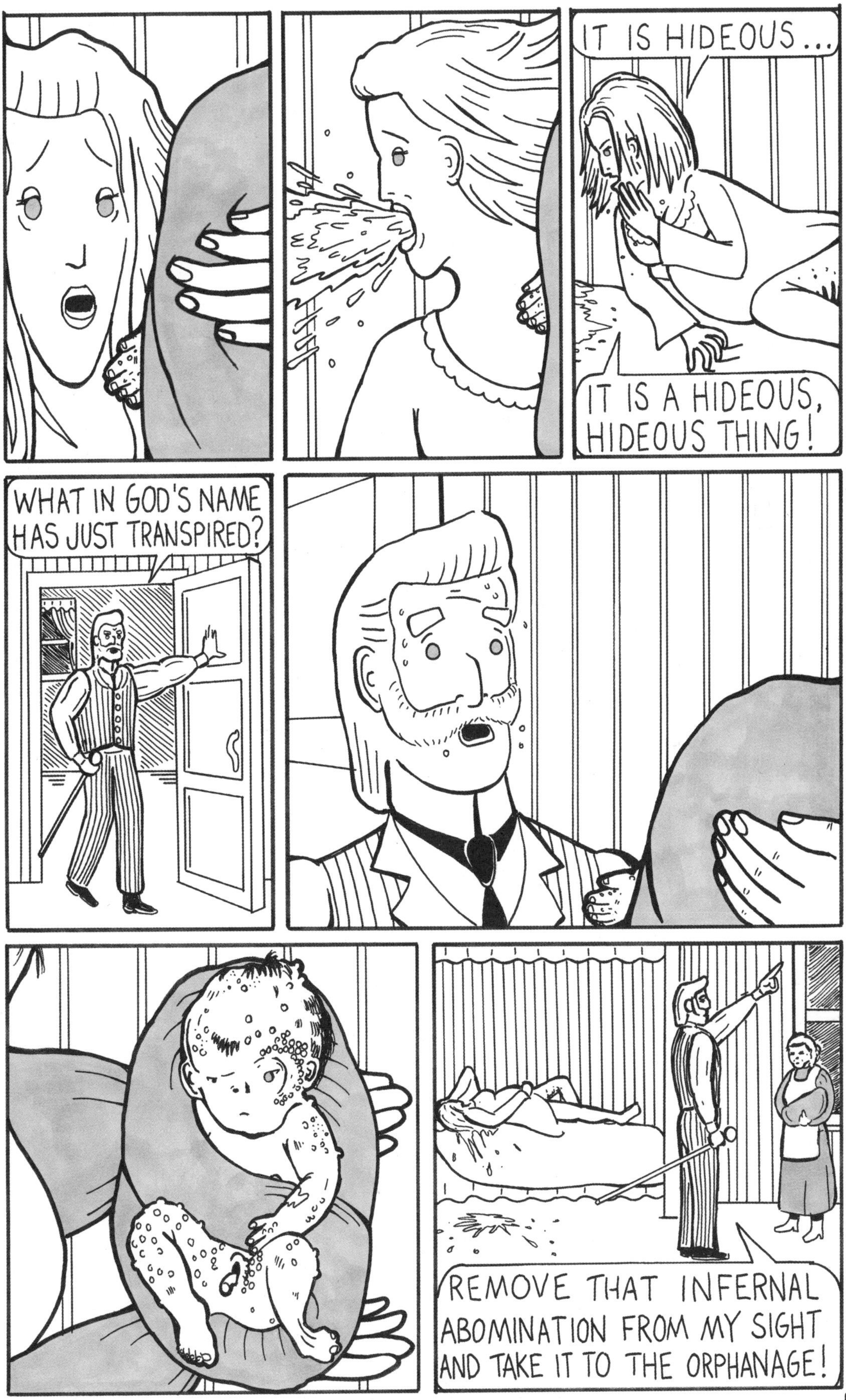
IT IS HIDEOUS...
IT IS A HIDEOUS, HIDEOUS THING!
WHAT IN GOD'S NAME HAS JUST TRANSPIRED?
REMOVE THAT INFERNAL ABOMINATION FROM MY SIGHT AND TAKE IT TO THE ORPHANAGE!

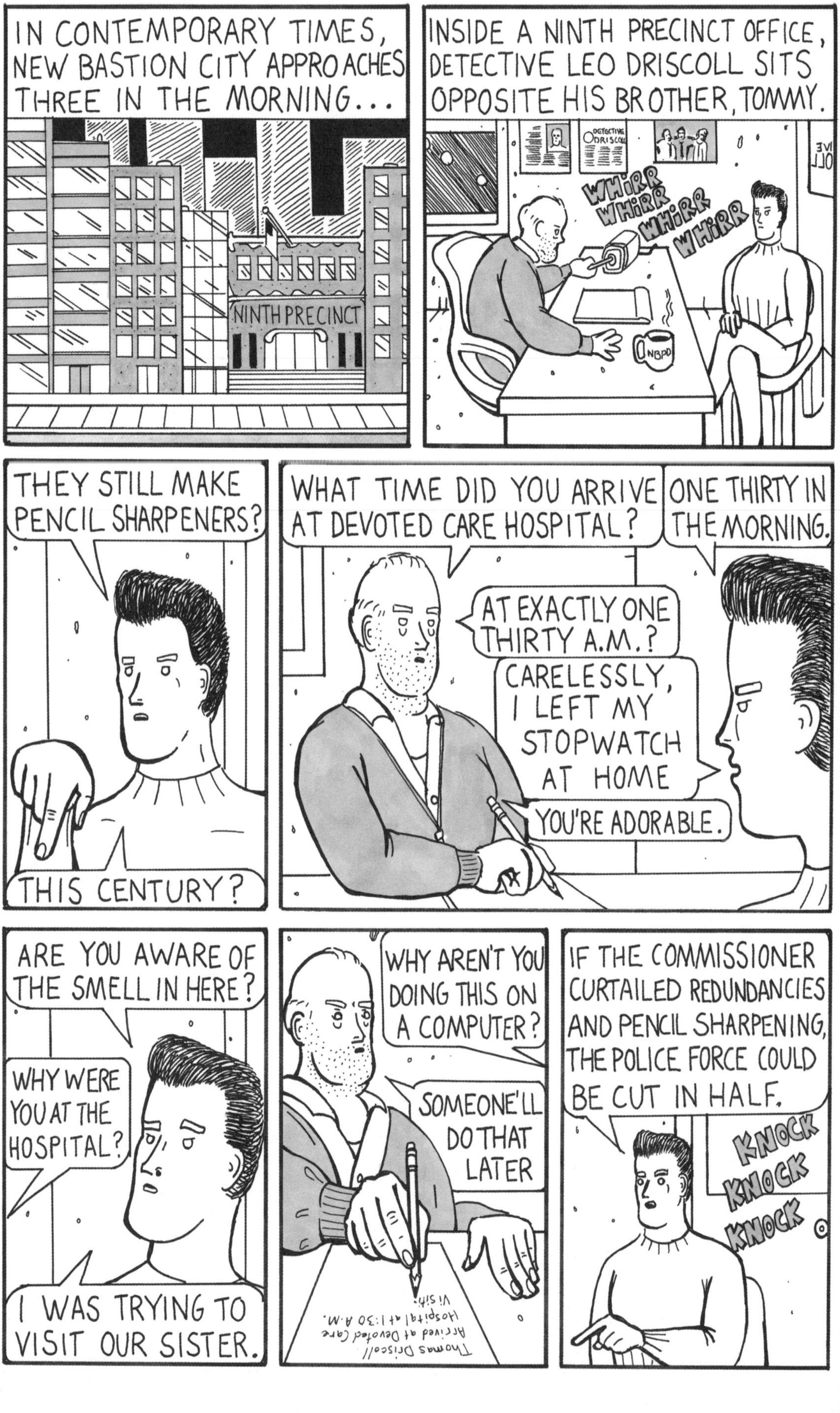
IN CONTEMPORARY TIMES, NEW BASTION CITY APPROACHES THREE IN THE MORNING...
NINTH PRECINCT
INSIDE A NINTH PRECINCT OFFICE, DETECTIVE LEO DRISCOLL SITS OPPOSITE HIS BROTHER, TOMMY.
DETECTIVE DRISCOLL
WHIRR
WHIRR
WHIRR
WHIRR
NBPD
THEY STILL MAKE PENCIL SHARPENERS?
THIS CENTURY?
WHAT TIME DID YOU ARRIVE AT DEVOTED CARE HOSPITAL?
ONE THIRTY IN THE MORNING.
AT EXACTLY ONE THIRTY A.M.?
CARELESSLY, I LEFT MY STOPWATCH AT HOME
YOU'RE ADORABLE.
ARE YOU AWARE OF THE SMELL IN HERE?
WHY WERE YOU AT THE HOSPITAL?
I WAS TRYING TO VISIT OUR SISTER.
WHY AREN'T YOU DOING THIS ON A COMPUTER?
SOMEONE'LL DO THAT LATER
Thomas Driscoll
Arrived at Devoted Care
Hospital at 1:30 A.M.
Visit:
IF THE COMMISSIONER CURTAILED REDUNDANCIES AND PENCIL SHARPENING, THE POLICE FORCE COULD BE CUT IN HALF.
KNOCK
KNOCK
KNOCK

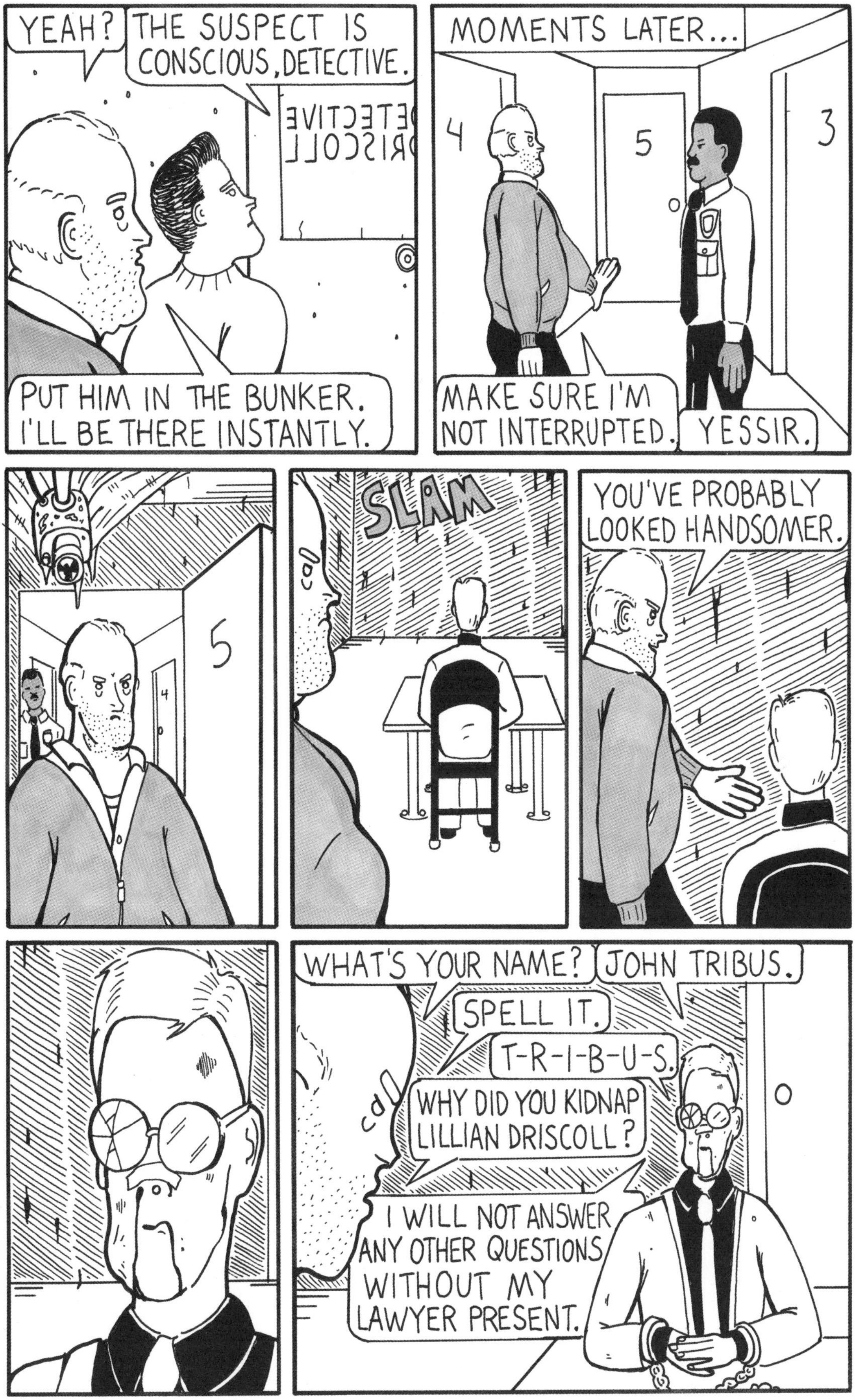
YEAH?
THE SUSPECT IS CONSCIOUS, DETECTIVE.
DETECTIVE DRISCOLL
PUT HIM IN THE BUNKER. I'LL BE THERE INSTANTLY.
MOMENTS LATER...
4
5
3
MAKE SURE I'M NOT INTERRUPTED.
YESSIR.
5
4
SLAM
YOU'VE PROBABLY LOOKED HANDSOMER.
WHAT'S YOUR NAME?
JOHN TRIBUS.
SPELL IT.
T-R-I-B-U-S.
WHY DID YOU KIDNAP LILLIAN DRISCOLL?
I WILL NOT ANSWER ANY OTHER QUESTIONS WITHOUT MY LAWYER PRESENT.

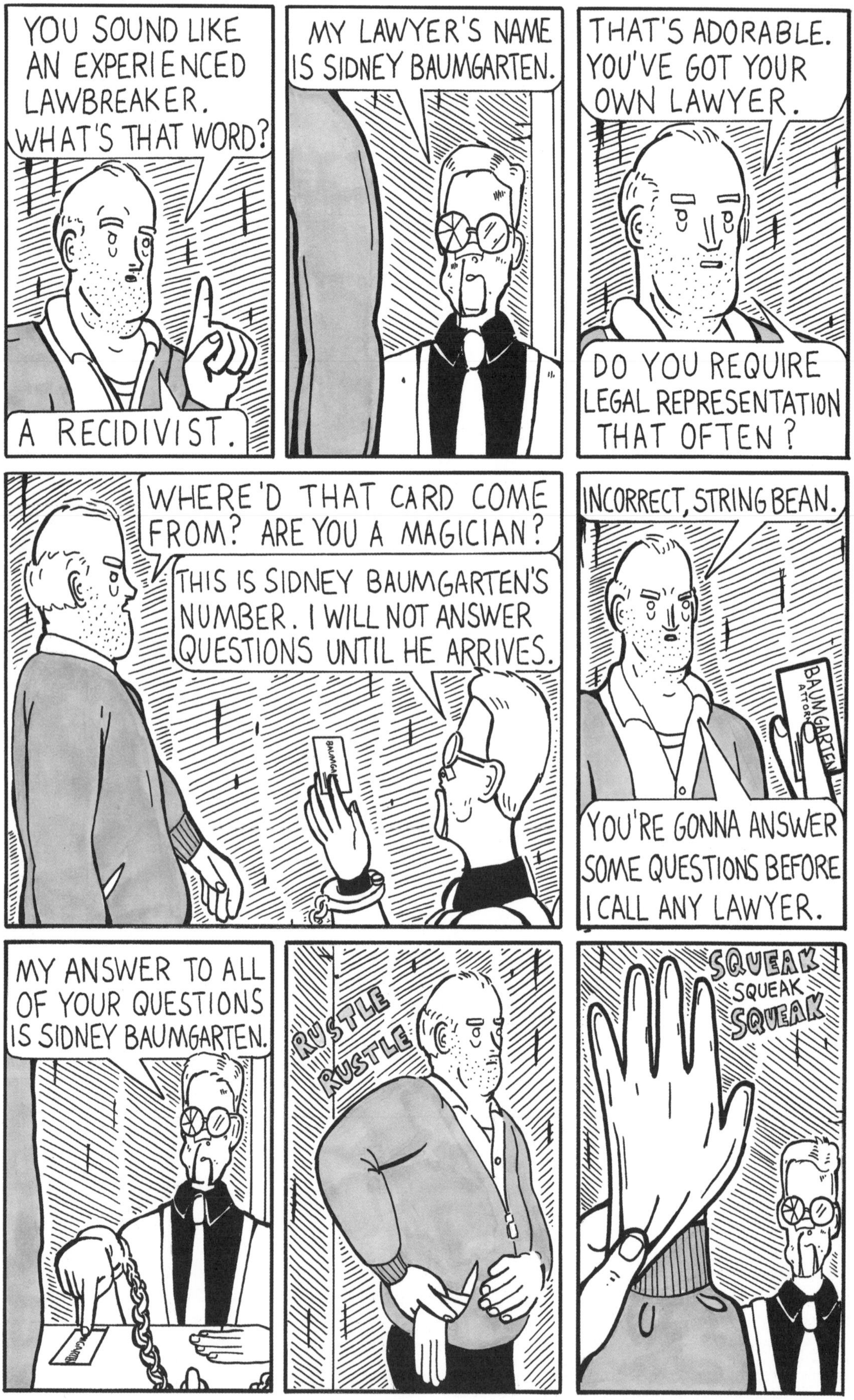
YOU SOUND LIKE AN EXPERIENCED LAWBREAKER. WHAT'S THAT WORD?
A RECIDIVIST.
MY LAWYER'S NAME IS SIDNEY BAUMGARTEN.
THAT'S ADORABLE. YOU'VE GOT YOUR OWN LAWYER.
DO YOU REQUIRE LEGAL REPRESENTATION THAT OFTEN?
WHERE'D THAT CARD COME FROM? ARE YOU A MAGICIAN?
THIS IS SIDNEY BAUMGARTEN'S NUMBER. I WILL NOT ANSWER QUESTIONS UNTIL HE ARRIVES.
INCORRECT, STRING BEAN.
BAUMGARTEN
YOU'RE GONNA ANSWER SOME QUESTIONS BEFORE I CALL ANY LAWYER.
MY ANSWER TO ALL OF YOUR QUESTIONS IS SIDNEY BAUMGARTEN.
RUSTLE
RUSTLE
SQUEAK
SQUEAK
SQUEAK

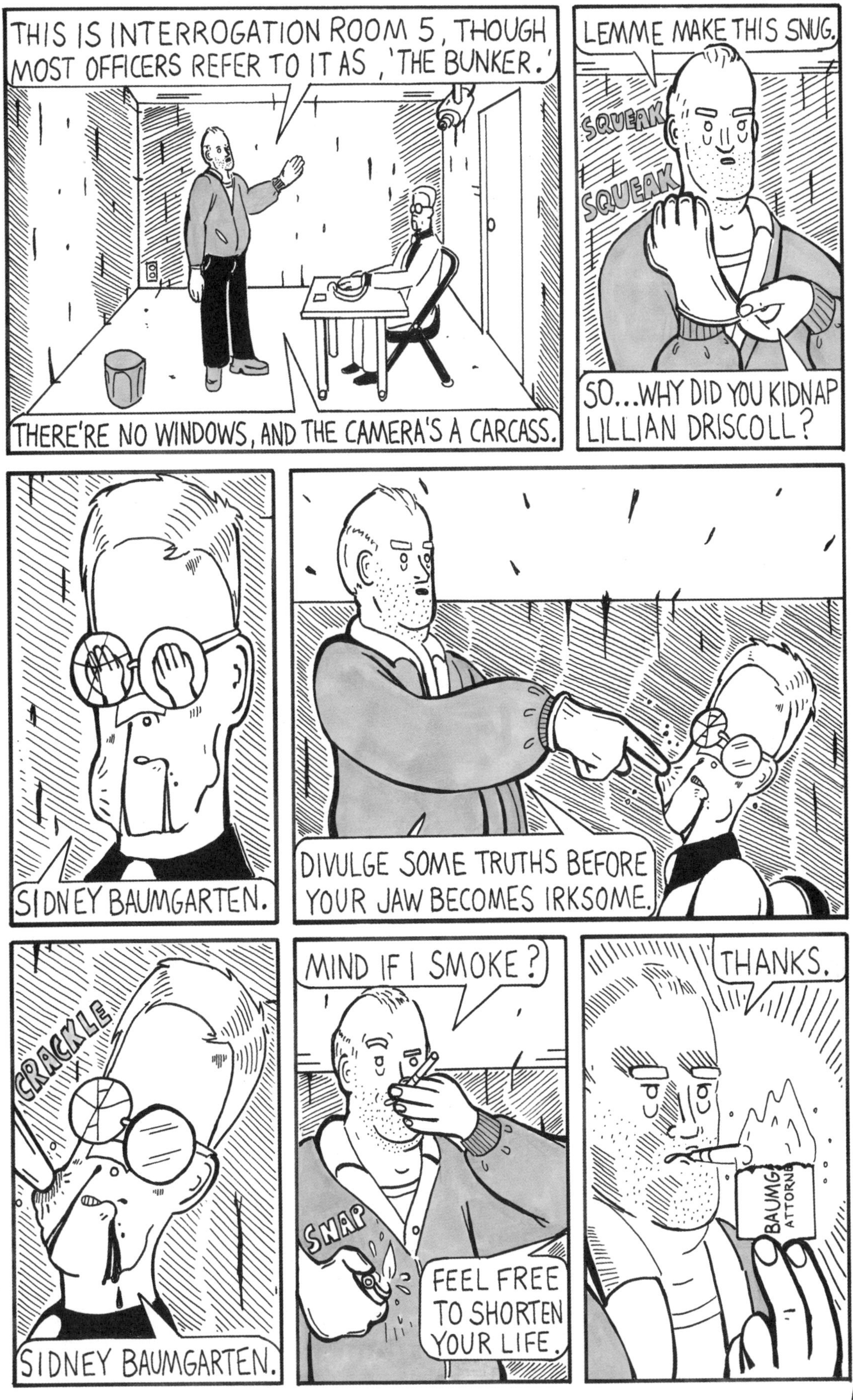
THIS IS INTERROGATION ROOM 5, THOUGH MOST OFFICERS REFER TO IT AS, 'THE BUNKER.'
THERE'RE NO WINDOWS, AND THE CAMERA'S A CARCASS.
LEMME MAKE THIS SNUG.
SQUEAK
SQUEAK
SO...WHY DID YOU KIDNAP LILLIAN DRISCOLL?
SIDNEY BAUMGARTEN.
DIVULGE SOME TRUTHS BEFORE YOUR JAW BECOMES IRKSOME.
CRACKLE
SIDNEY BAUMGARTEN.
MIND IF I SMOKE?
SNAP
FEEL FREE TO SHORTEN YOUR LIFE.
THANKS.

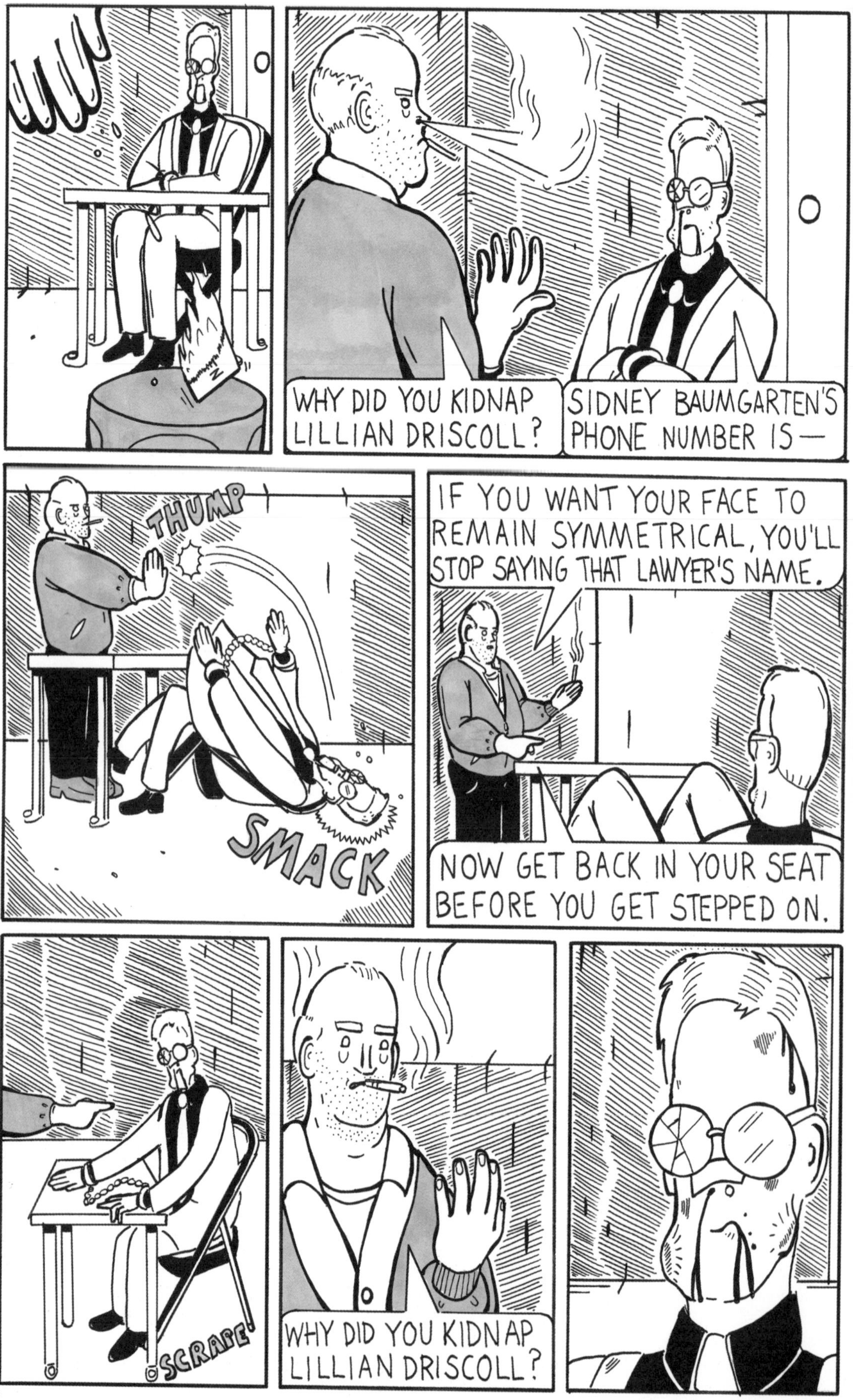
WHY DID YOU KIDNAP LILLIAN DRISCOLL?
SIDNEY BAUMGARTEN'S PHONE NUMBER IS—
THUMP
SMACK
IF YOU WANT YOUR FACE TO REMAIN SYMMETRICAL, YOU'LL STOP SAYING THAT LAWYER'S NAME.
NOW GET BACK IN YOUR SEAT BEFORE YOU GET STEPPED ON.
SCRAPE
WHY DID YOU KIDNAP LILLIAN DRISCOLL?

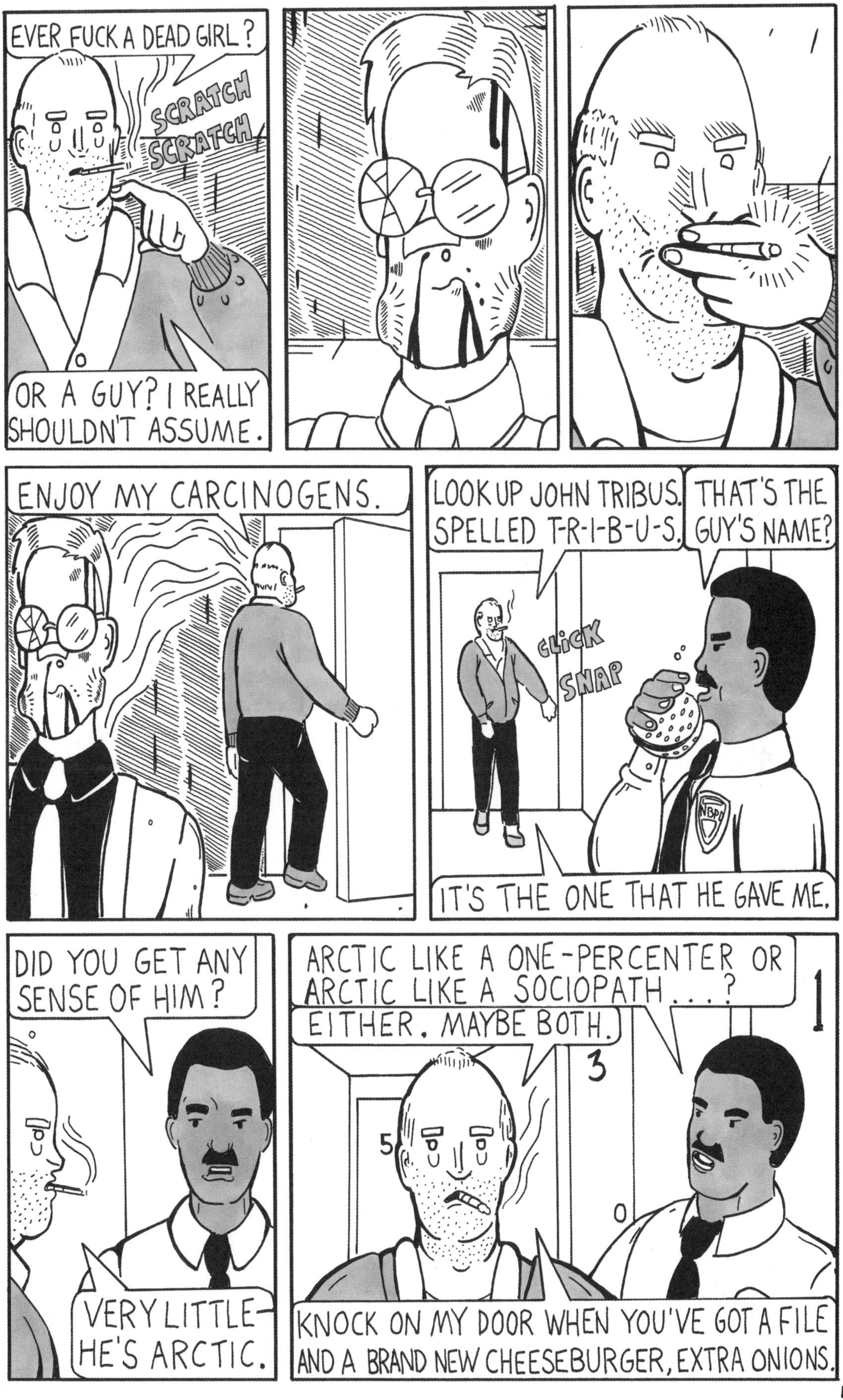
EVER FUCK A DEAD GIRL?
SCRATCH SCRATCH
OR A GUY? I REALLY SHOULDN'T ASSUME.
ENJOY MY CARCINOGENS.
LOOK UP JOHN TRIBUS. SPELLED T-R-I-B-U-S.
THAT'S THE GUY'S NAME?
CLICK
SNAP
NBPD
IT'S THE ONE THAT HE GAVE ME.
DID YOU GET ANY SENSE OF HIM?
VERY LITTLE- HE'S ARCTIC.
ARCTIC LIKE A ONE-PERCENTER OR ARCTIC LIKE A SOCIOPATH...?
EITHER. MAYBE BOTH.
1
3
5
KNOCK ON MY DOOR WHEN YOU'VE GOT A FILE AND A BRAND NEW CHEESEBURGER, EXTRA ONIONS.

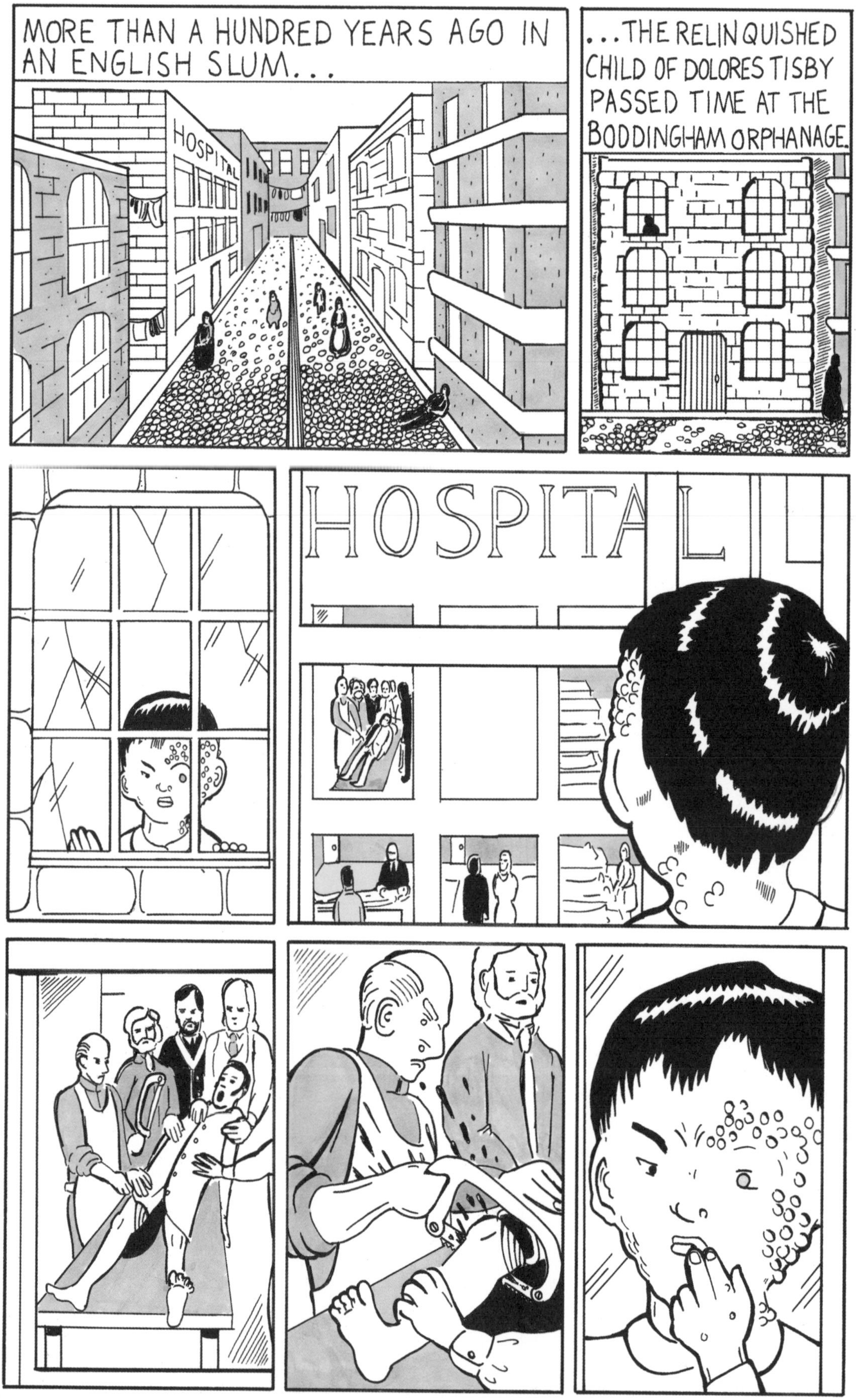
MORE THAN A HUNDRED YEARS AGO IN AN ENGLISH SLUM...
HOSPITAL
...THE RELINQUISHED CHILD OF DOLORES TISBY PASSED TIME AT THE BODDINGHAM ORPHANAGE.
HOSPITAL

TWO DAYS PASSED.

HOSPITAL

GO

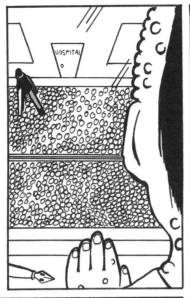

HOSPITAL

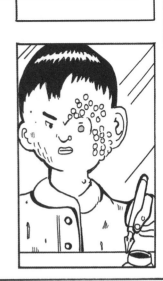

CLASS RESUMED AT THE BODDINGHAM ORPHANAGE THE FOLLOWING MORNING.

Bible Study
42:10

CHIRP CHIRP CHIRP

CHIRP CHIRP

PAY ATTENTION TO THE LESSON!

YOU CANNOT IMPROVE YOUR APPEARANCE, BUT YOU CAN BETTER YOUR MIND.

49

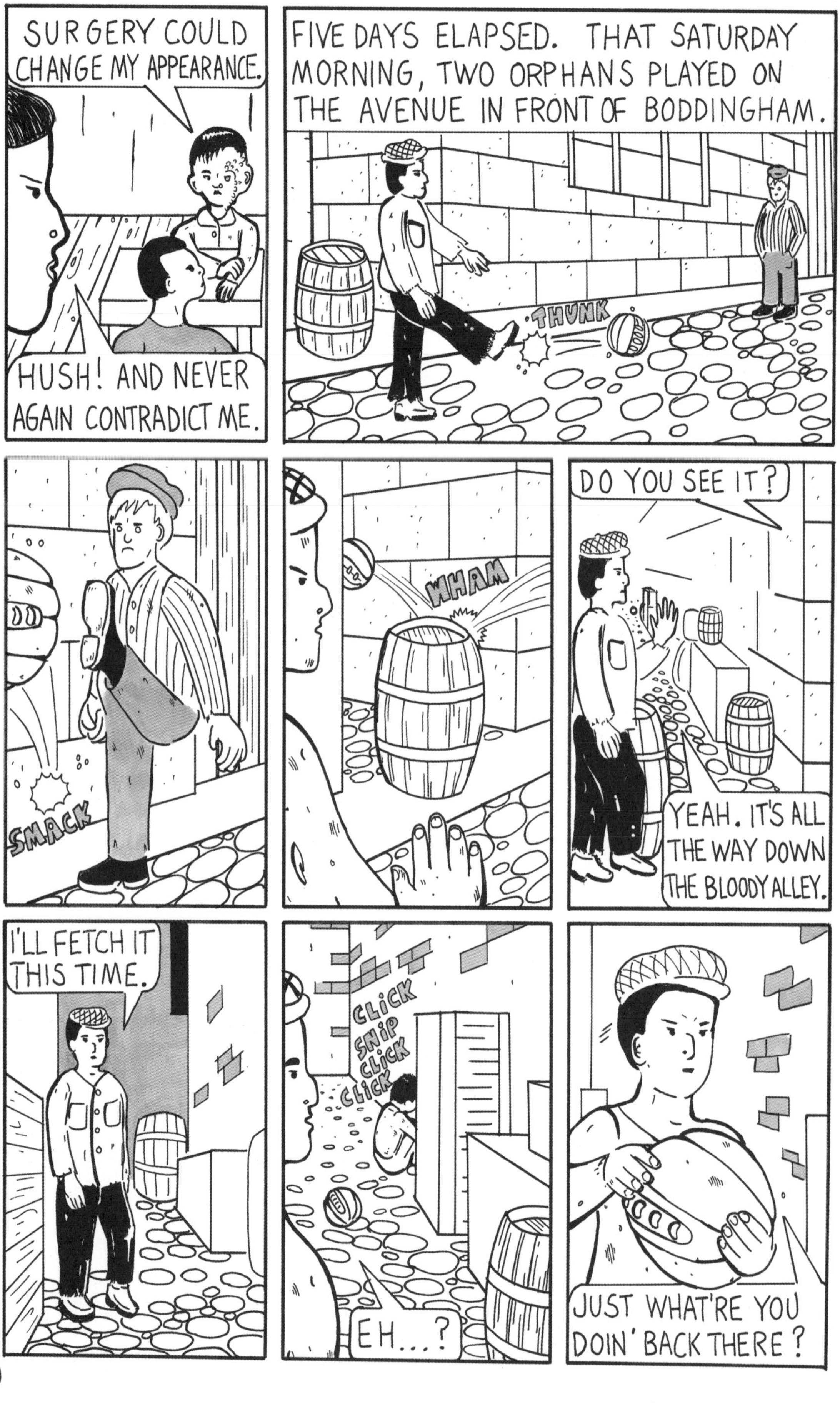

SURGERY COULD CHANGE MY APPEARANCE.
HUSH! AND NEVER AGAIN CONTRADICT ME.
FIVE DAYS ELAPSED. THAT SATURDAY MORNING, TWO ORPHANS PLAYED ON THE AVENUE IN FRONT OF BODDINGHAM.
THUNK
SMACK
WHAM
DO YOU SEE IT?
YEAH. IT'S ALL THE WAY DOWN THE BLOODY ALLEY.
I'LL FETCH IT THIS TIME.
CLICK
SNIP
CLICK
CLICK
EH...?
JUST WHAT'RE YOU DOIN' BACK THERE?

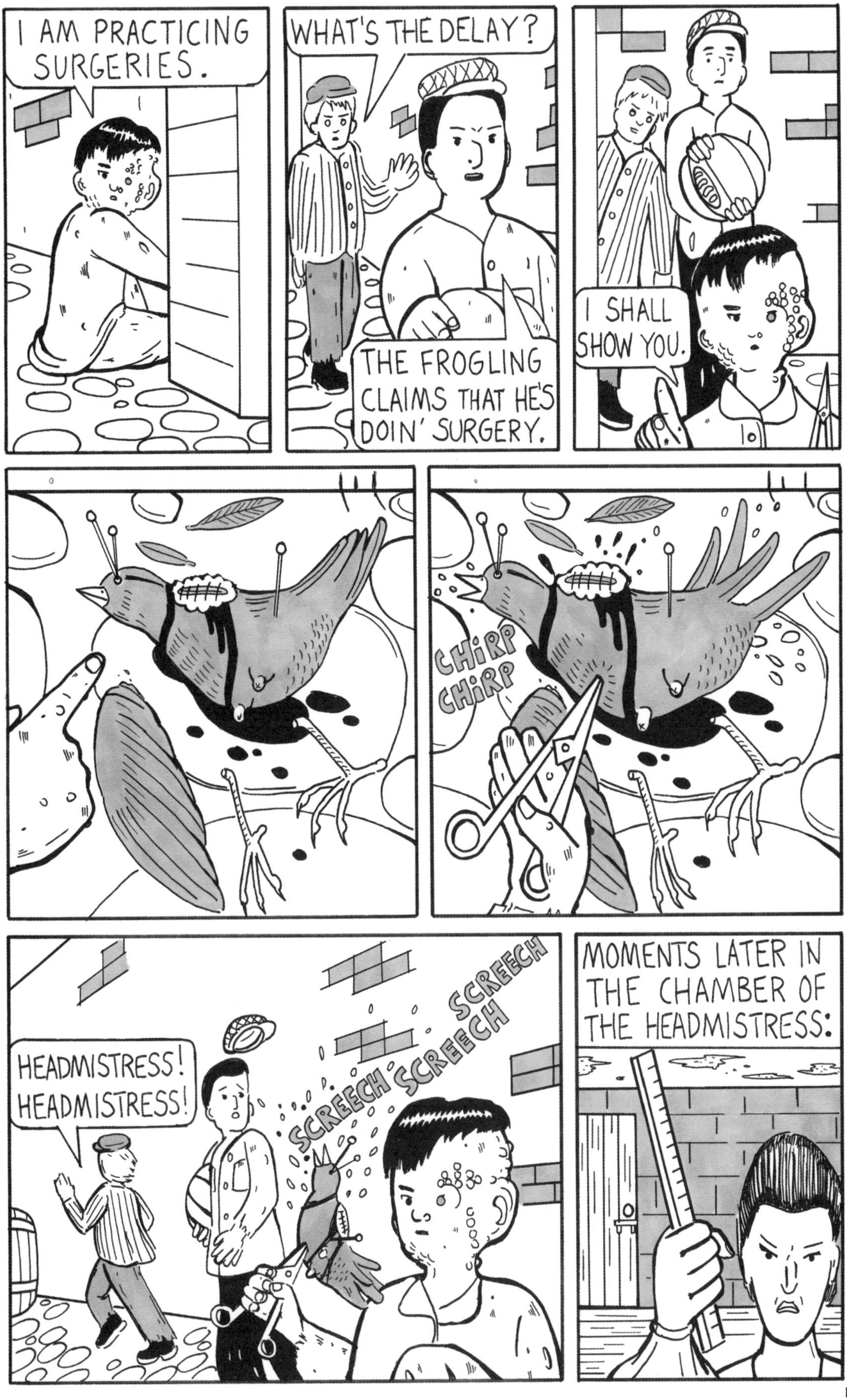
I AM PRACTICING SURGERIES.
WHAT'S THE DELAY?
THE FROGLING CLAIMS THAT HE'S DOIN' SURGERY.
I SHALL SHOW YOU.
CHIRP CHIRP
HEADMISTRESS! HEADMISTRESS!
SCREECH SCREECH SCREECH SCREECH
MOMENTS LATER IN THE CHAMBER OF THE HEADMISTRESS:

YOU WARTY DEGENERATE!

SMACK

YOU SHOULD BE ASHAMED OF DOING SOMETHING SO WICKED TO ONE OF GOD'S CREATURES.

SMACK

BUT MY SURGERIES WERE SUCCESSFUL: THE BIRD STILL LIVES.

SIX MORE YEARS ELAPSED AT THE BODDINGHAM ORPHANAGE.

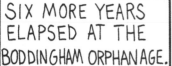

IT WAS AFTER MIDNIGHT AND ALL OF THE CHILDREN BUT ONE WERE ABED.

HOWL HOWL

DIDJA HEAR THAT DOG?

YEAH—HE SOUNDS HURT ... AND THE FROGLING AIN'T IN BED.

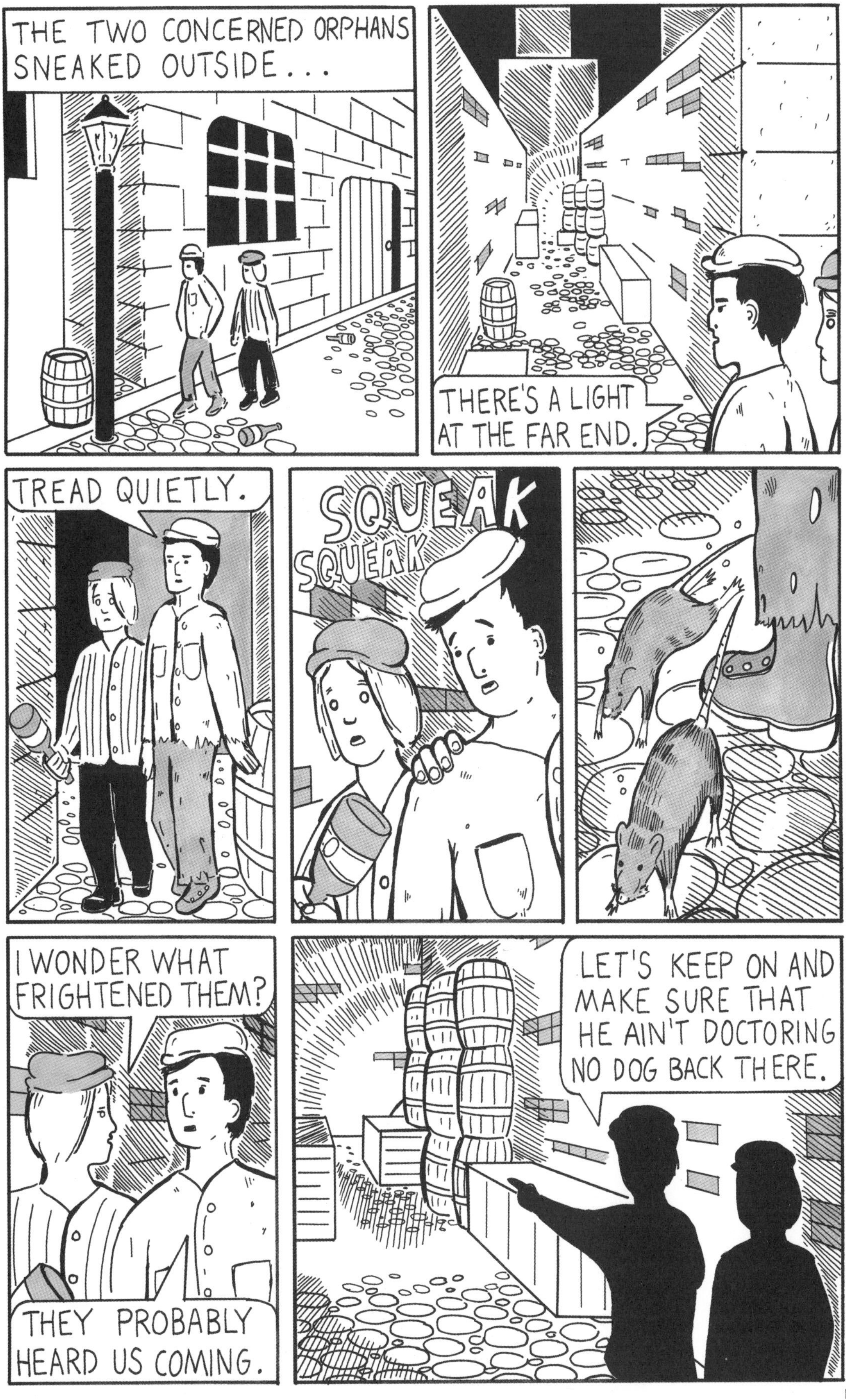
THE TWO CONCERNED ORPHANS SNEAKED OUTSIDE...
THERE'S A LIGHT AT THE FAR END.
TREAD QUIETLY.
SQUEAK
SQUEAK
I WONDER WHAT FRIGHTENED THEM?
THEY PROBABLY HEARD US COMING.
LET'S KEEP ON AND MAKE SURE THAT HE AIN'T DOCTORING NO DOG BACK THERE.

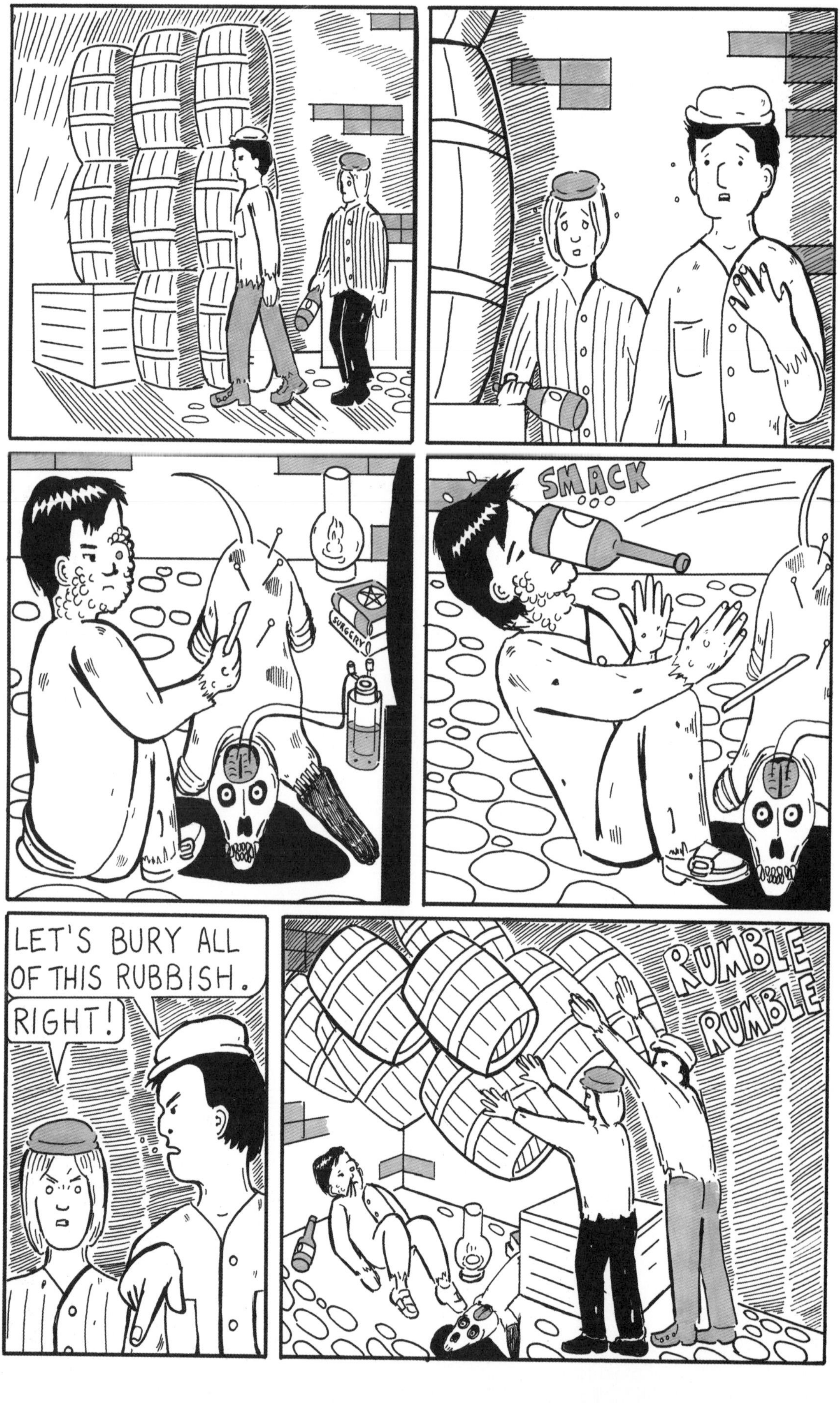
SURGERY
SMACK
LET'S BURY ALL OF THIS RUBBISH.
RIGHT!
RUMBLE
RUMBLE

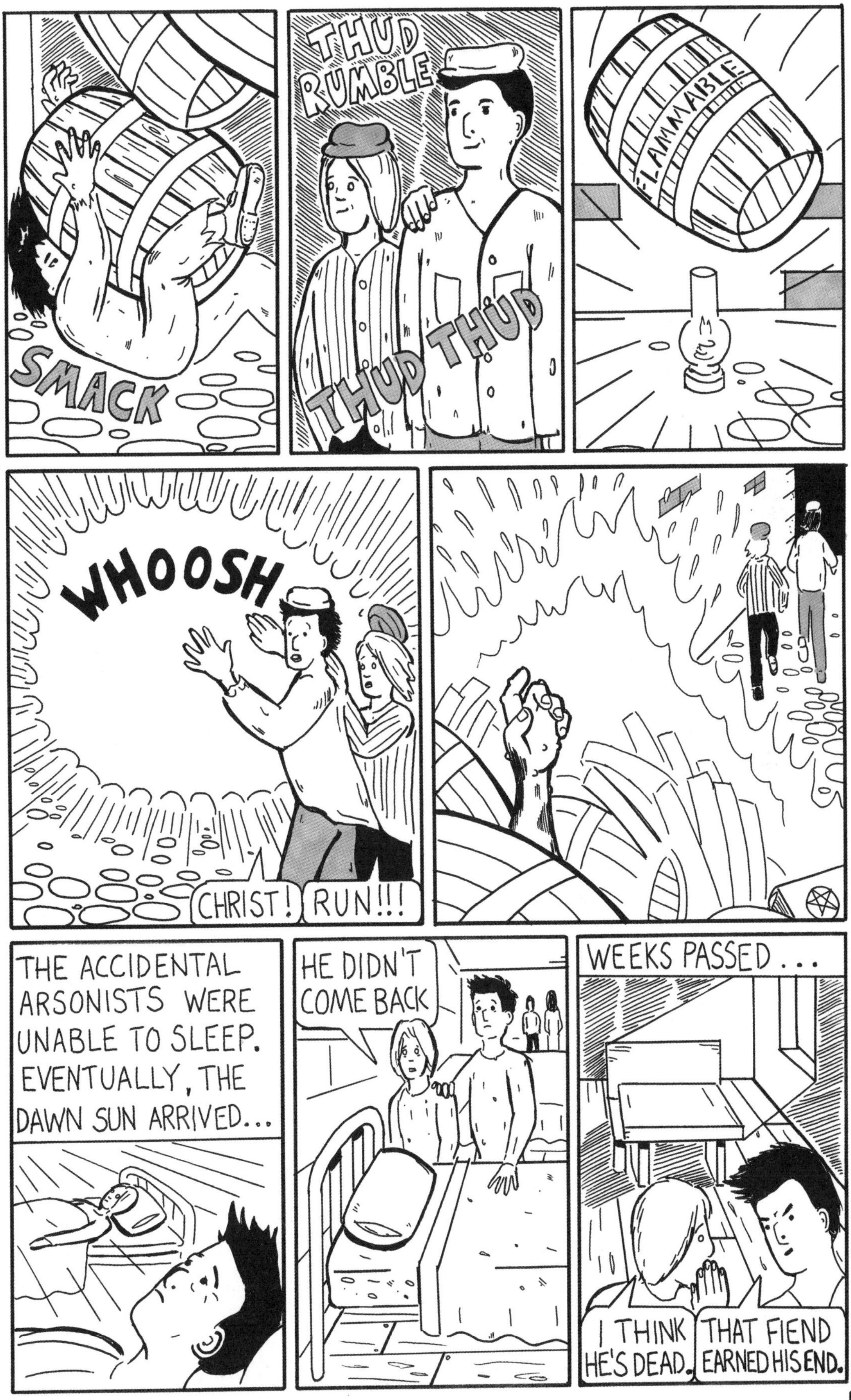
SMACK
THUD
RUMBLE
THUD THUD
FLAMMABLE
WHOOSH
CHRIST!
RUN!!!
THE ACCIDENTAL ARSONISTS WERE UNABLE TO SLEEP. EVENTUALLY, THE DAWN SUN ARRIVED...
HE DIDN'T COME BACK
WEEKS PASSED...
I THINK HE'S DEAD.
THAT FIEND EARNED HIS END.

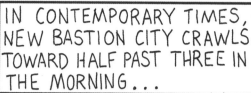
IN CONTEMPORARY TIMES, NEW BASTION CITY CRAWLS TOWARD HALF PAST THREE IN THE MORNING...

NINTH PRECINCT

HAVE YOU EVER HEARD OF A GUY NAMED SIDNEY BAUMGARTEN?

NO, I HAVEN'T. DOCTOR, LAWYER OR RABBI?

LAWYER. TRIBUS ASKED FOR HIM BY NAME. HAD HIS BUSINESS CARD.

THEY MANUFACTURE BUSINESS CARDS THIS MILLENNIUM?

KNOCK KNOCK

YOU GOT THE FILE ON JOHN TRIBUS?

YEAH, BUT THE BURGER PLACE IS OUT OF PATTIES.

SIGH

COME IN.

JOHN TRIBUS IS THE GUY'S REAL NAME?

IT LOOKS LIKE IT IS. THE WORD MEANS 'THREE' IN LATIN.

FASCINATING. NOW TELL ME SOMETHING WORTH REMEMBERING.

TRIBUS WAS TRIED FOR MURDER SIX YEARS AGO, BUT FOUND INNOCENT.

JURIES ARE ADORABLE. WHAT ELSE?

HE WAS BORN IN NEW BASTION. WAS IN THE MARINES. WENT TO IRAQ. HONORABLY DISCHARGED THEN DISAPPEARED FOR THREE YEARS ACCORDING TO THE I.R.S.

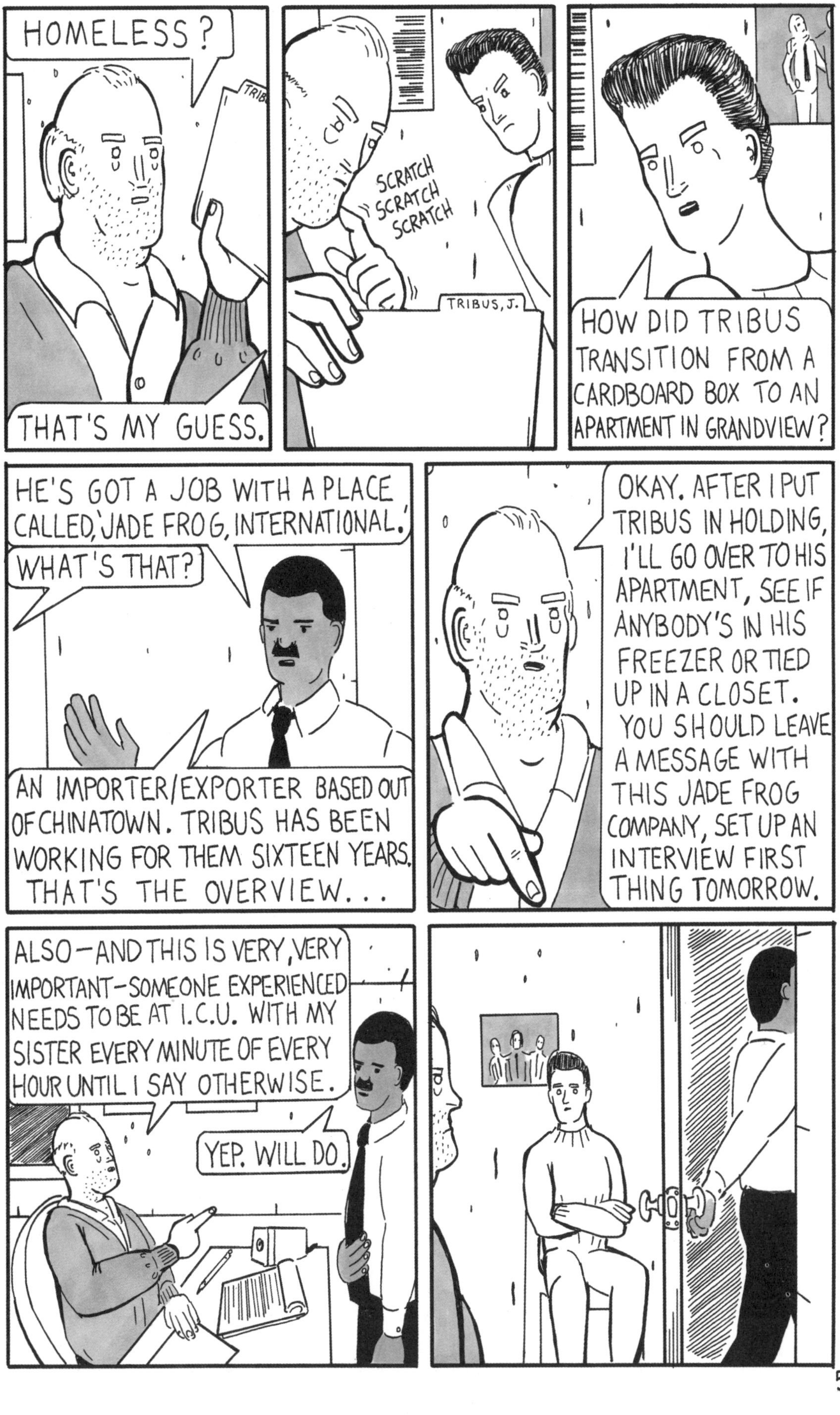
HOMELESS?
THAT'S MY GUESS.
TRIB
SCRATCH SCRATCH SCRATCH
TRIBUS, J.
HOW DID TRIBUS TRANSITION FROM A CARDBOARD BOX TO AN APARTMENT IN GRANDVIEW?
HE'S GOT A JOB WITH A PLACE CALLED, 'JADE FROG, INTERNATIONAL.'
WHAT'S THAT?
AN IMPORTER/EXPORTER BASED OUT OF CHINATOWN. TRIBUS HAS BEEN WORKING FOR THEM SIXTEEN YEARS. THAT'S THE OVERVIEW...
OKAY. AFTER I PUT TRIBUS IN HOLDING, I'LL GO OVER TO HIS APARTMENT, SEE IF ANYBODY'S IN HIS FREEZER OR TIED UP IN A CLOSET. YOU SHOULD LEAVE A MESSAGE WITH THIS JADE FROG COMPANY, SET UP AN INTERVIEW FIRST THING TOMORROW.
ALSO—AND THIS IS VERY, VERY IMPORTANT—SOMEONE EXPERIENCED NEEDS TO BE AT I.C.U. WITH MY SISTER EVERY MINUTE OF EVERY HOUR UNTIL I SAY OTHERWISE.
YEP. WILL DO.

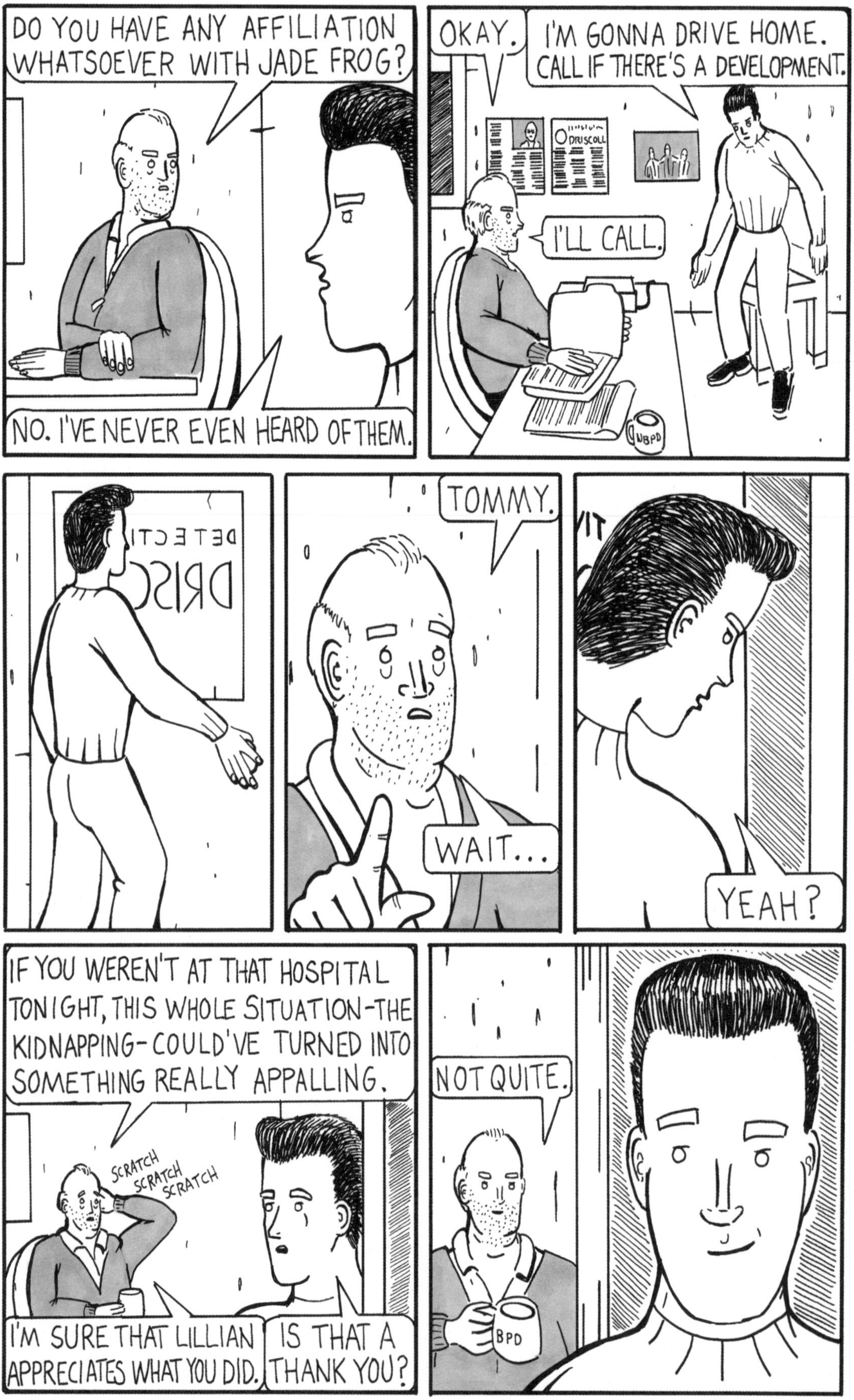
DO YOU HAVE ANY AFFILIATION WHATSOEVER WITH JADE FROG?
NO. I'VE NEVER EVEN HEARD OF THEM.
OKAY.
I'M GONNA DRIVE HOME. CALL IF THERE'S A DEVELOPMENT.
I'LL CALL.
TOMMY.
WAIT...
YEAH?
IF YOU WEREN'T AT THAT HOSPITAL TONIGHT, THIS WHOLE SITUATION-THE KIDNAPPING-COULD'VE TURNED INTO SOMETHING REALLY APPALLING.
SCRATCH SCRATCH SCRATCH
I'M SURE THAT LILLIAN APPRECIATES WHAT YOU DID.
IS THAT A THANK YOU?
NOT QUITE.
BPD

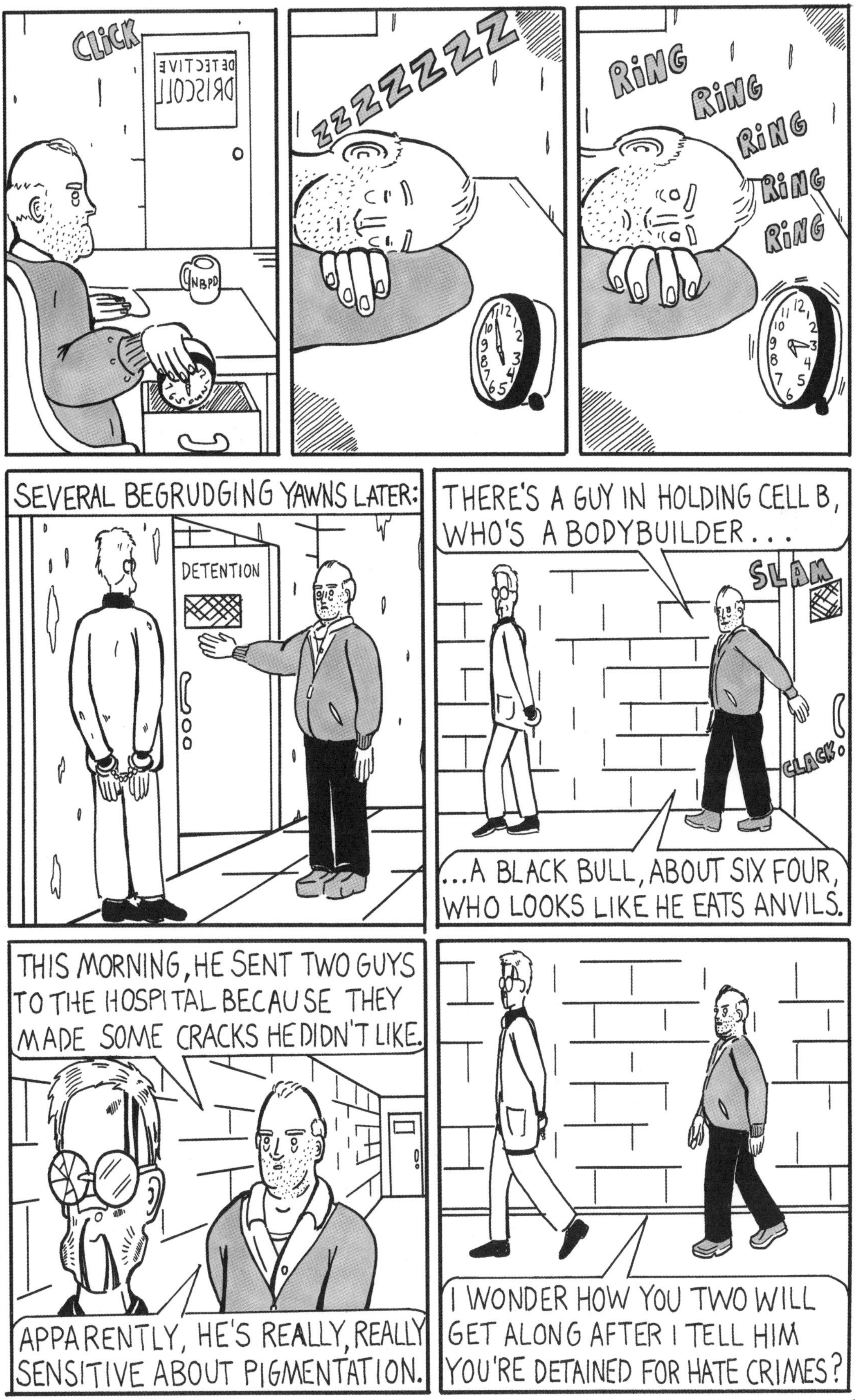
CLICK
DETECTIVE DRISCOLL
NBPD
ZZZZZZZZ
RING RING RING RING RING
SEVERAL BEGRUDGING YAWNS LATER:
DETENTION
THERE'S A GUY IN HOLDING CELL B, WHO'S A BODYBUILDER . . .
SLAM
CLACK
...A BLACK BULL, ABOUT SIX FOUR, WHO LOOKS LIKE HE EATS ANVILS.
THIS MORNING, HE SENT TWO GUYS TO THE HOSPITAL BECAUSE THEY MADE SOME CRACKS HE DIDN'T LIKE.
APPARENTLY, HE'S REALLY, REALLY SENSITIVE ABOUT PIGMENTATION.
I WONDER HOW YOU TWO WILL GET ALONG AFTER I TELL HIM YOU'RE DETAINED FOR HATE CRIMES?

HARMONIOUSLY?

MAY I PRESUME THAT THERE ARE NO WORKING CAMERAS IN THIS AREA?

THEY BROKE DOWN A FEW YEARS AGO.

CLACK

KEEP WALKING, STRING BEAN.

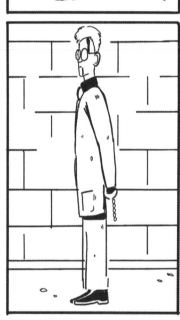

OKAY...

TIME TO GET CATALYTIC.

THUMP

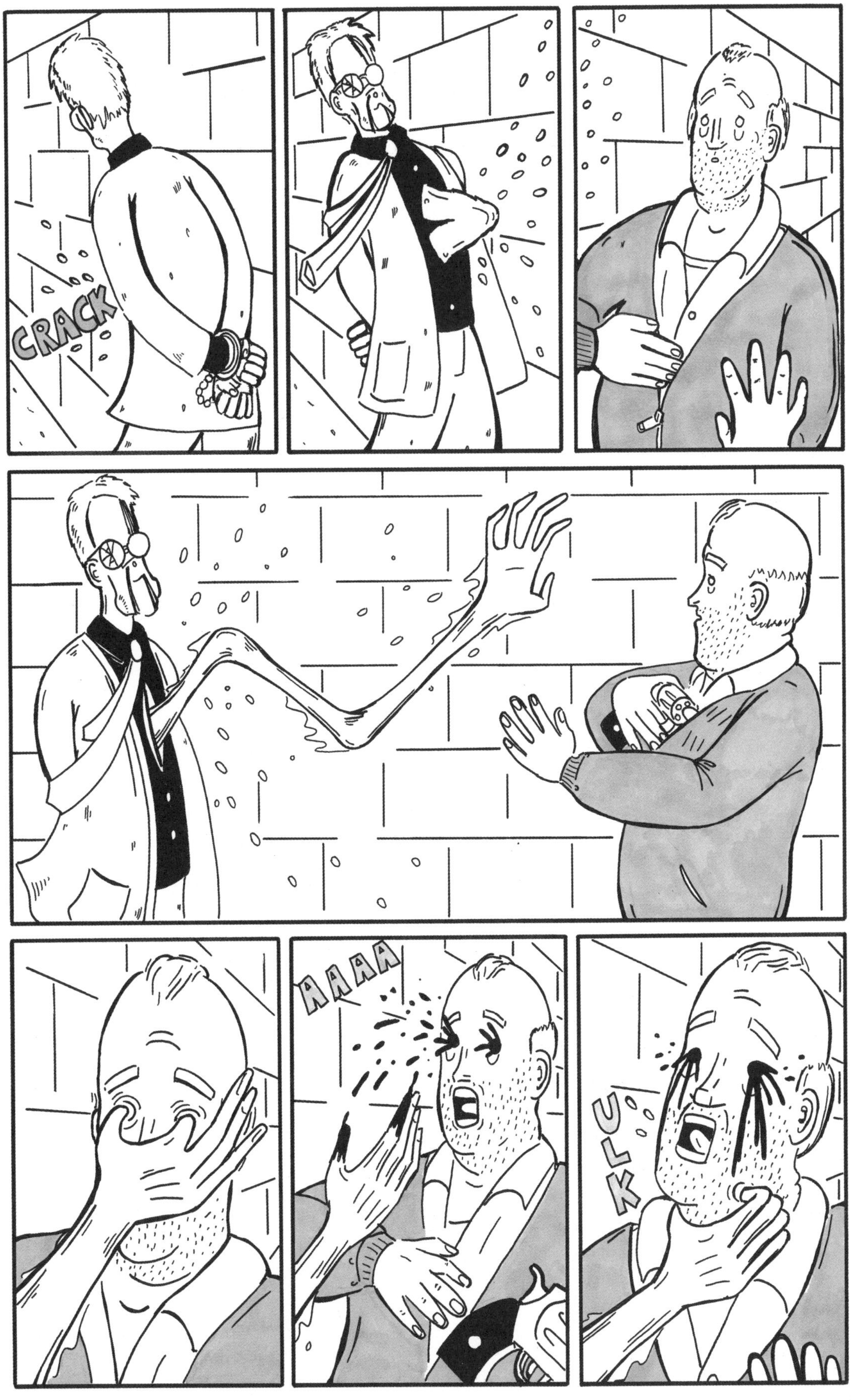
CRACK
AAAA
ULK

DAWN DRAWS NEARER, BUT TOMMY DRISCOLL CANNOT SLEEP.

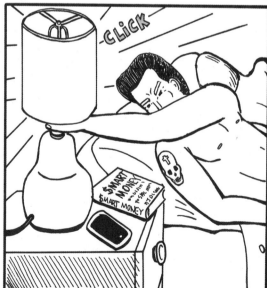

CLICK

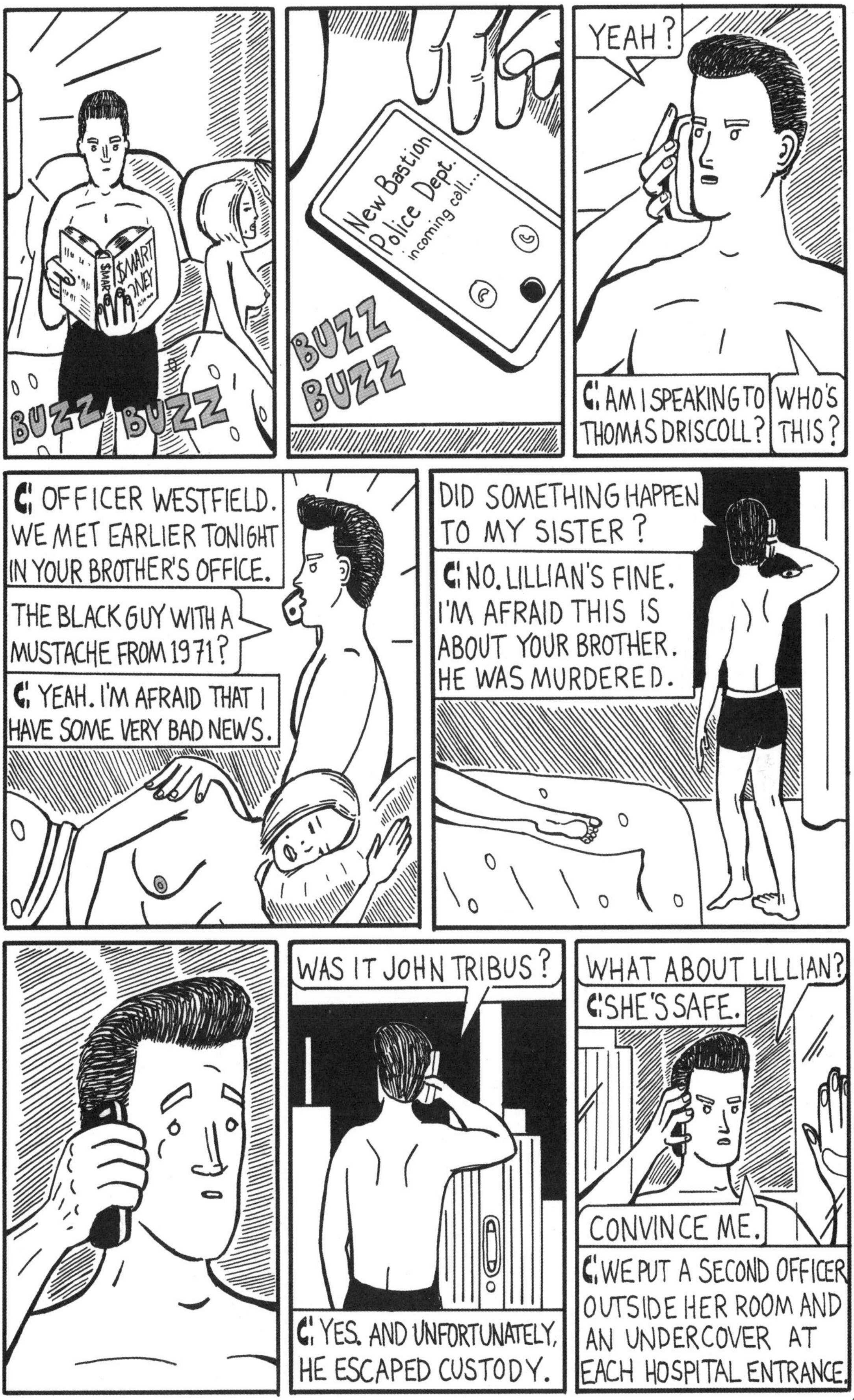
BUZZ BUZZ
$MART MONEY
New Bastion Police Dept.
incoming call...
BUZZ BUZZ
YEAH?
C: AM I SPEAKING TO THOMAS DRISCOLL?
WHO'S THIS?
C: OFFICER WESTFIELD. WE MET EARLIER TONIGHT IN YOUR BROTHER'S OFFICE.
THE BLACK GUY WITH A MUSTACHE FROM 1971?
C: YEAH. I'M AFRAID THAT I HAVE SOME VERY BAD NEWS.
DID SOMETHING HAPPEN TO MY SISTER?
C: NO. LILLIAN'S FINE. I'M AFRAID THIS IS ABOUT YOUR BROTHER. HE WAS MURDERED.
WAS IT JOHN TRIBUS?
C: YES. AND UNFORTUNATELY, HE ESCAPED CUSTODY.
WHAT ABOUT LILLIAN?
C: SHE'S SAFE.
CONVINCE ME.
C: WE PUT A SECOND OFFICER OUTSIDE HER ROOM AND AN UNDERCOVER AT EACH HOSPITAL ENTRANCE.

YOU GUYS'RE LOOKING FOR TRIBUS?

C: YES WE ARE.

DID YOU CHECK OUT HIS APARTMENT IN GRANDVIEW?

C: IT TURNED OUT TO BE A FAKE ADDRESS.

THE BUILDING DOESN'T EXIST?

C: THE BUILDING'S REAL, BUT THE APARTMENT NUMBER ISN'T.

HOW THE FUCK DID A CAPTIVE PRISONER KILL MY BROTHER INSIDE OF A POLICE PRECINCT AND ESCAPE?

C: THE DETAILS AREN'T CLEAR AT THIS TIME, MR. DRISCOLL. WE'RE SORRY. LEO WAS A GREAT—

EVERY BAD THING I'VE SAID ABOUT COPS DURING THE COURSE OF MY ENTIRE LIFE HAS JUST BEEN VALIDATED.

C: WE'RE ANGRY TOO.

SO WHAT'RE YOU BLUE CLOWNS DOING NOW?

C: WE'VE SENT HIS DESCRIPTION TO AIRPORTS, BUS DEPOTS, TRAIN STATIONS, AND HIGHWAY PATROL, AND WE'VE CALLED IN EVERY OFFICER.

ARE YOU LOOKING FOR THAT LAWYER WHO TRIBUS KEPT ASKING FOR?

C: WHAT LAWYER?

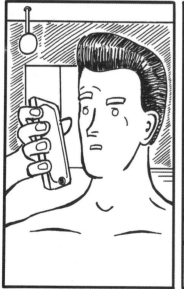

SORRY... I DON'T RECALL HIS NAME...

C: OKAY.

C: IF YOU REMEMBER, CALL THE STATION.

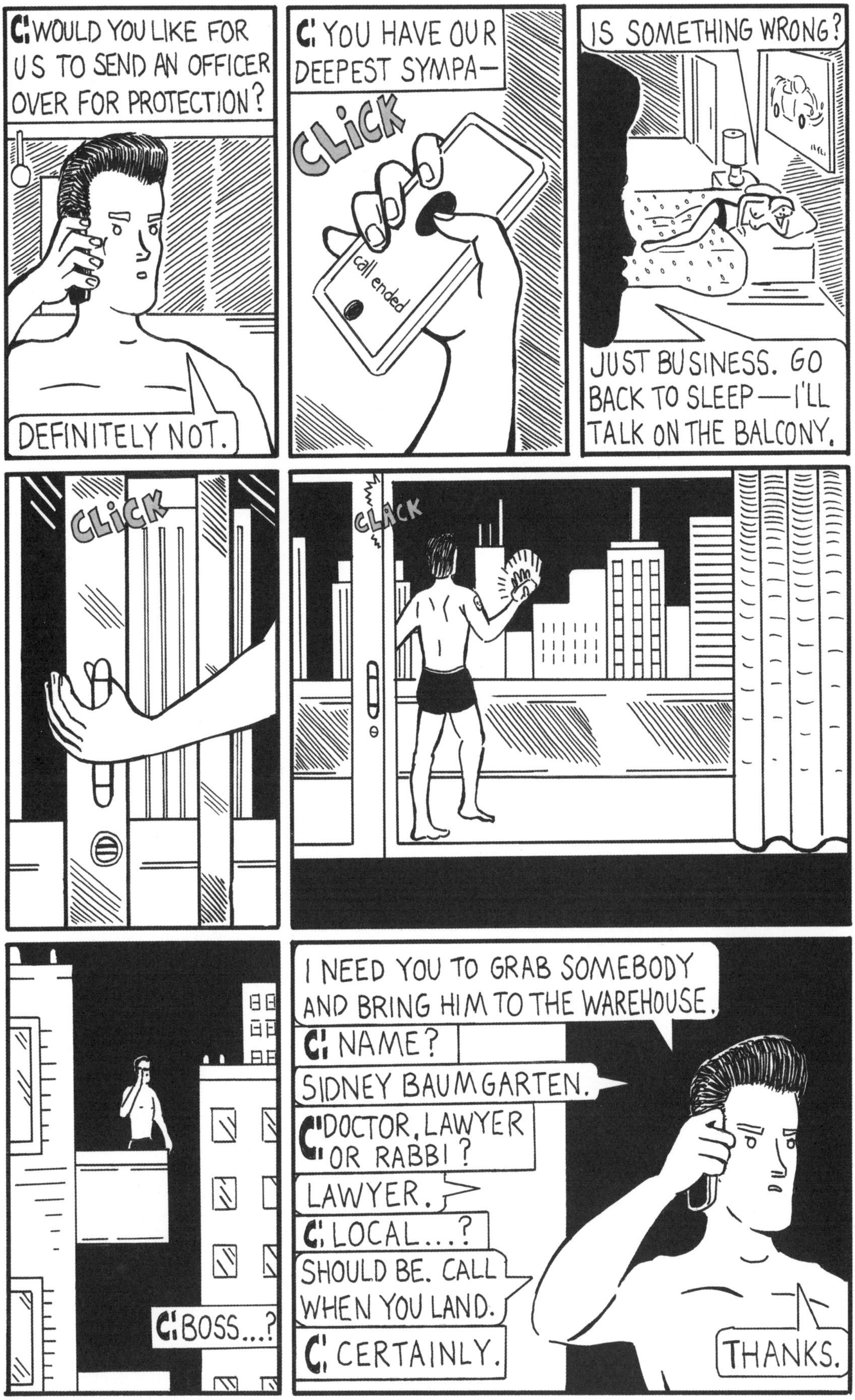
C: WOULD YOU LIKE FOR US TO SEND AN OFFICER OVER FOR PROTECTION?
DEFINITELY NOT.
C: YOU HAVE OUR DEEPEST SYMPA—
CLICK
call ended
IS SOMETHING WRONG?
JUST BUSINESS. GO BACK TO SLEEP—I'LL TALK ON THE BALCONY.
CLICK
CLACK
C: BOSS...?
I NEED YOU TO GRAB SOMEBODY AND BRING HIM TO THE WAREHOUSE.
C: NAME?
SIDNEY BAUMGARTEN.
C: DOCTOR, LAWYER OR RABBI?
LAWYER.
C: LOCAL...?
SHOULD BE. CALL WHEN YOU LAND.
C: CERTAINLY.
THANKS.

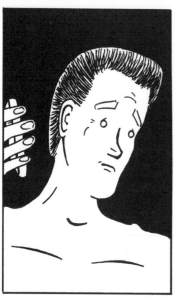

THIRTY—FIVE MINUTES LATER...

...ON THE EAST SIDE OF NEW BASTION...

SIDNEY BAUMGARTEN'S MINIATURE SPOUSE MAKES A REQUEST...

MEOW

YOU'VE ALREADY APPRISED ME OF YOUR HUNGER, MY INAMORATA.

MROWR MEOW

WITH YOUR PERMISSION, I SHALL SURVEY THE ICEBOX.

MEOW MRRR

HOW DOES LIVERWURST SOUND? WOULD THAT BE ACCEPTABLE?

OR SHALL I CHARTER A FISHING BOAT SO THAT I MIGHT REEL IN A TUNA?

ROWR ?

CLICK CLACK

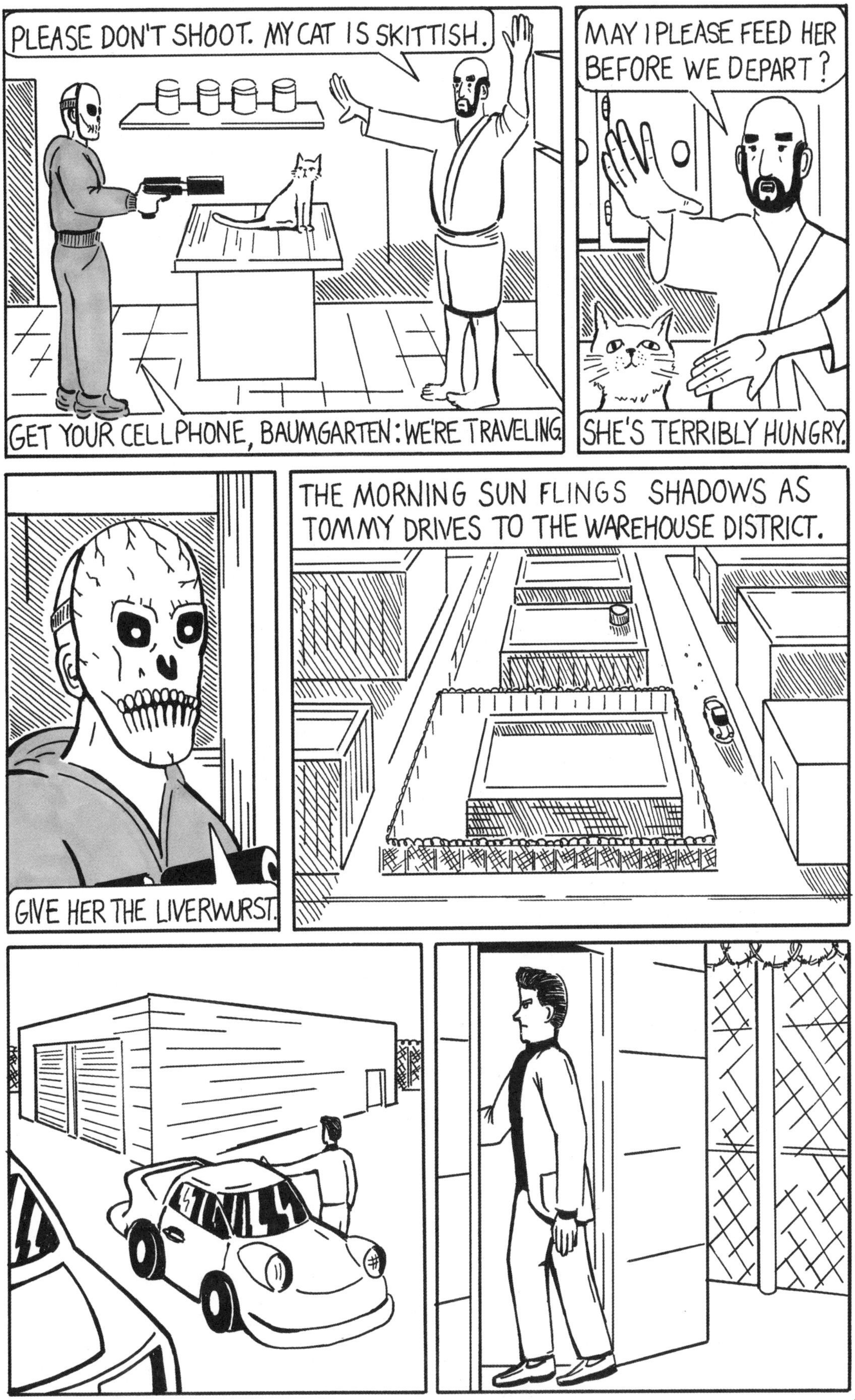
PLEASE DON'T SHOOT. MY CAT IS SKITTISH.
GET YOUR CELLPHONE, BAUMGARTEN: WE'RE TRAVELING.
MAY I PLEASE FEED HER BEFORE WE DEPART?
SHE'S TERRIBLY HUNGRY.
GIVE HER THE LIVERWURST.
THE MORNING SUN FLINGS SHADOWS AS TOMMY DRIVES TO THE WAREHOUSE DISTRICT.

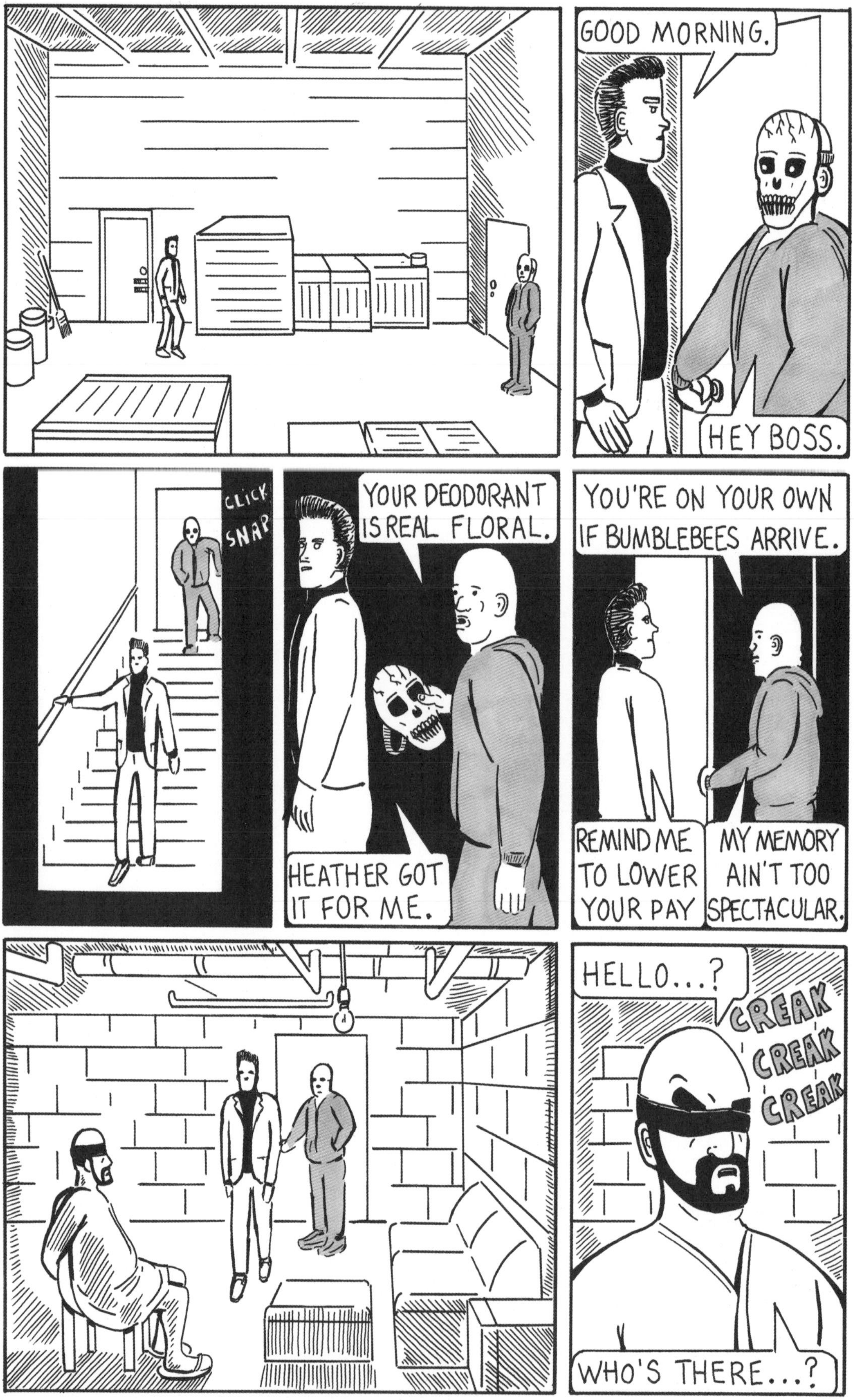
GOOD MORNING.
HEY BOSS.
CLICK
SNAP
YOUR DEODORANT IS REAL FLORAL.
HEATHER GOT IT FOR ME.
YOU'RE ON YOUR OWN IF BUMBLEBEES ARRIVE.
REMIND ME TO LOWER YOUR PAY
MY MEMORY AIN'T TOO SPECTACULAR.
HELLO...?
CREAK
CREAK
CREAK
WHO'S THERE...?

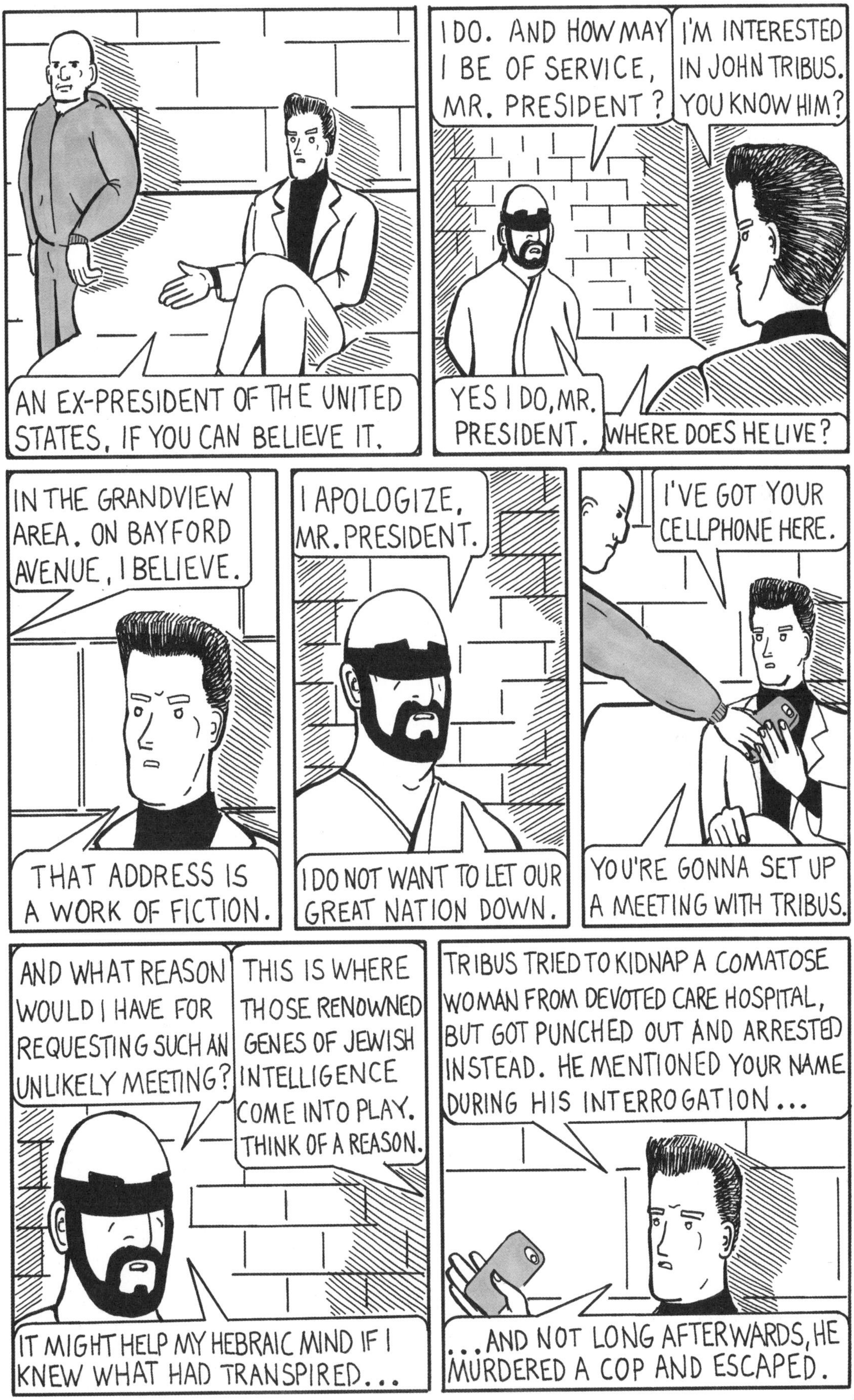
AN EX-PRESIDENT OF THE UNITED STATES, IF YOU CAN BELIEVE IT.
I DO. AND HOW MAY I BE OF SERVICE, MR. PRESIDENT?
I'M INTERESTED IN JOHN TRIBUS. YOU KNOW HIM?
YES I DO, MR. PRESIDENT.
WHERE DOES HE LIVE?
IN THE GRANDVIEW AREA. ON BAYFORD AVENUE, I BELIEVE.
THAT ADDRESS IS A WORK OF FICTION.
I APOLOGIZE, MR. PRESIDENT.
I DO NOT WANT TO LET OUR GREAT NATION DOWN.
I'VE GOT YOUR CELLPHONE HERE.
YOU'RE GONNA SET UP A MEETING WITH TRIBUS.
AND WHAT REASON WOULD I HAVE FOR REQUESTING SUCH AN UNLIKELY MEETING?
THIS IS WHERE THOSE RENOWNED GENES OF JEWISH INTELLIGENCE COME INTO PLAY. THINK OF A REASON.
IT MIGHT HELP MY HEBRAIC MIND IF I KNEW WHAT HAD TRANSPIRED...
TRIBUS TRIED TO KIDNAP A COMATOSE WOMAN FROM DEVOTED CARE HOSPITAL, BUT GOT PUNCHED OUT AND ARRESTED INSTEAD. HE MENTIONED YOUR NAME DURING HIS INTERROGATION...
...AND NOT LONG AFTERWARDS, HE MURDERED A COP AND ESCAPED.

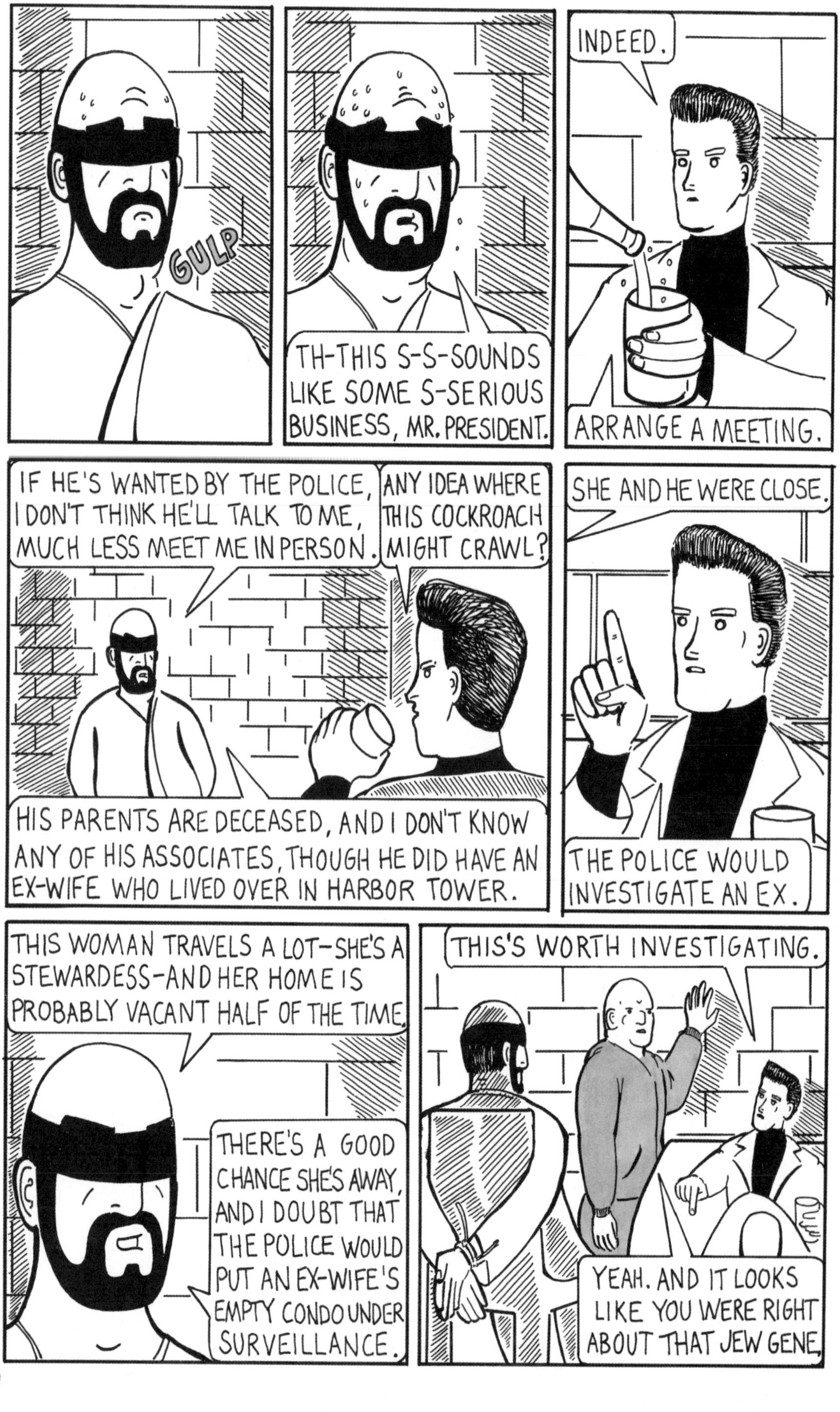
GULP
TH-THIS S-S-SOUNDS LIKE SOME S-SERIOUS BUSINESS, MR. PRESIDENT.
INDEED.
ARRANGE A MEETING.
IF HE'S WANTED BY THE POLICE, I DON'T THINK HE'LL TALK TO ME, MUCH LESS MEET ME IN PERSON.
ANY IDEA WHERE THIS COCKROACH MIGHT CRAWL?
HIS PARENTS ARE DECEASED, AND I DON'T KNOW ANY OF HIS ASSOCIATES, THOUGH HE DID HAVE AN EX-WIFE WHO LIVED OVER IN HARBOR TOWER.
SHE AND HE WERE CLOSE.
THE POLICE WOULD INVESTIGATE AN EX.
THIS WOMAN TRAVELS A LOT—SHE'S A STEWARDESS—AND HER HOME IS PROBABLY VACANT HALF OF THE TIME.
THERE'S A GOOD CHANCE SHE'S AWAY, AND I DOUBT THAT THE POLICE WOULD PUT AN EX-WIFE'S EMPTY CONDO UNDER SURVEILLANCE.
THIS'S WORTH INVESTIGATING.
YEAH. AND IT LOOKS LIKE YOU WERE RIGHT ABOUT THAT JEW GENE.

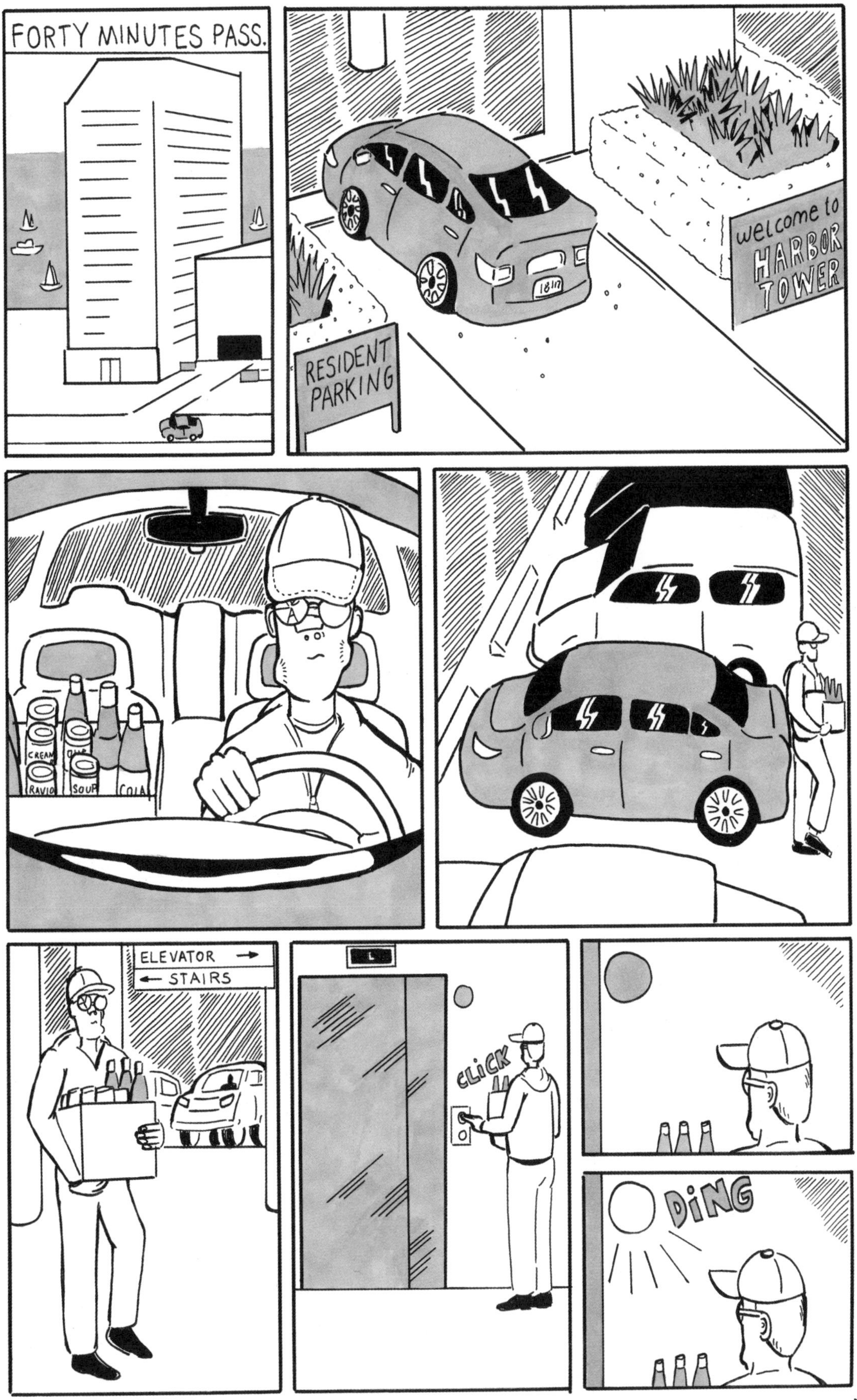
FORTY MINUTES PASS.
welcome to
HARBOR
TOWER
RESIDENT
PARKING
1817
CREAM
RAVIO
SOUP
COLA
ELEVATOR
STAIRS
CLICK
DiNG

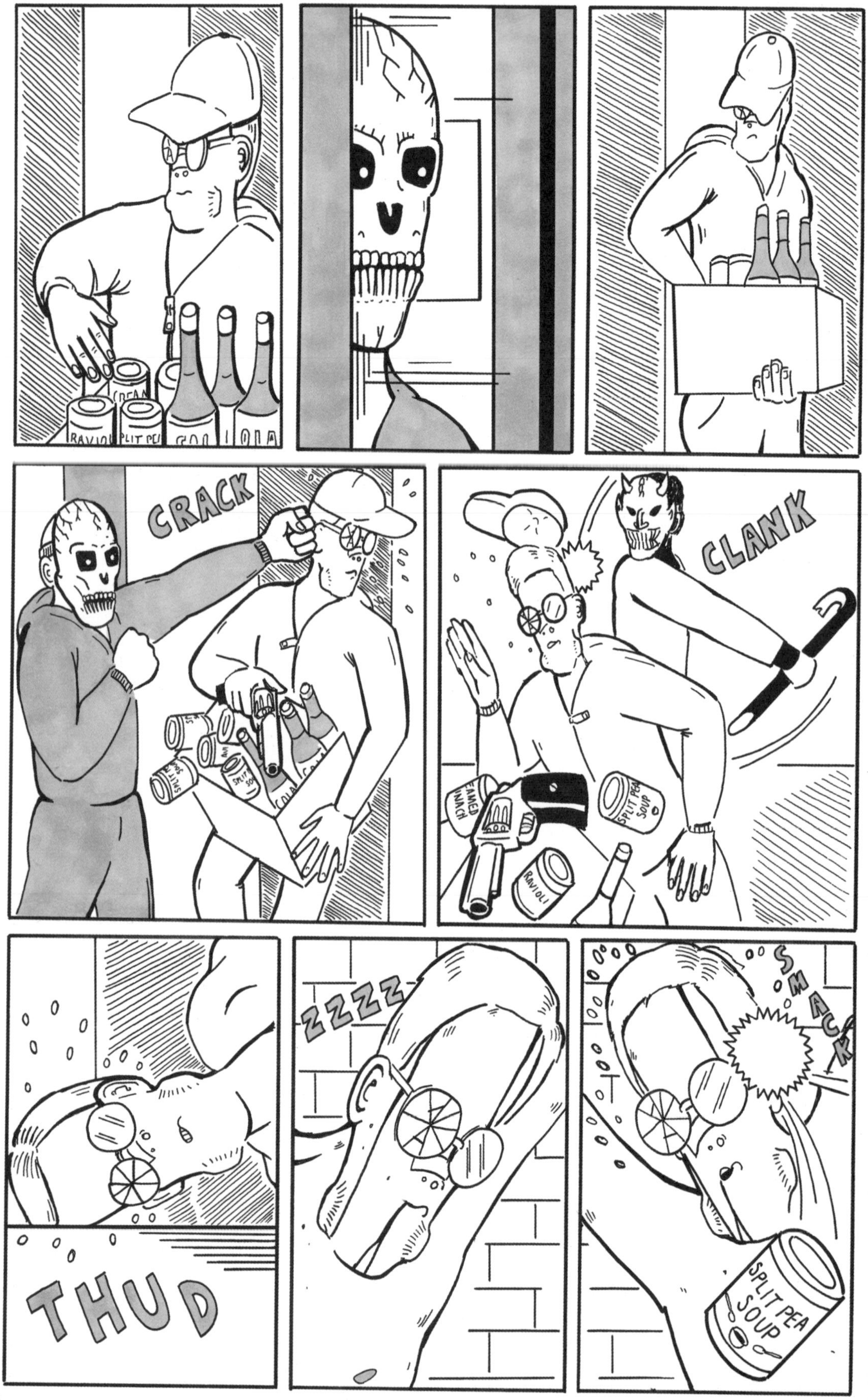
CRACK
CLANK
SPLIT PEA SOUP
RAVIOLI
THUD
ZZZZ
SMACK
SPLIT PEA SOUP

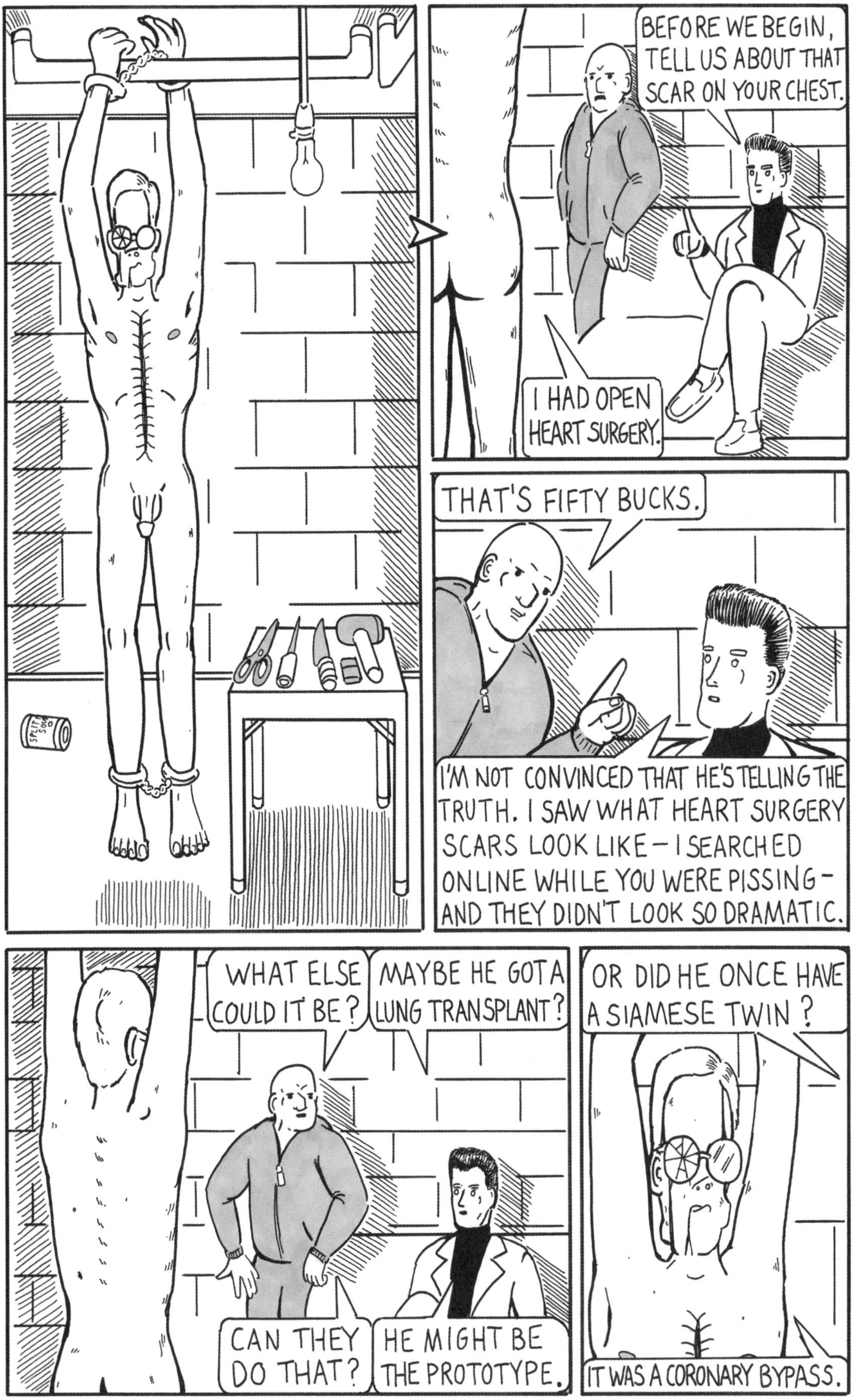
SPLIT SOUP
BEFORE WE BEGIN, TELL US ABOUT THAT SCAR ON YOUR CHEST.
I HAD OPEN HEART SURGERY.
THAT'S FIFTY BUCKS.
I'M NOT CONVINCED THAT HE'S TELLING THE TRUTH. I SAW WHAT HEART SURGERY SCARS LOOK LIKE – I SEARCHED ONLINE WHILE YOU WERE PISSING – AND THEY DIDN'T LOOK SO DRAMATIC.
WHAT ELSE COULD IT BE?
MAYBE HE GOT A LUNG TRANSPLANT?
CAN THEY DO THAT?
HE MIGHT BE THE PROTOTYPE.
OR DID HE ONCE HAVE A SIAMESE TWIN?
IT WAS A CORONARY BYPASS.

FINE. THANKS.

OKAY, TRIBUS... ...TELL ME WHY YOU ABDUCTED LILLIAN DRISCOLL.

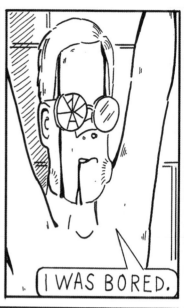

I WAS BORED.

BOSS...?

HURT HIM A LITTLE.

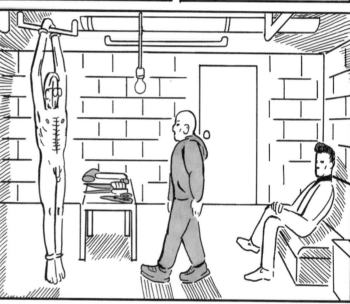

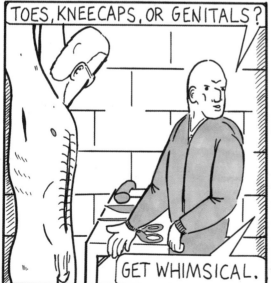

TOES, KNEECAPS, OR GENITALS?

GET WHIMSICAL.

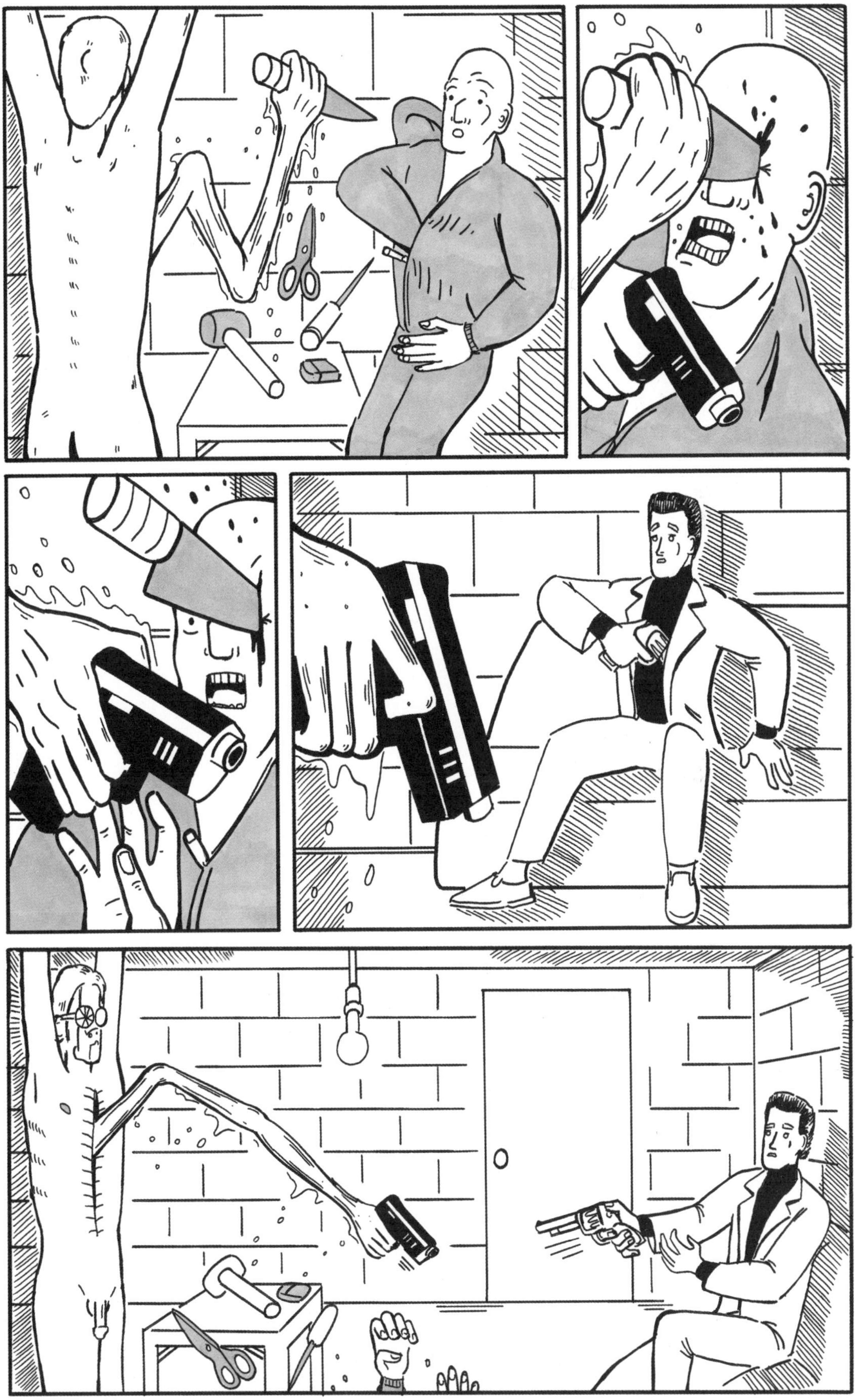

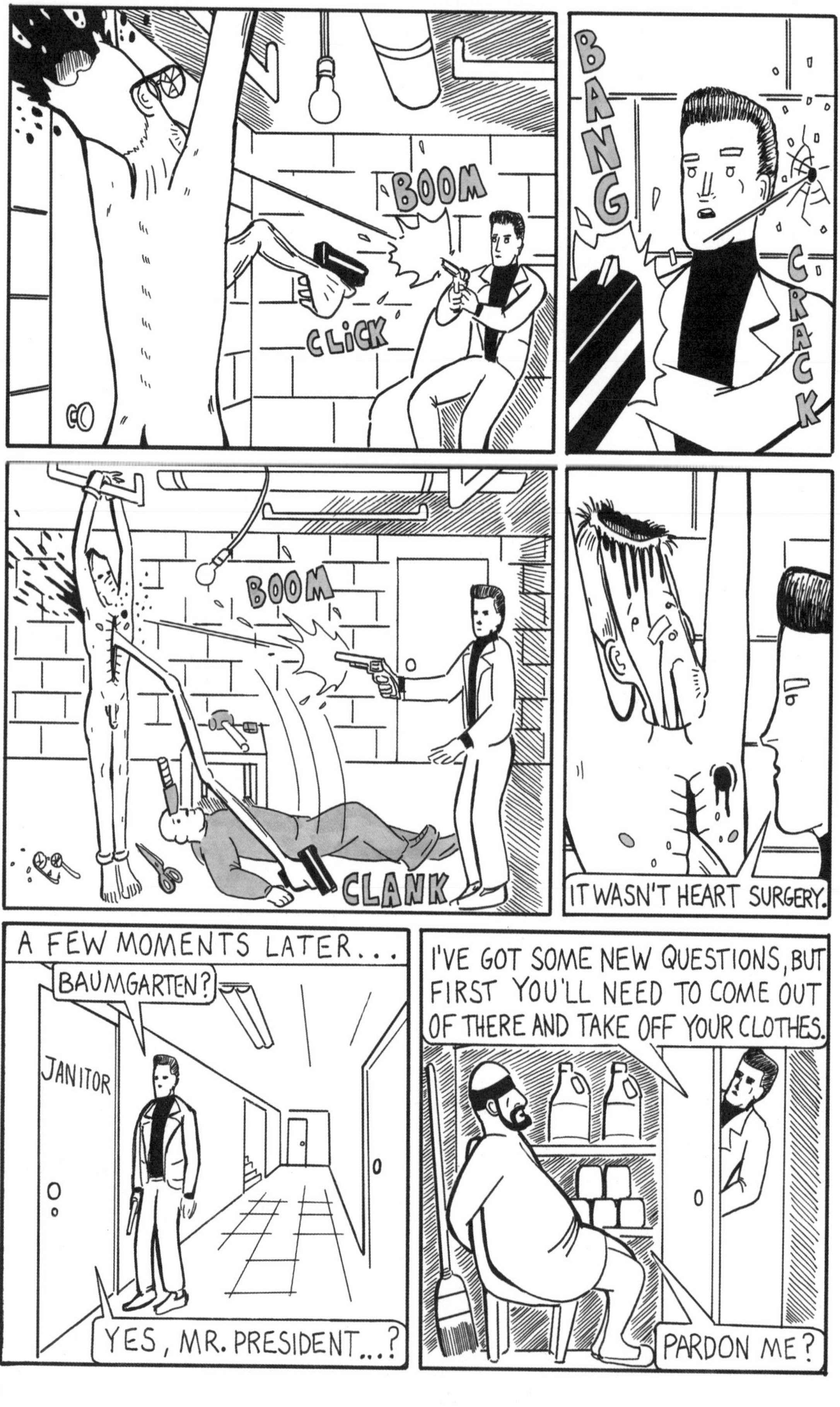
BOOM
CLICK
BANG
CRACK
BOOM
CLANK
IT WASN'T HEART SURGERY.
A FEW MOMENTS LATER...
BAUMGARTEN?
JANITOR
YES, MR. PRESIDENT...?
I'VE GOT SOME NEW QUESTIONS, BUT FIRST YOU'LL NEED TO COME OUT OF THERE AND TAKE OFF YOUR CLOTHES.
PARDON ME?

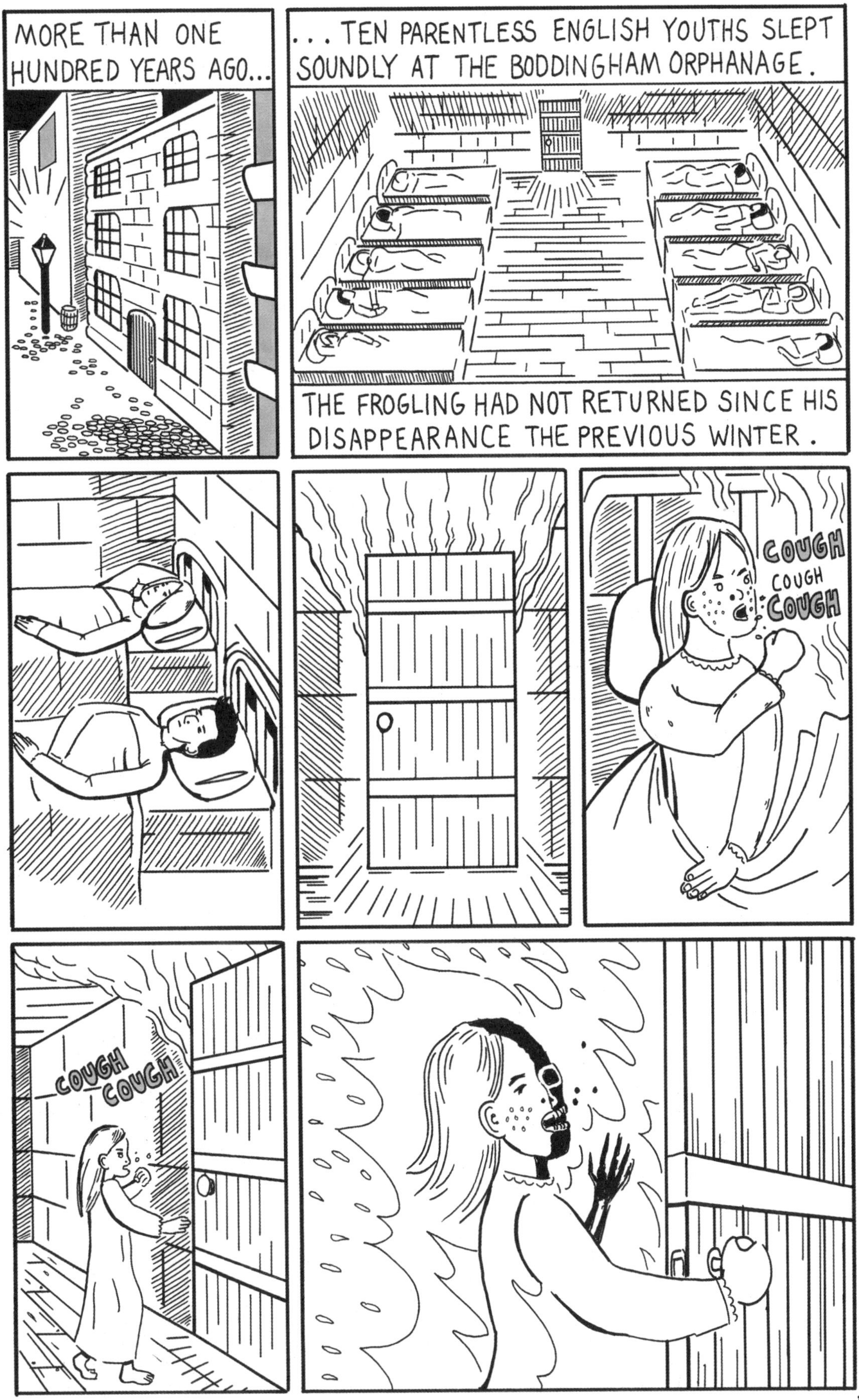
MORE THAN ONE HUNDRED YEARS AGO...
...TEN PARENTLESS ENGLISH YOUTHS SLEPT SOUNDLY AT THE BODDINGHAM ORPHANAGE.
THE FROGLING HAD NOT RETURNED SINCE HIS DISAPPEARANCE THE PREVIOUS WINTER.
COUGH
COUGH
COUGH
COUGH
COUGH

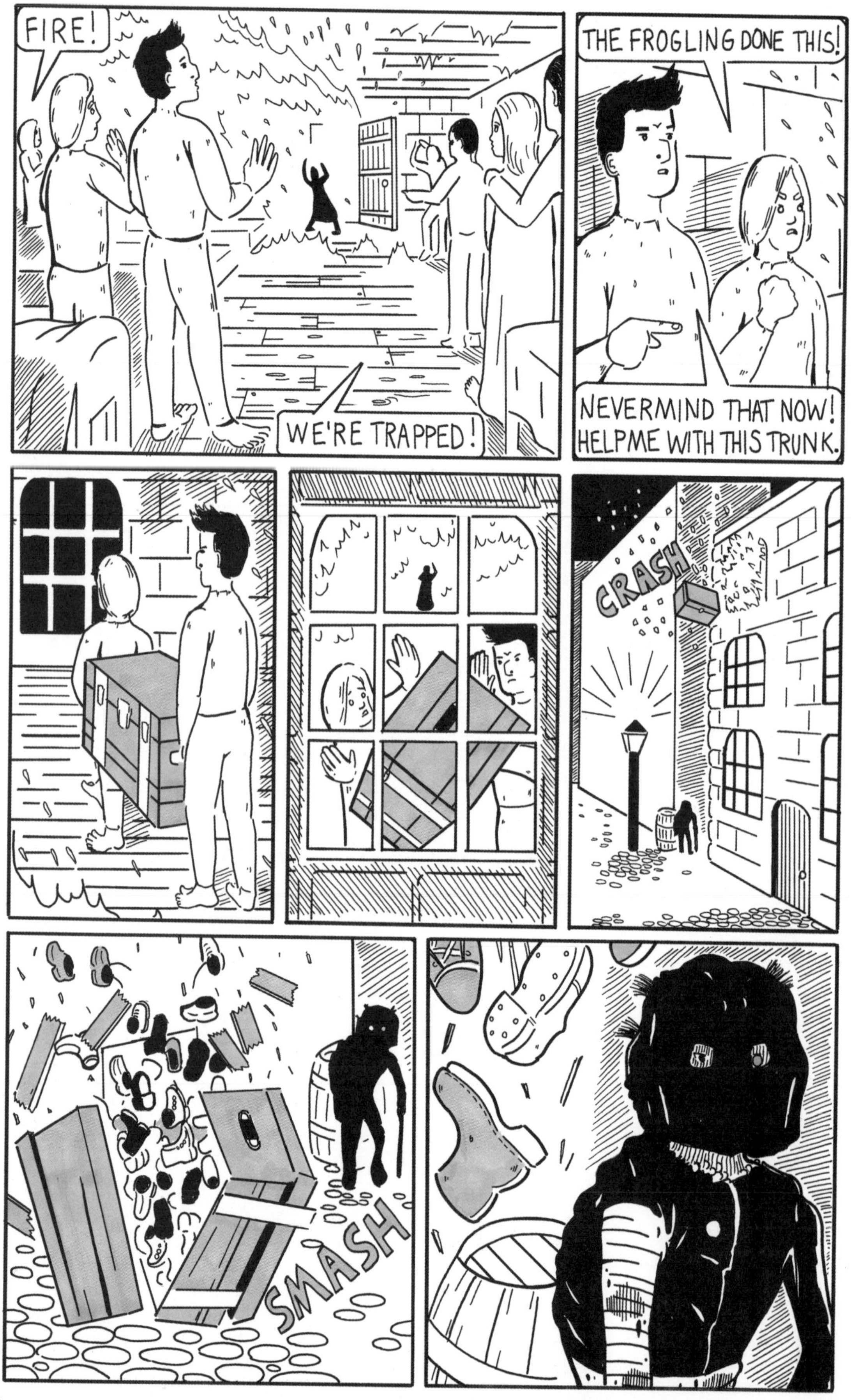
FIRE!
WE'RE TRAPPED!
THE FROGLING DONE THIS!
NEVERMIND THAT NOW! HELPME WITH THIS TRUNK.
CRASH
SMASH

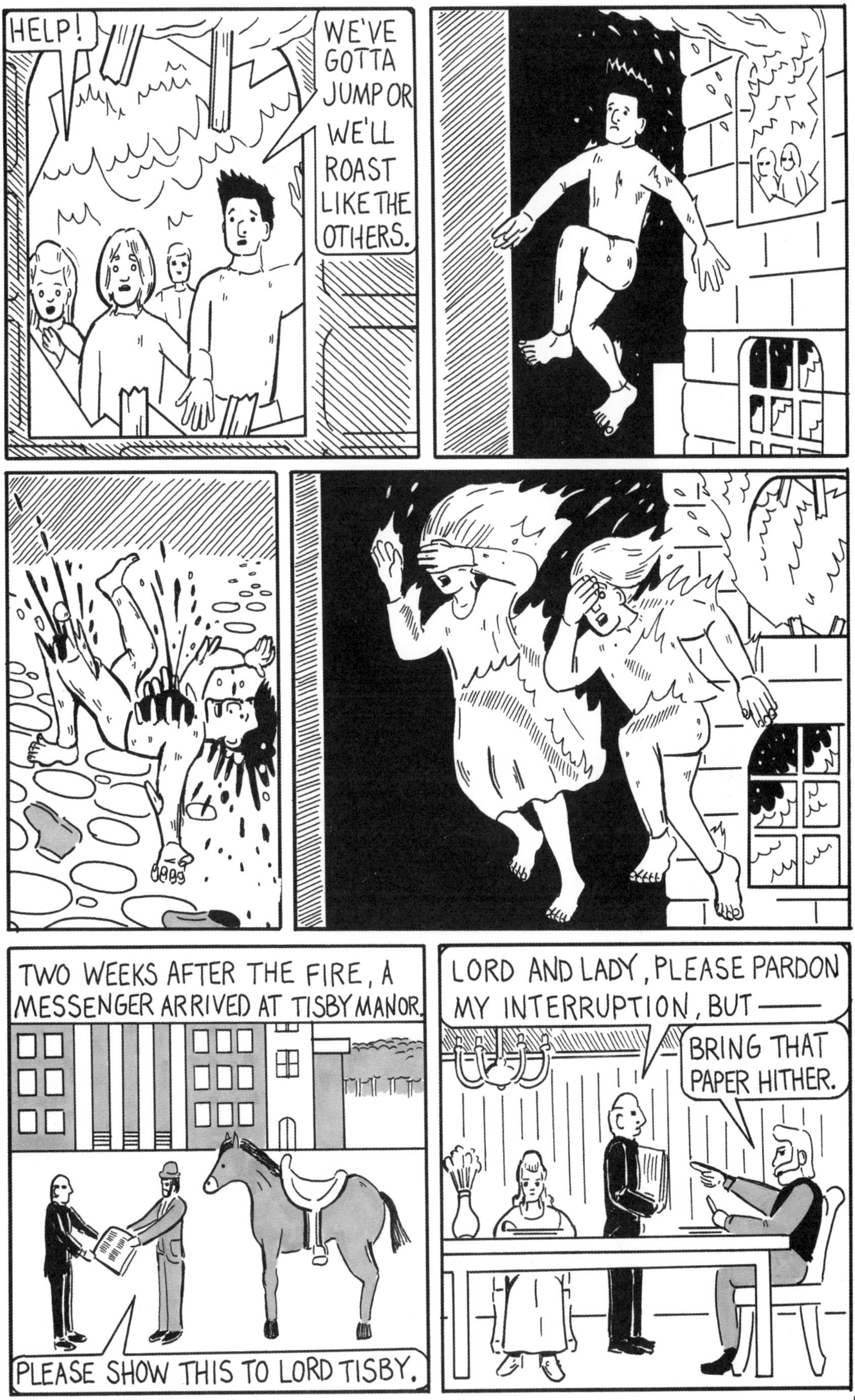
HELP!
WE'VE GOTTA JUMP OR WE'LL ROAST LIKE THE OTHERS.
TWO WEEKS AFTER THE FIRE, A MESSENGER ARRIVED AT TISBY MANOR.
PLEASE SHOW THIS TO LORD TISBY.
LORD AND LADY, PLEASE PARDON MY INTERRUPTION, BUT ——
BRING THAT PAPER HITHER.

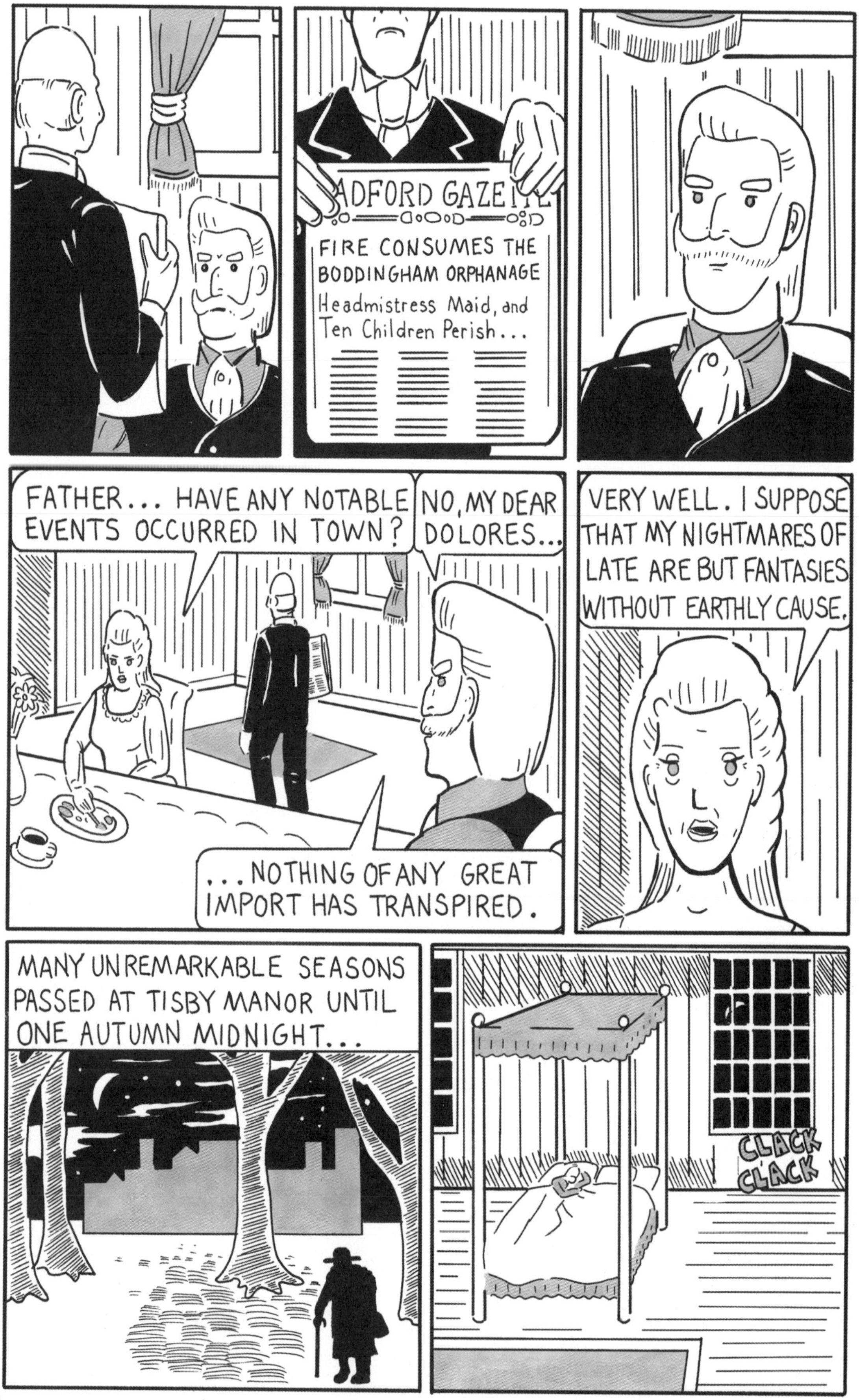
ADFORD GAZETTE
FIRE CONSUMES THE BODDINGHAM ORPHANAGE
Headmistress Maid, and Ten Children Perish...
FATHER... HAVE ANY NOTABLE EVENTS OCCURRED IN TOWN?
NO, MY DEAR DOLORES...
...NOTHING OF ANY GREAT IMPORT HAS TRANSPIRED.
VERY WELL. I SUPPOSE THAT MY NIGHTMARES OF LATE ARE BUT FANTASIES WITHOUT EARTHLY CAUSE.
MANY UNREMARKABLE SEASONS PASSED AT TISBY MANOR UNTIL ONE AUTUMN MIDNIGHT...
CLACK
CLACK

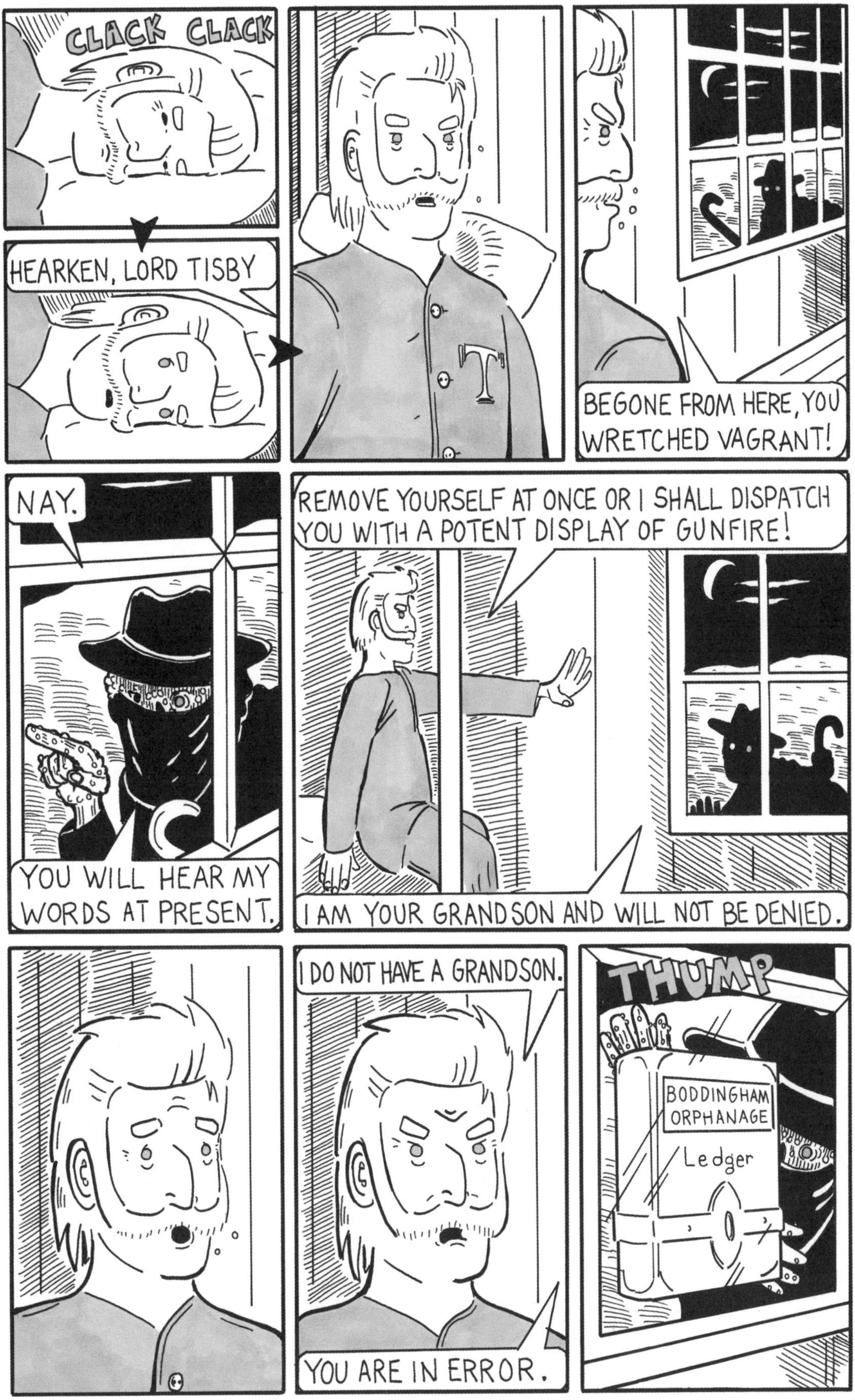

CLACK CLACK
HEARKEN, LORD TISBY
BEGONE FROM HERE, YOU WRETCHED VAGRANT!
NAY.
YOU WILL HEAR MY WORDS AT PRESENT.
REMOVE YOURSELF AT ONCE OR I SHALL DISPATCH YOU WITH A POTENT DISPLAY OF GUNFIRE!
I AM YOUR GRANDSON AND WILL NOT BE DENIED.
I DO NOT HAVE A GRANDSON.
YOU ARE IN ERROR.
THUMP
BODDINGHAM ORPHANAGE
Ledger

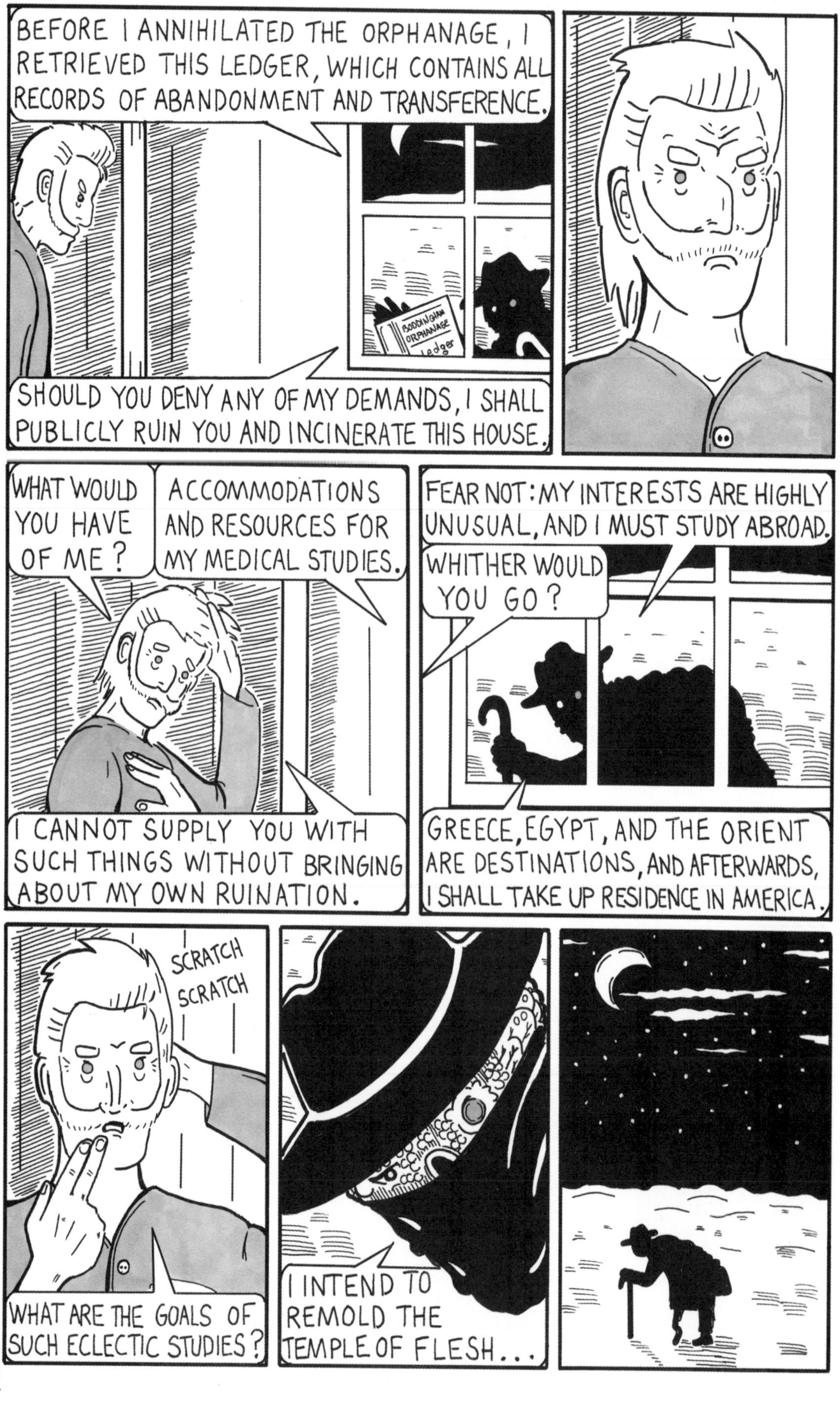
BEFORE I ANNIHILATED THE ORPHANAGE, I RETRIEVED THIS LEDGER, WHICH CONTAINS ALL RECORDS OF ABANDONMENT AND TRANSFERENCE.
BODDINGHAM ORPHANAGE Ledger
SHOULD YOU DENY ANY OF MY DEMANDS, I SHALL PUBLICLY RUIN YOU AND INCINERATE THIS HOUSE.
WHAT WOULD YOU HAVE OF ME?
ACCOMMODATIONS AND RESOURCES FOR MY MEDICAL STUDIES.
I CANNOT SUPPLY YOU WITH SUCH THINGS WITHOUT BRINGING ABOUT MY OWN RUINATION.
FEAR NOT: MY INTERESTS ARE HIGHLY UNUSUAL, AND I MUST STUDY ABROAD.
WHITHER WOULD YOU GO?
GREECE, EGYPT, AND THE ORIENT ARE DESTINATIONS, AND AFTERWARDS, I SHALL TAKE UP RESIDENCE IN AMERICA.
SCRATCH SCRATCH
WHAT ARE THE GOALS OF SUCH ECLECTIC STUDIES?
I INTEND TO REMOLD THE TEMPLE OF FLESH...

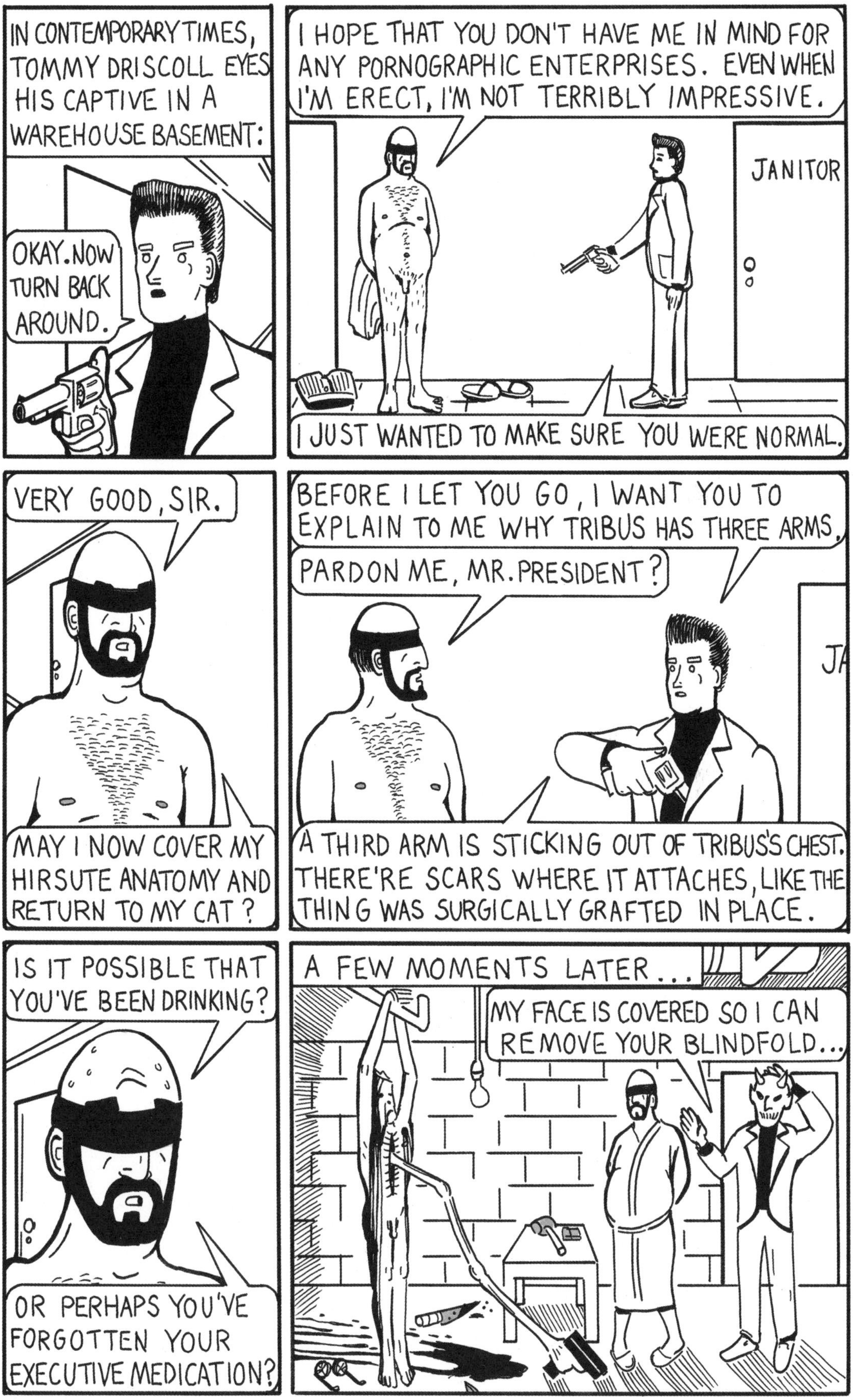
IN CONTEMPORARY TIMES, TOMMY DRISCOLL EYES HIS CAPTIVE IN A WAREHOUSE BASEMENT:
OKAY. NOW TURN BACK AROUND.
I HOPE THAT YOU DON'T HAVE ME IN MIND FOR ANY PORNOGRAPHIC ENTERPRISES. EVEN WHEN I'M ERECT, I'M NOT TERRIBLY IMPRESSIVE.
JANITOR
I JUST WANTED TO MAKE SURE YOU WERE NORMAL.
VERY GOOD, SIR.
MAY I NOW COVER MY HIRSUTE ANATOMY AND RETURN TO MY CAT?
BEFORE I LET YOU GO, I WANT YOU TO EXPLAIN TO ME WHY TRIBUS HAS THREE ARMS.
PARDON ME, MR. PRESIDENT?
A THIRD ARM IS STICKING OUT OF TRIBUS'S CHEST. THERE'RE SCARS WHERE IT ATTACHES, LIKE THE THING WAS SURGICALLY GRAFTED IN PLACE.
IS IT POSSIBLE THAT YOU'VE BEEN DRINKING?
OR PERHAPS YOU'VE FORGOTTEN YOUR EXECUTIVE MEDICATION?
A FEW MOMENTS LATER...
MY FACE IS COVERED SO I CAN REMOVE YOUR BLINDFOLD...

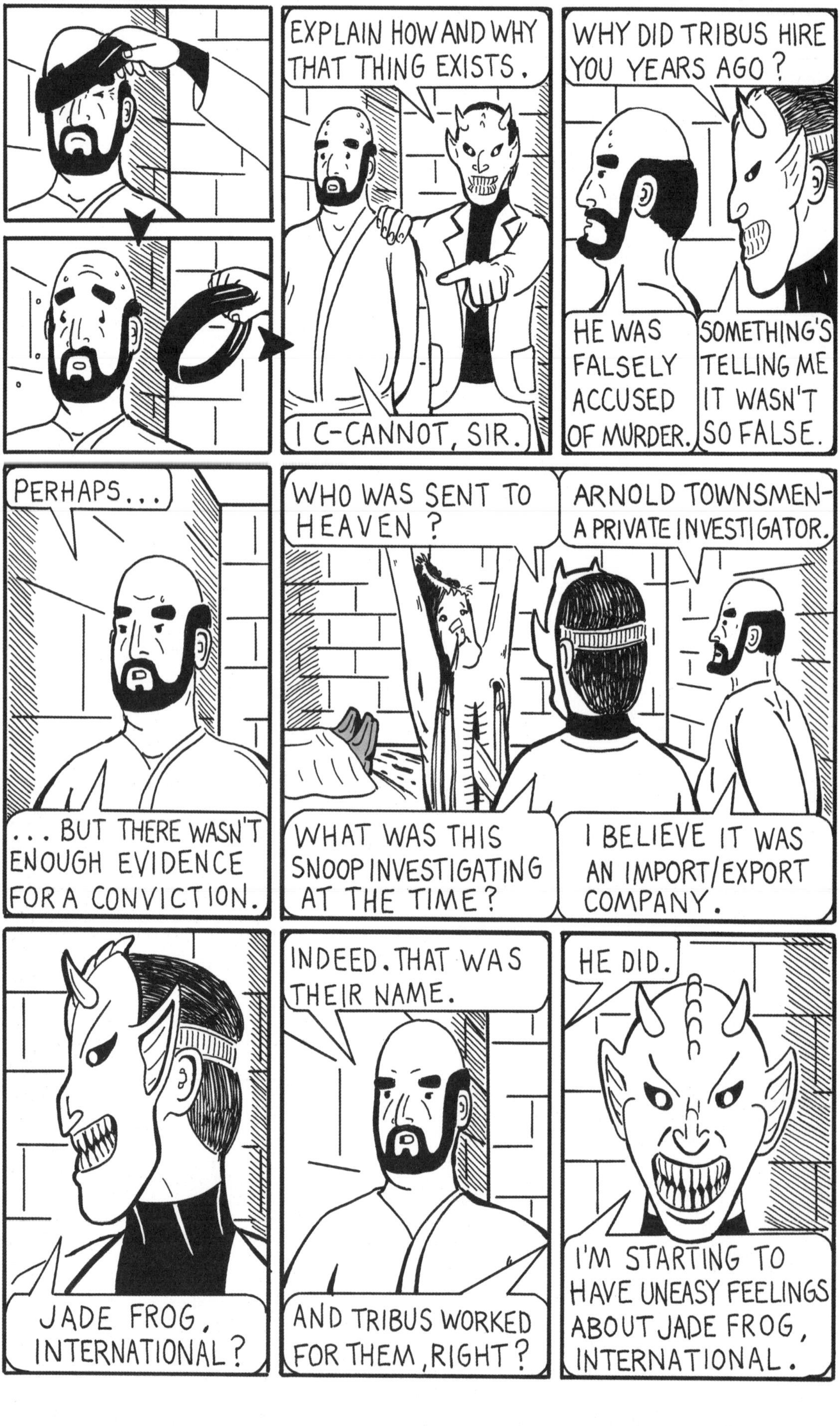
EXPLAIN HOW AND WHY THAT THING EXISTS.
I C-CANNOT, SIR.
WHY DID TRIBUS HIRE YOU YEARS AGO?
HE WAS FALSELY ACCUSED OF MURDER.
SOMETHING'S TELLING ME IT WASN'T SO FALSE.
PERHAPS...
...BUT THERE WASN'T ENOUGH EVIDENCE FOR A CONVICTION.
WHO WAS SENT TO HEAVEN?
ARNOLD TOWNSMEN- A PRIVATE INVESTIGATOR.
WHAT WAS THIS SNOOP INVESTIGATING AT THE TIME?
I BELIEVE IT WAS AN IMPORT/EXPORT COMPANY.
JADE FROG, INTERNATIONAL?
INDEED. THAT WAS THEIR NAME.
AND TRIBUS WORKED FOR THEM, RIGHT?
HE DID.
I'M STARTING TO HAVE UNEASY FEELINGS ABOUT JADE FROG, INTERNATIONAL.

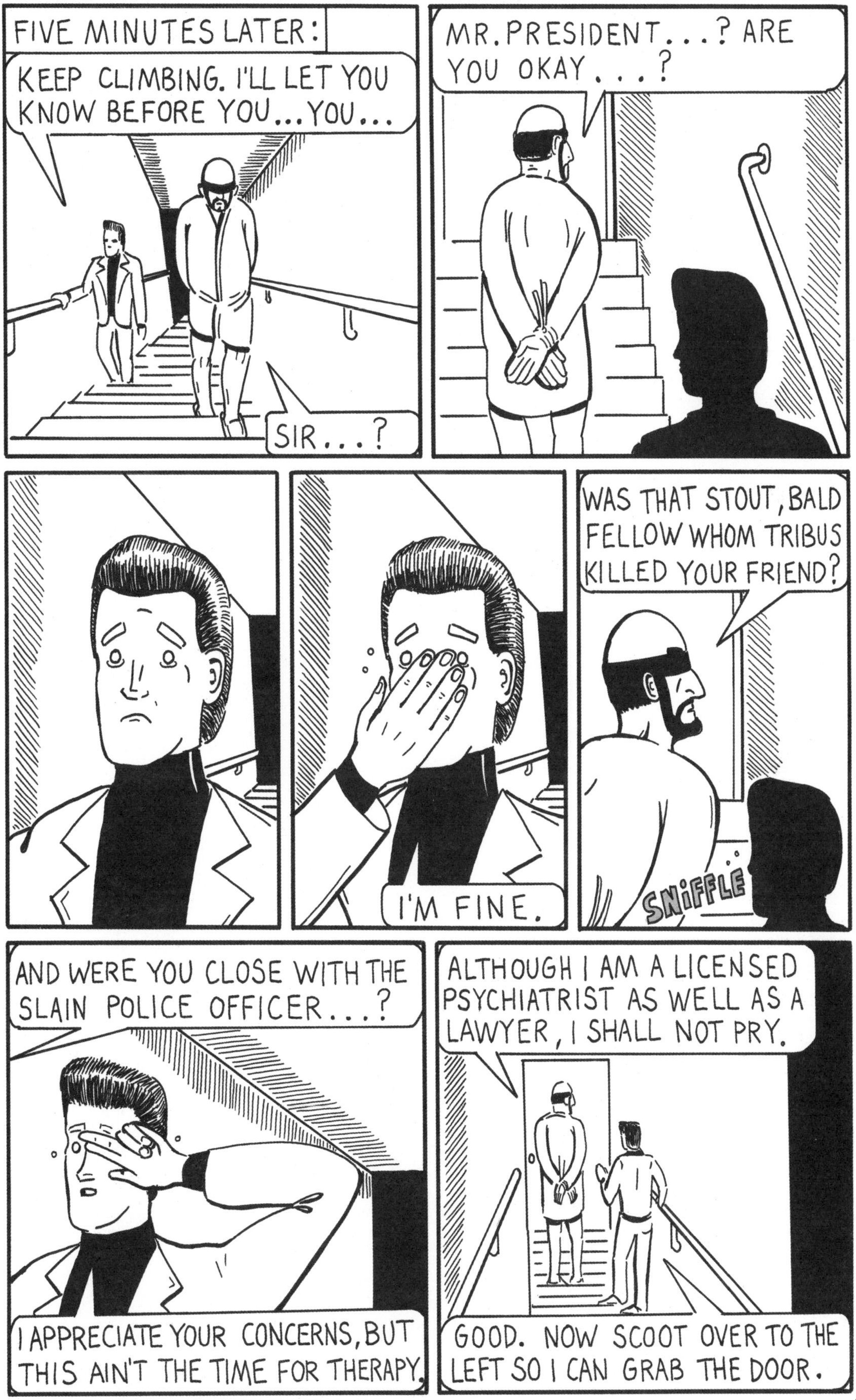
FIVE MINUTES LATER:
KEEP CLIMBING. I'LL LET YOU KNOW BEFORE YOU...YOU...
SIR...?
MR. PRESIDENT...? ARE YOU OKAY...?
I'M FINE.
WAS THAT STOUT, BALD FELLOW WHOM TRIBUS KILLED YOUR FRIEND?
SNIFFLE
AND WERE YOU CLOSE WITH THE SLAIN POLICE OFFICER...?
I APPRECIATE YOUR CONCERNS, BUT THIS AIN'T THE TIME FOR THERAPY.
ALTHOUGH I AM A LICENSED PSYCHIATRIST AS WELL AS A LAWYER, I SHALL NOT PRY.
GOOD. NOW SCOOT OVER TO THE LEFT SO I CAN GRAB THE DOOR.

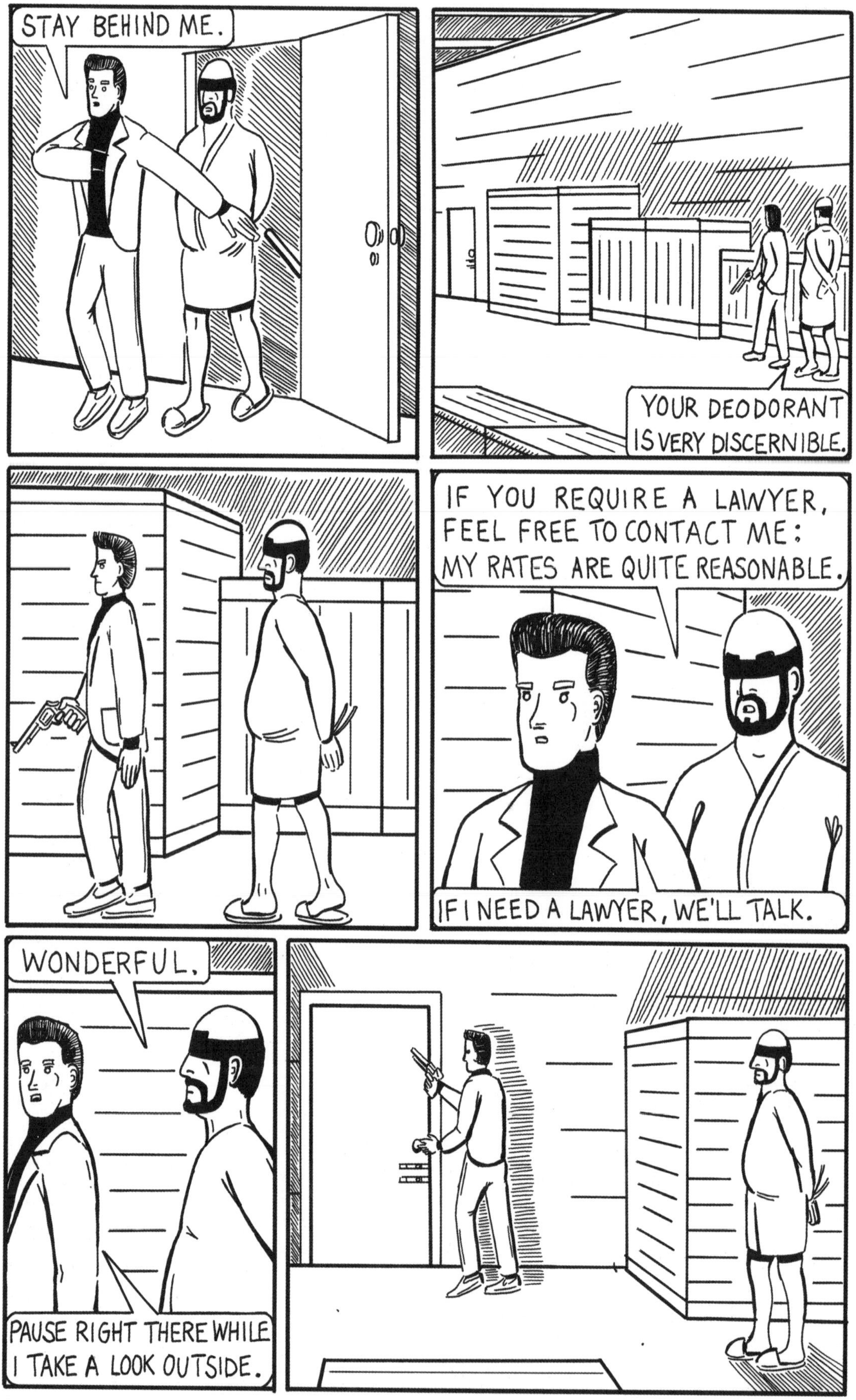
STAY BEHIND ME.
YOUR DEODORANT IS VERY DISCERNIBLE.
IF YOU REQUIRE A LAWYER, FEEL FREE TO CONTACT ME: MY RATES ARE QUITE REASONABLE.
IF I NEED A LAWYER, WE'LL TALK.
WONDERFUL.
PAUSE RIGHT THERE WHILE I TAKE A LOOK OUTSIDE.

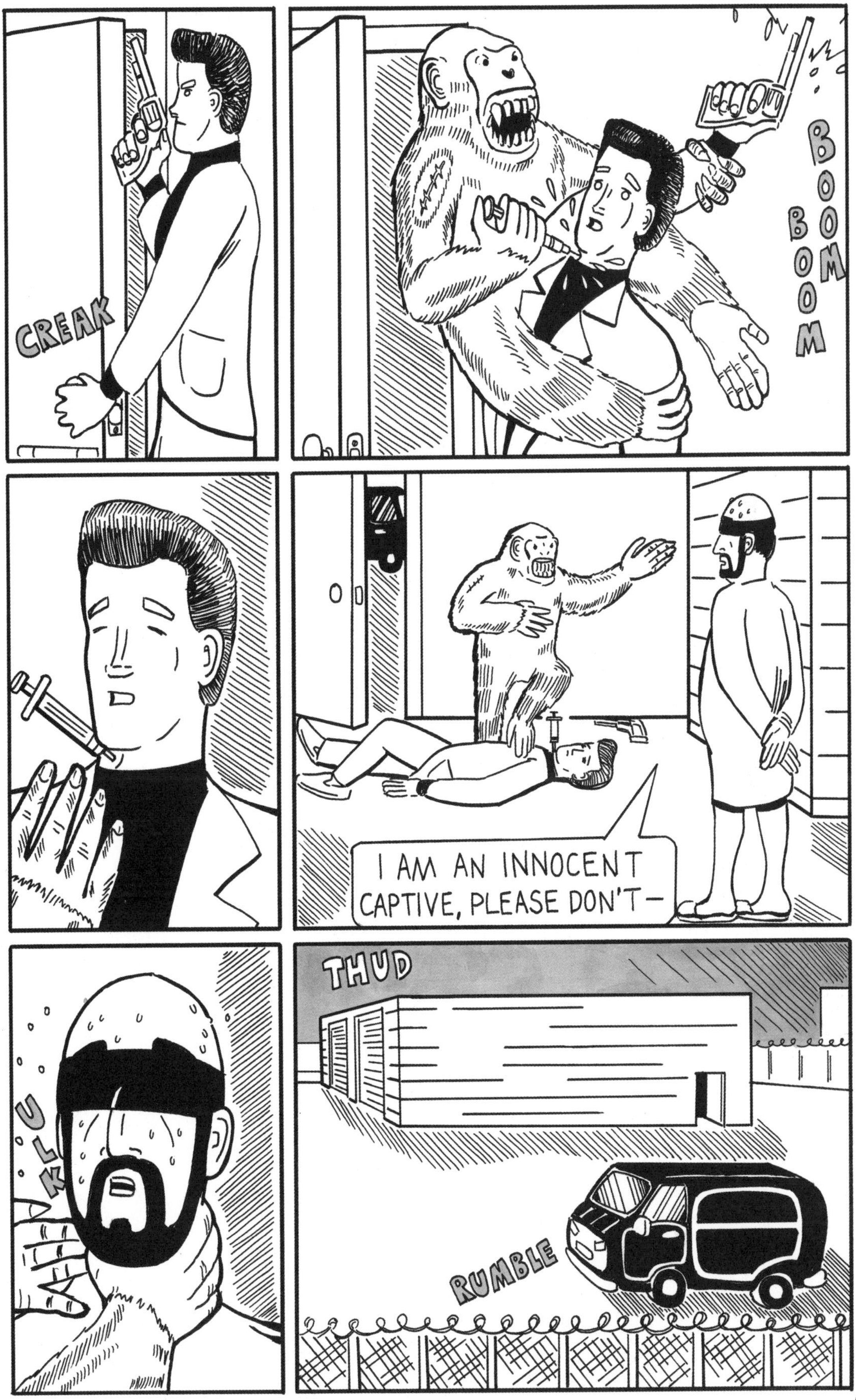
CREAK
BOOM
BOOM
I AM AN INNOCENT CAPTIVE, PLEASE DON'T—
ULK
THUD
RUMBLE

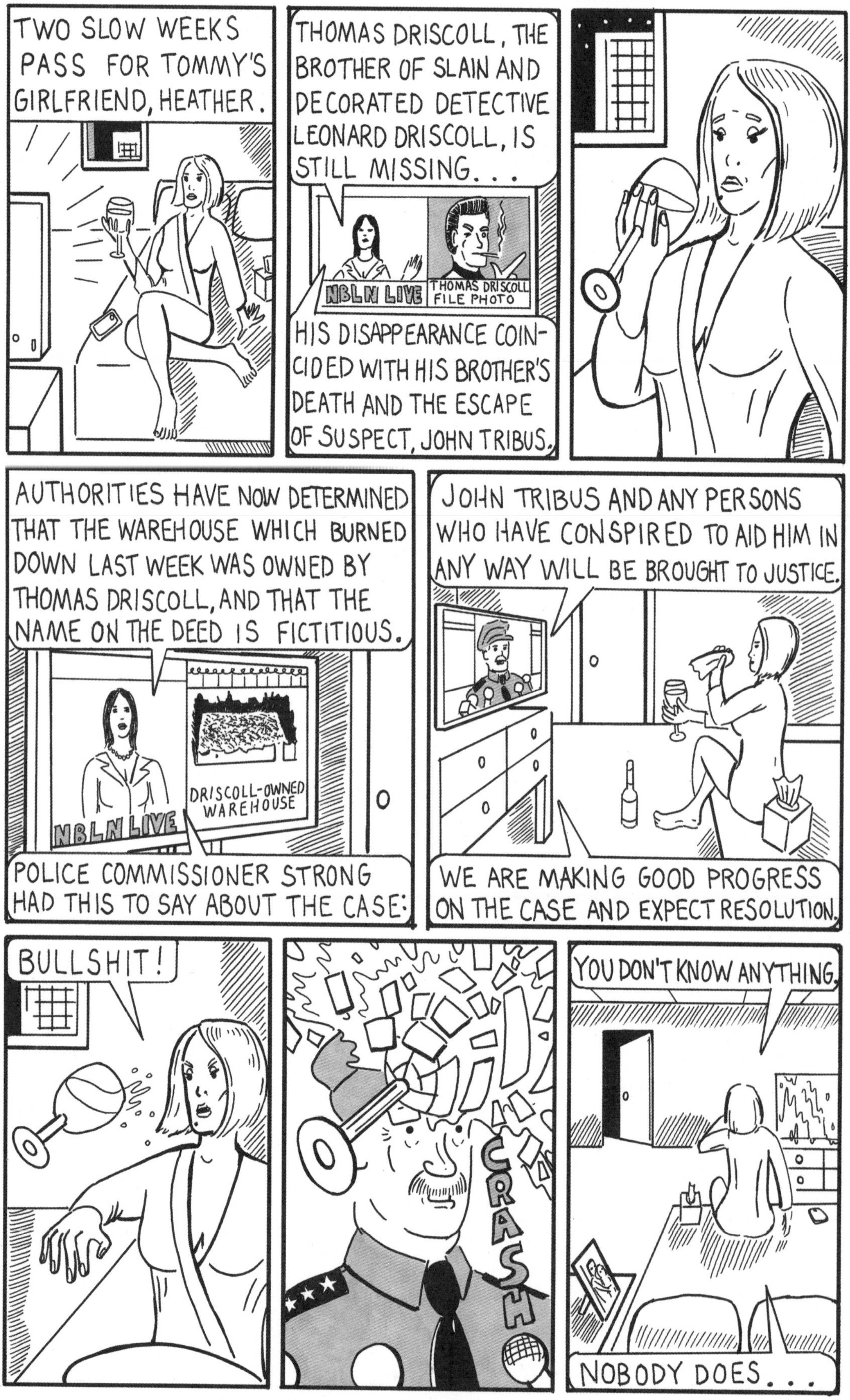
TWO SLOW WEEKS PASS FOR TOMMY'S GIRLFRIEND, HEATHER.
THOMAS DRISCOLL, THE BROTHER OF SLAIN AND DECORATED DETECTIVE LEONARD DRISCOLL, IS STILL MISSING...
NBLN LIVE
THOMAS DRISCOLL FILE PHOTO
HIS DISAPPEARANCE COINCIDED WITH HIS BROTHER'S DEATH AND THE ESCAPE OF SUSPECT, JOHN TRIBUS.
AUTHORITIES HAVE NOW DETERMINED THAT THE WAREHOUSE WHICH BURNED DOWN LAST WEEK WAS OWNED BY THOMAS DRISCOLL, AND THAT THE NAME ON THE DEED IS FICTITIOUS.
DRISCOLL-OWNED WAREHOUSE
NBLN LIVE
POLICE COMMISSIONER STRONG HAD THIS TO SAY ABOUT THE CASE:
JOHN TRIBUS AND ANY PERSONS WHO HAVE CONSPIRED TO AID HIM IN ANY WAY WILL BE BROUGHT TO JUSTICE.
WE ARE MAKING GOOD PROGRESS ON THE CASE AND EXPECT RESOLUTION.
BULLSHIT!
CRASH
YOU DON'T KNOW ANYTHING.
NOBODY DOES...

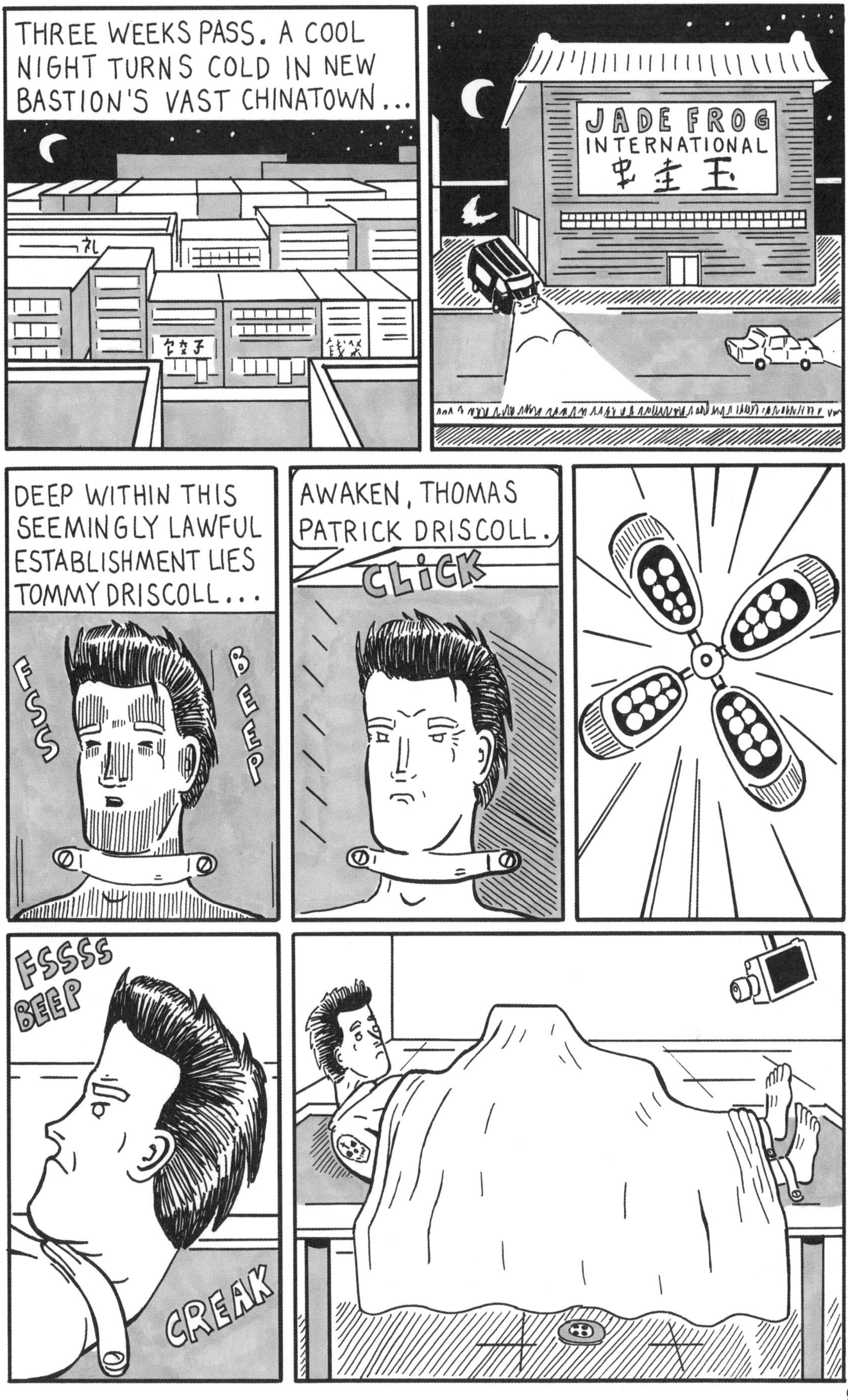
THREE WEEKS PASS. A COOL NIGHT TURNS COLD IN NEW BASTION'S VAST CHINATOWN...
JADE FROG INTERNATIONAL
DEEP WITHIN THIS SEEMINGLY LAWFUL ESTABLISHMENT LIES TOMMY DRISCOLL...
FSS
BEEP
AWAKEN, THOMAS PATRICK DRISCOLL.
CLICK
FSSSS
BEEP
CREAK

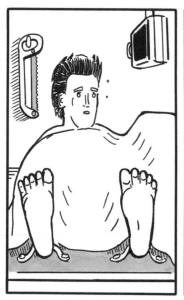

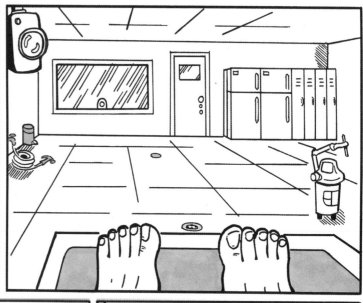

HOW ARE YOU FEELING AT PRESENT?

VERY, VERY FUCKING ANGRY. YOU'D BETTER UNTIE ME RIGHT NOW.

I HAVE SOME SOME GOOD NEWS FOR YOU.

FSSSS

BEEP

DON'T BE OFFENDED IF I'M DOUBTFUL.

YOU HAVE SAVED YOUR SISTER'S LIFE.

WHAT ARE YOU TALKING ABOUT?

YOUR BLOOD AND HER BLOOD ARE THE SAME TYPE, AND YOUR HLA TISSUE CLASSIFICATION ALSO MATCHES.

ADDITIONALLY, YOUR SYSTEM IS VIRILE WHEREAS HERS HAS DEGRADED. YOU ARE A FAR BETTER CHOICE.

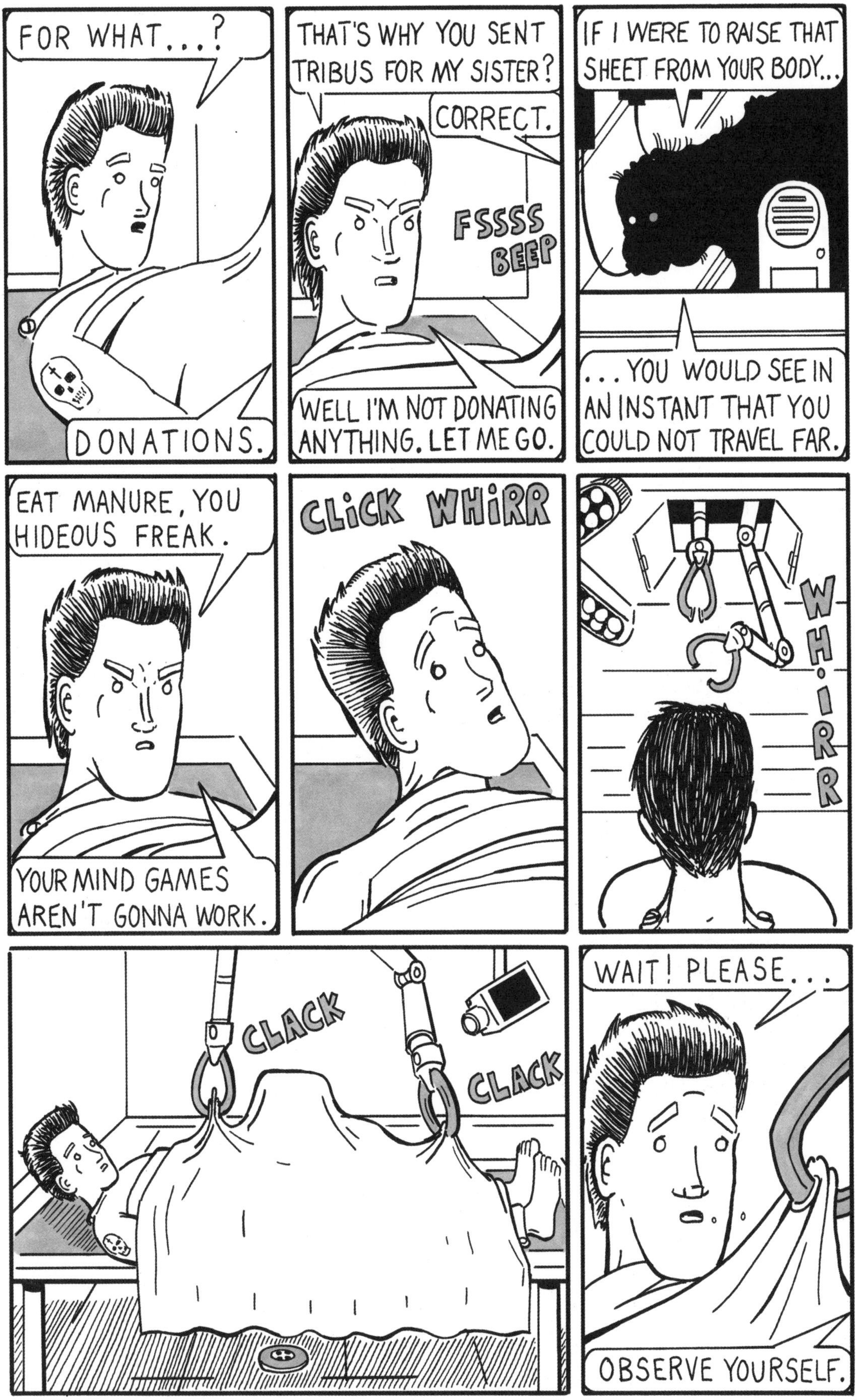
FOR WHAT...?
DONATIONS.
THAT'S WHY YOU SENT TRIBUS FOR MY SISTER?
CORRECT.
FSSSS
BEEP
WELL I'M NOT DONATING ANYTHING. LET ME GO.
IF I WERE TO RAISE THAT SHEET FROM YOUR BODY...
...YOU WOULD SEE IN AN INSTANT THAT YOU COULD NOT TRAVEL FAR.
EAT MANURE, YOU HIDEOUS FREAK.
YOUR MIND GAMES AREN'T GONNA WORK.
CLICK WHIRR
WHIRR
CLACK
CLACK
WAIT! PLEASE...
OBSERVE YOURSELF.

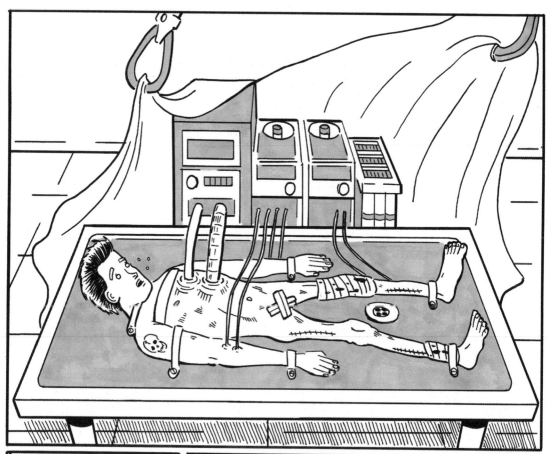

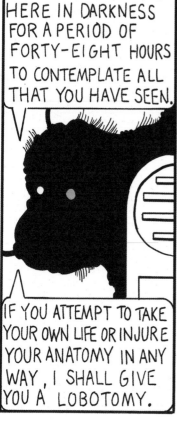

I SHALL LEAVE YOU HERE IN DARKNESS FOR A PERIOD OF FORTY-EIGHT HOURS TO CONTEMPLATE ALL THAT YOU HAVE SEEN.

IF YOU ATTEMPT TO TAKE YOUR OWN LIFE OR INJURE YOUR ANATOMY IN ANY WAY, I SHALL GIVE YOU A LOBOTOMY.

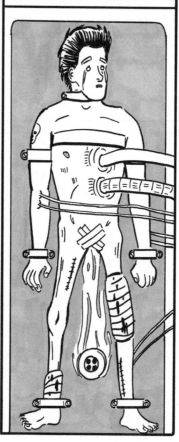

P-PLEASE DON'T DO THIS... PLEASE.

I HAVE MONEY—MILLIONS IN CASH—AND CAN GET MORE.

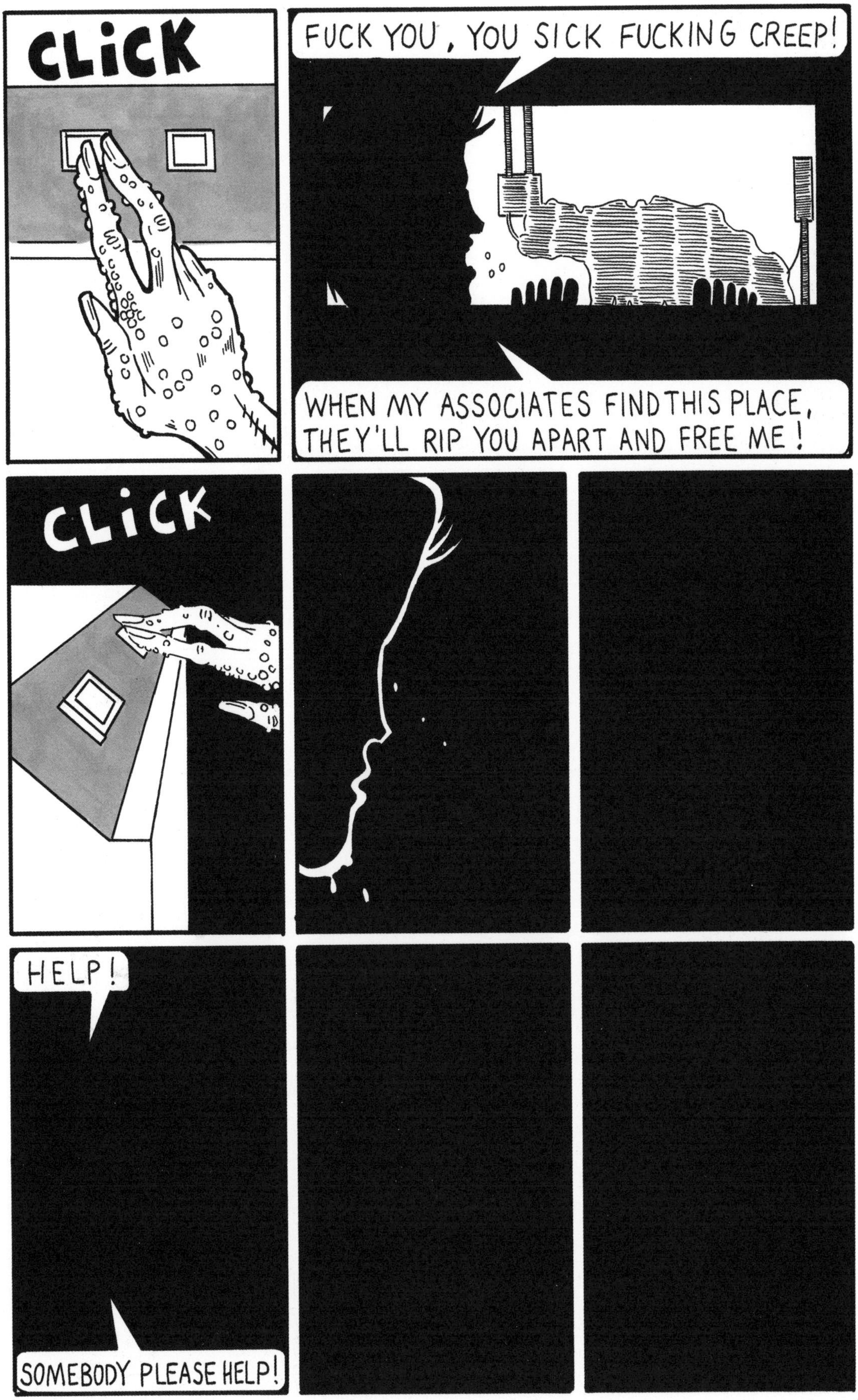
CLICK
FUCK YOU, YOU SICK FUCKING CREEP!
WHEN MY ASSOCIATES FIND THIS PLACE, THEY'LL RIP YOU APART AND FREE ME!
CLICK
HELP!
SOMEBODY PLEASE HELP!

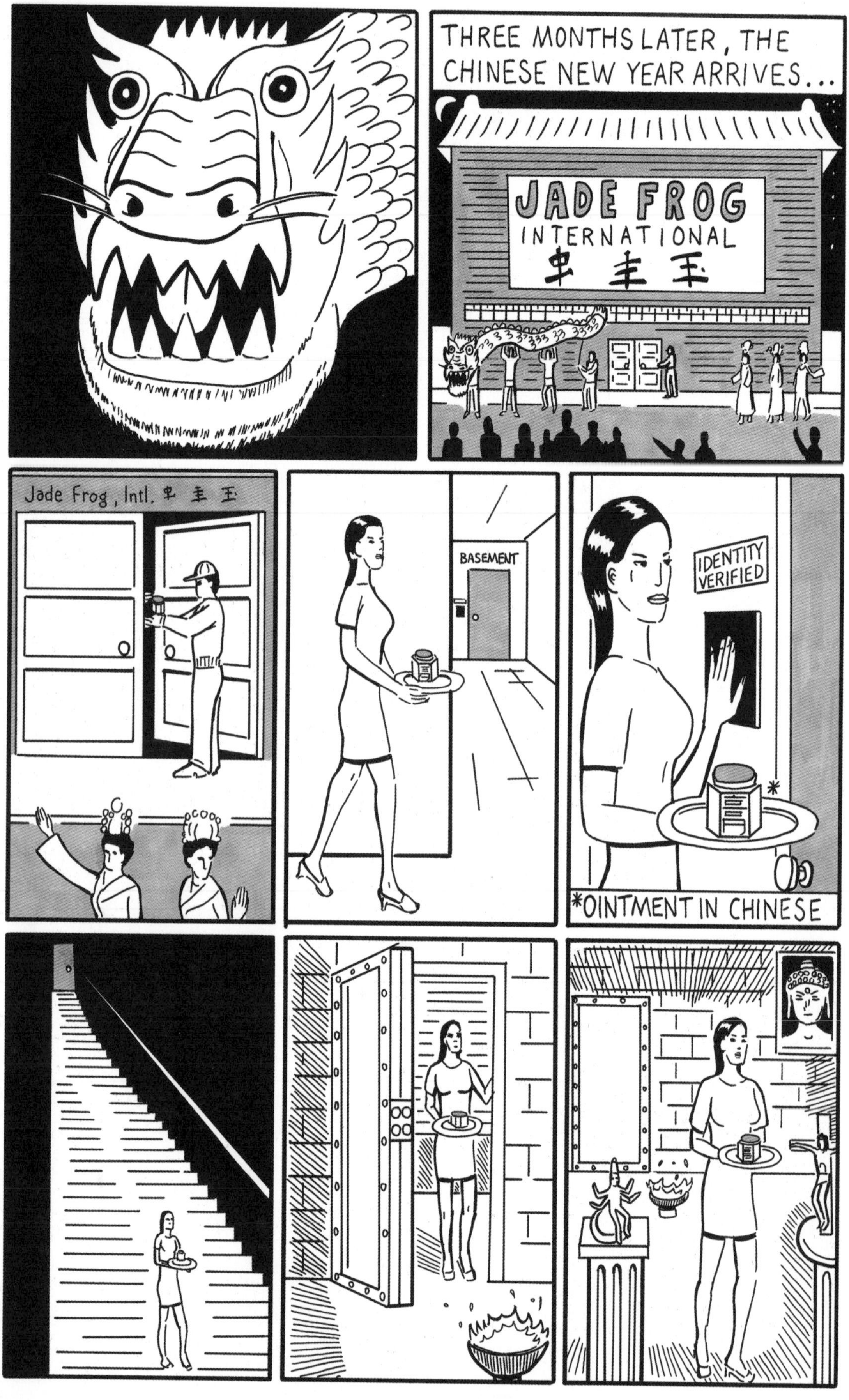
THREE MONTHS LATER, THE CHINESE NEW YEAR ARRIVES...
JADE FROG
INTERNATIONAL
Jade Frog, Intl.
BASEMENT
IDENTITY VERIFIED
*OINTMENT IN CHINESE

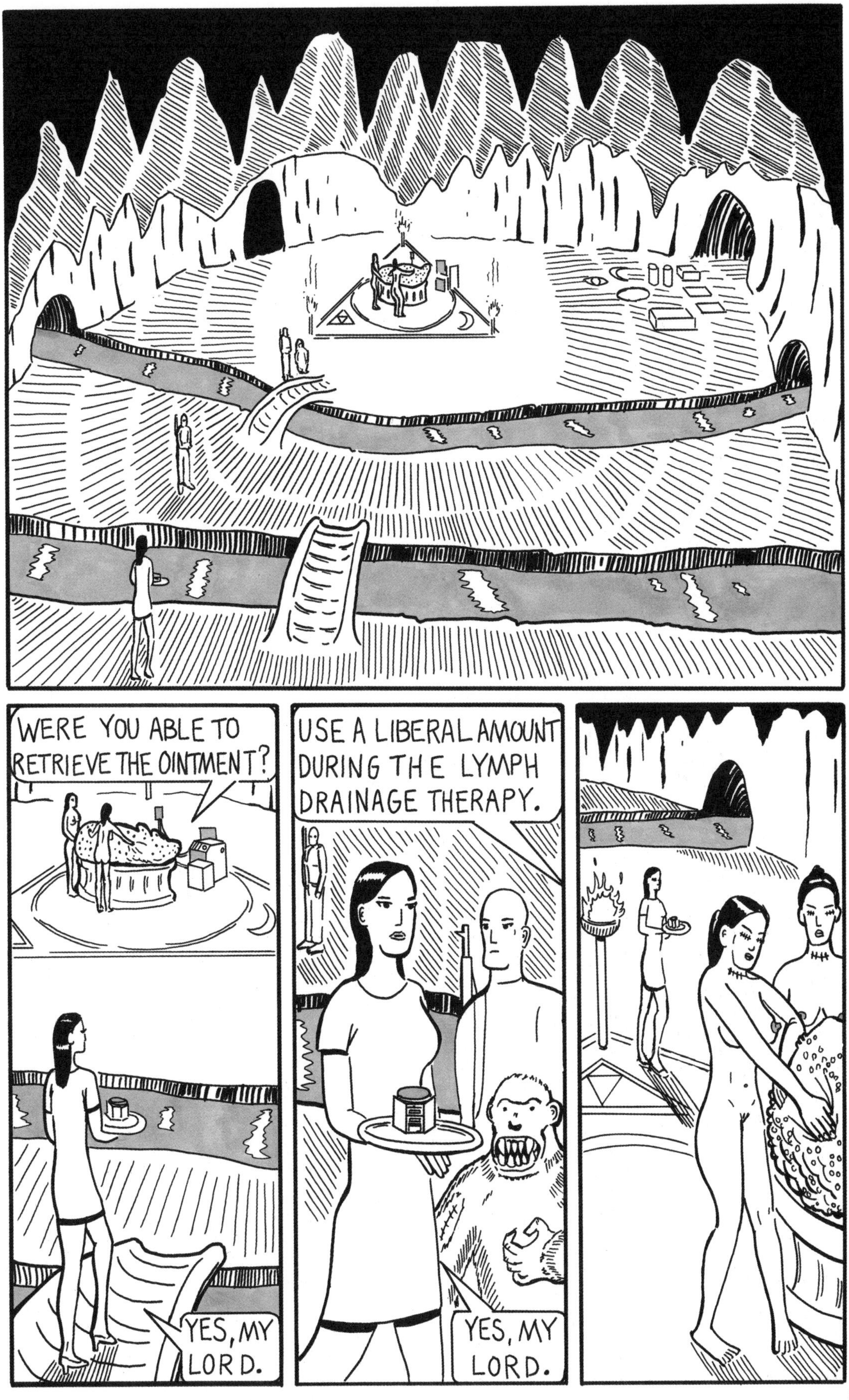
WERE YOU ABLE TO RETRIEVE THE OINTMENT?
YES, MY LORD.
USE A LIBERAL AMOUNT DURING THE LYMPH DRAINAGE THERAPY.
YES, MY LORD.

THE ROAD TO GODHOOD IS PAINFUL...

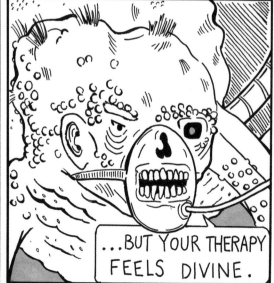

...BUT YOUR THERAPY FEELS DIVINE.

S. CRAIG ZAHLER is a novelist, screenwriter, director, composer, musician, and tyro cartoonist who was born in Florida and lives in New York. His debut western novel *A Congregation of Jackals* was nominated for both the Peacemaker and the Spur awards. His 2014 crime novel *Mean Business on North Ganson Street* received a starred review for excellence in Booklist who said the book was "bizarrely mean... mordantly funny... and not to be missed," while *Kirkus* review called it "a gripping story." His science fiction novel, *Corpus Chrome, Inc.* was praised by sci-fi grandmaster Larry Niven and called, "a bravura literary performance," by *Booklist*, and his other novels, the horrific western *Wraiths of the Broken Land* and the gothic orphan tale *Hug Chickenpenny: The Panegyric of an Anomalous Childwere* were similarly well received. His newest novel is a nasty and intricately plotted crime piece entitled, *The Slanted Gutter.*

Zahler wrote and directed (and co-composed the score for) the 2015 film *Bone Tomahawk*, an Independent Spirit Award nominated picture for Best Screenplay, starring Kurt Russell, Patrick Wilson, and Richard Jenkins. The film garnered praise from critics and fans alike, including the *New York Times*, who called *Bone Tomahawk*, "[a] witty fusion of western, horror and comedy that gallops to its own beat" and Conan O'Brien, who named it the single best motion picture of the decade.

Zahler then wrote and directed *Brawl in Cell Block 99*, starring Vince Vaughn, Jennifer Carpenter, and Don Johnson, which premiered at the prestigious Venice Film Festival and went on to be a New York Times critics' pick and even wider critical acclaim.

Zahler's third movie was *Dragged Across Concrete*, a crime film that stars Mel Gibson, Vince Vaughn, and Tory Kittles. This picture premiered at the 75th Venice Film Festival in 2018 and showed at the London Film Festival and also to a sold-out crowd for the closing night of Beyond Fest. *The Guardian* called it, "Inventive and nasty," and *Birth.Movies.Death.* said it was "[A]n idiosyncratic cop movie masterstroke," while Indiewire named the director, "One of genre's most exciting filmmakers."

His movies have been added to the permanent collection at the Museum of Modern Art in New York City.

Zahler has released three albums with his doomy epic metal band Realmbuilder (wherein he sings and plays drums as well) and a pair of black metal platters with Charnel Valley, and he co-composed the soundtracks to all three of his movies, two of which contain original songs that were performed by soul music legends, The O'Jays and Butch Tavares.

Forbidden Surgeries of the Hideous Dr. Divinus is Zahler's debut graphic novel, and he is already at work on his second story in this medium, which he has adored since childhood.